Delphi Challenge

Delphi in Space
Book Nine

Bob Blanton

Cover by Momir Borocki
momir.borocki@gmail.com

D1739320

Delphi Publishing

Copyright © 2019 by Robert D. Blanton

Cover by Momir Borocki

momir.borocki@gmail.com

https://www.facebook.com/StarshipSakira/

Table of Contents

1 Chili Powder

"Oh my," Marc said, rubbing his face with his hands. "You sure know how to spice up a guy's day." Samantha, his girlfriend, had just told him she was pregnant five minutes after he had been informed that the aliens heading toward Artemis were the same ones that had attacked the Paraxean colony mission some seventy-odd years before.

"Why now?" he asked.

"Well, Governor McCormack, I thought I'd time it for late summer, just after the harvest," Samantha said. "I didn't know we had killer aliens coming."

"Why after the harvest?"

"Things will slow down then. It'll be easier to get help with the baby."

Marc poured himself a glass of scotch. "And does that mean you've decided to marry me?" He'd been proposing to Samantha every couple of months for the last year.

"What do you think?"

"I have no clue," Marc said. "We left Earth, almost two months ago, and you didn't want to get married then."

"That's because I wanted to avoid a state wedding," Samantha said. Marc was the president and monarch of Delphi Nation, and a huge wedding would have been expected.

"And you don't think one will be expected here?"

"It won't be that big a deal. We only have twenty-five hundred colonists, and most of them are not that interested in social gatherings. I think we can get away with a small affair."

"Oh boy, a wedding and a baby," ADI piped in. ADI was the digital intelligence that came with the starship Marc had discovered three years ago.

"ADI!"

"I know, private conversation," ADI said then she whispered "A baby shower and a bridal shower," as she closed the Comm channel. Of course, she was still recording the conversation, but it was being stored in a private area of her memory, only to be accessed under an emergency or court order.

"And Catie?"

"She's stuck at the Academy," Samantha said. "I wish she could be here, but the timing doesn't work."

"No it doesn't. You know she'll think you did it on purpose."

"What, get pregnant, or set it up so she couldn't attend the wedding?"

"She'll know you got pregnant on purpose; but avoiding the big wedding looks suspicious," Marc said.

"And she'd be right."

"And she'll probably want to get even after the big birthday party you forced on her last year."

"I'm sure Catie and I will be able to come to terms," Samantha said. Catie had already gotten even for the birthday party by spreading rumors that Marc and Samantha were getting married. After Samantha called her out on it, they'd reached a truce. "I'll work with ADI and Catie on the wedding, you should start figuring out what you're going to do about the arrival of our alien friends."

"Come in," Catie called out after her Comm announced a visitor outside her dorm room.

"Hi, Alex," Cadet Colonel Miranda Cordova said after she entered. Catie was attending the Academy as Alex MacGregor. Her appearance had been altered along with her name to give her a real Academy experience instead of one marked by the fact that she was Princess Catie.

"Welcome, ma'am!" Catie said as she jumped up and snapped to attention.

"Hey, it's just me, Miranda. I came by to thank you for all your help on the ship design class. I just finished the final."

"So, you did okay?"

"I think I did. I'm sure I'll be able to maintain my top-of-class ranking."

"Hi, Yvette," Catie said as her roommate came in behind Miranda. "How'd you do?"

"Good, I think," Yvette said. "I'm glad it's over. Three more tests and I'm done."

"I only have two more," Catie said. "What about you, Miranda?"

"I've also got three left."

"Did you see those four schooners arrive?" Catie asked.

"Yes, I think they're for us," Miranda said.

"For *us*?" Yvette asked, shocked at the assertion.

"They said we're going to have a two-week cruise after our week off. I was thinking it would be aboard one of the frigates our Navy has, but I'm guessing it's going to be on those schooners."

"Why?"

"Lots of academies like to put their cadets on a sailing ship. Without all the technology, things get pretty basic. And there is a lot more coordination needed on a sailing ship. Sails don't set themselves."

"Oh, that sounds like as much fun as two weeks in Guatemala," Catie said.

"Oh it won't be that bad. I have to go. Thanks again, Alex; I'll see you after the break."

"Sailing?" Yvette asked after Miranda left the room. "Who would think of that?"

"Sadists," Catie replied.

"You're pregnant?!" Catie asked in disbelief. She was in a study room in the library so she would have privacy to talk with Marc and Samantha.

"Yes," Samantha replied.

"Congratulations," Blake said. "When's the big day?"

"You mean the wedding or the birth?" Marc asked.

"Let's start with the wedding."

"No fair!" Catie squealed.

"Ah, the penny drops," Marc said. "What's not fair?"

"She's getting out of the big wedding!"

"And what does that have to do with fair?" Marc asked.

"She . . . she," Catie sputtered. "And I can't even be there!"

"I'm sorry about the timing, we could hold off on the wedding until you can be here," Samantha said.

"Nooo, that would mess up your wedding. I can be there virtually," Catie acquiesced. "You deserve a nice wedding. But you deserve a huge, royal wedding more!"

"Have you told Linda yet?" Blake asked.

"No, we'll call her right after this," Marc said.

"And the date?" Blake asked.

"Next week, on Tuesday."

"Just before Christmas?"

"Yep, I'll be able to combine presents," Marc said. Samantha slapped him on the back of the head just as he finished.

"Apparently not," Blake said. "And the baby is due when?"

"First week of September," Samantha said. "I don't know what that's going to be here."

"We have to get the calendar figured out," Marc said.

"June, so you're only a few weeks along?"

"Yes," Samantha said.

"But you're sure?"

"Oh, I'm sure," Samantha said. "The Paraxeans have this pregnancy thing down."

"Well, *congratulations*," Catie said with minimal enthusiasm.

"We'll talk to you later," Marc said.

"Blake?" Marc had called his brother to discuss plans.

"Hey, Bro. How did Linda take the news?"

"She says she's fine with it," Marc replied.

"She would, but how did she sound?"

"She seemed to be okay. Ask Catie, I'm sure they've talked by now."

"I will. Now, what did you want?"

"I'd like to discuss options on how to deal with our impending guests. What have you got?"

"Me, I've got nothing," Blake said, "and I see you're drinking, it's not that bad. They won't make it there until June."

"Oh, this," Marc swirled his glass of scotch. "Just trying to loosen up the brain cells. Come on, you must have some thoughts."

"The first one is, you would have received their message by now. That means, you need to decide about a reply," Blake said.

"*Au contraire*, dear brother. They won't expect to receive a reply for another four months. That gives me loads of time."

"Oh, duh, forgot about that. Well, since we know they're inclined to be violent, and they tried to look intimidating in their message, you might just want to tell them to stay away."

"And how would we do that?"

"The Victory will be there; you could just make a point that your ship is bigger than their ship."

"And if they ignore that?"

"Well, with the Victory, your ship will be bigger than theirs."

"So, we start a war?"

"A police action," Blake said.

"We need to analyze possible tactics. We still don't know much about them."

"We'll start running simulations."

"Okay, keep me posted," Marc said.

"What are you going to do?"

"Get married, build that governor's house, and get this colony established."

"Sounds like a full plate. Have fun."

"Captain, they should be getting our reply about now," the first officer said. He was stationed at the navigation console on the alien starship heading toward Artemis.

"They should," the captain said. "I will be very interested to see how they will react to it."

"How could they have beaten us to the planet? We've been observing it for two and a half years while we approach," the first mate said.

"Who knows from which direction they came. And if they have gravity drives like us, we wouldn't have seen an exhaust plume, and even if there was one, we could easily have missed it."

"Do you think they're going to be willing to share the resources?"

"They're going to have to," the captain said. "I have not spent three years of my life on this mission to have to return home with nothing. I will not accept no for an answer!"

"Shouldn't we consider looking for another system?"

"What are the odds that we would find one within four years' travel?" the captain said. "We need those resources. I'm going back into stasis; I'll see you in a month. Now, get back to work."

2 Winter Break

"Alex, what are your plans for the break?" Yvette asked.

"I've got some personal things to attend to until Wednesday," Catie said. "After that, I guess I'll hang around with my Academy Family." Academy families were local families that provided the cadet a chance for a home experience on the weekends and such.

"I've been invited to a party on New Year's Eve, would you like to come?"

"What kind of people will be there?"

"My Academy Family is hosting it as a mixer," Yvette said. "Just a few ladies from the Academy and some men from Delphi University; the husband teaches there."

"Might be fun, what should I wear?"

"Something pretty," Yvette said.

"So a dress?"

"That should go without saying."

"Okay, but you have to help me pick it out."

"Of course, Chérie," Yvette said. "I was also planning to stay at The Four Seasons."

"Why?"

"Because, Chérie, in just over two weeks, we will be living on one of those schooners, in a small bunk that we will have to get out of just to scratch our nose."

"So?"

"A few days in a nice big bed, and a few trips to the spa, will make that so much more bearable."

Catie shrugged her shoulders. "Why not. Are we going to share a room?"

"But of course. Too bad they don't have a casino," Yvette said, harkening back to their stay in Monaco, where Catie paid all their expenses with her winnings from playing cards.

"What are you going to do for Christmas week?" Catie asked.

"I am flying home to stay with my Mama and Papa. They tell me they are missing me. Maybe, that means I will get a nice present," Yvette said.

Catie met Liz for breakfast Monday morning.

"What do you have lined up for the week?" she asked.

"This week, we need to hire the crew for the Dutchman," Liz said.

"How many?" Catie asked.

"I count fifty-one," Liz said.

"What about the pilots and ground crew for all those Foxes?"

"That's Blake's problem. We're just ferrying them. We just need to make sure we have enough pilots to handle our four Lynxes. The engineering section should be able to handle the maintenance on them."

"Okay, so how do you get to fifty-one?"

"Chief engineer, one engineer and three specialists each for environmental, reactors, propulsion, robotics, and electronics."

"Who's fixing the plumbing if it breaks?"

"The robotics guys."

"Oh, that reminds me, we need to build a bunch of bots."

"Definitely. Nobody wants to have to clean all the flooring, and no one wants to have to go outside and check the hull for damage and repair all those pock marks."

"Okay, okay, I'll get on it. You've covered engineering, what about the command deck?"

"A first mate and a second mate who can cover communications. Then three specialists and a third mate who can handle security and watch standing. Plus two marine types," Liz said. "A navigator, two specialists learning to navigate, a weapons officer and three gunners, and three gofers."

"What about a cook?" Catie asked.

"One chief steward and four bottle washers."

"Cargo?"

"We have one supply chief and four specialists to handle loading and unloading."

"Doctor?"

"A medic and one nurse should be enough."

"How are we going to choose them?"

"Good old-fashioned interviews," Liz said. "We have a bunch of applicants. We have their service records; ADI was kind enough to sort out the best ones for us."

"You're welcome," ADI said.

Liz shook her head at ADI's interjection. "We'll do a quick filter, and invite the ones we like back for a second interview with the other one of us."

"Fifty-one interviews?"

"It's going to take more than that; we'll probably interview four or five per position, but we're only looking for the officers this week. Once we select them, we'll let them do the main interviews for the rest of the crew; you and I will just do the second filter."

Catie sighed. "Whew, I can probably manage that."

"I've got us set up with an office in ring two, an outer office for the reception, and an inner office for each of us. We'll give them a time slot for coming back for the second interview, we'll do that together. You do the filter for the engineers, and I'll cover the rest."

"We should probably try to get the first mate and chief engineer figured out so they can sit in on the second interviews," Catie suggested. "And what are you thinking about for the reactor engineer? We'll probably have to get a Paraxean to deal with the antimatter reactor."

"I don't know; Blake's been putting a few engineers through an accelerated class, and I'm hoping to poach one of them."

"Uncle Blake will love you for that."

"He can't blame us if they like us better."

"Hey, Barty," Liz said as she and Catie entered the office she'd rented for the week. "This is my partner Alex MacGregor." Catie was staying with her undercover identity to avoid anyone tying Catie McCormack to her new look.

"Hello, Ms. Farmer, Ms. MacGregor" Barty said. Catie remembered him as the son of one of the chemists who worked in the Vancouver Integrated plant in the city.

"What's he, like *twelve*?" Catie whispered.

"Yes. And I remember you being twelve once. It's a pretty simple job. I'm sure he will be able to handle it."

Barty smiled. "I've already got the applicants' packets ready. I'll send you the packet for the next interviewee right after you finish each interview. How long do you want to review it, five minutes?"

"He also has good hearing," Liz said. "Barty, give us two minutes."

"Yes, ma'am."

Barty sent Catie the packet on her first interviewee. An Arlean Griggs, formerly chief engineer on a U.S. frigate; retired after twenty years at the rank of commander; just completed Delphi Forces accelerated indoctrination course for experienced officers; two children, a boy fifteen and a girl twelve. Married, husband teaches applied engineering at Delphi University.

Once Catie had finished scanning the package, she buzzed Barty to send Commander Griggs in. Barty was a gentleman and opened the door for the commander. Catie figured he must have been a bit awed by her, she had an imposing presence and résumé.

"Hello, Commander," Catie said, "please have a seat."

Commander Griggs did a short double-take when she realized how young Catie must be. "Ms. MacGregor, thanks for seeing me."

"Call me Alex, and thank you for interviewing with us," Catie said.

"Certainly, Alex, and please call me Arlean."

"Arlean, I see you retired from the U.S. Navy two years ago. What has kept you busy since then?"

"I've got two kids whom I've been spending time with," Commander Griggs said. "I also took a few courses at Cornell, where my husband was teaching."

"Obviously, you were deployed while you were in the Navy. I see you served aboard several frigates, which means you were away from your family quite a bit. Are you comfortable with our projected time in space versus shore time?"

"My kids are used to it. My husband has been the primary caregiver since our first was born. I keep up with them via chat and video calls. Actually, your schedule would be nice. I see you're projecting an in-port stay of one to two weeks, with deployment of eight to twelve weeks. I assume the eight weeks is for deliveries out to the asteroid belt."

"Oh, those would only be two weeks," Catie said.

"For a cargo ship?"

"With our powerplants, we should be able to maintain constant acceleration."

Commander Griggs' eyes unfocused as she did some quick calculations in her head. "Ah, I guess that's right. I assume the ship has gravity drives?"

"It does."

"And I've just heard a little about the jump drive, and based on your statement about the duration of a run, I assume that you can jump while underway."

"That's correct. You have to stabilize the ship so it doesn't yaw about its vector, but you can jump at full velocity."

"Do you match the velocity for the system you're traveling to?"

"Yes, but you can use the intermediate systems to adjust your speed, so the navigation officer will bleed off excess velocity or add velocity in those systems while you're recharging the capacitors for the next jump."

"I see you like to keep your reactor crew busy."

15

"We do. Tell me what you know about the antimatter reactor."

"I took a twelve-week course from Professor Pollard on it. I think I know about as much as he does. The Paraxeans don't seem to get too deep into the theory," Commander Griggs said.

"Professor Pollard?"

"I can't pronounce his Paraxean name; he's adopted Pollard for us humans."

"How about the fusion reactors?"

"Oh, I've been studying those for a couple of years now. Cornell has been developing a class on them as fast as Delphi has released information. I helped to integrate it into their course work."

"I thought you were a student?"

"I was, but I happen to have a familial relationship with the professor of nuclear science at Cornell."

"Your husband?"

"No, my father."

After another ten minutes of questions, Catie decided she really liked the commander. "Would you be available for another interview this evening at 1800?"

"Does that mean I've passed the first filter?"

"Yes, you did. We're in a hurry to get the chief engineer selected so they can participate in the final interviews for the rest of the engineering officers," Catie said.

"I'd be delighted to come back, and I'm glad to hear that you want the chief engineer involved with the other interviews."

◆ ◆ ◆

"Mr. George Calderon," Barty said as he let the man into the room.

The guy stopped dead in his tracks after he got through the door. "How old are you?"

"I don't think that's relevant," Catie replied. "If you would, please have a seat?"

"I came here for an interview to be chief engineer, what kind of questions are you going to ask me?"

"Mostly engineering questions," Catie said. "This is the preliminary interview. We'll go into more depth if we invite you back for the second interview."

"Why don't you just invite me back when you have a real engineer to interview me? I really don't want to waste my time."

Catie keyed her Comm, "Barty, Mr. Calderon is finished."

"Should I schedule him for a second interview?" Barty asked.

"No, we don't want to waste our time," Catie said.

"Wha . . .," Mr. Calderon gaped. "Who do you think you are?"

"I'm Alex MacGregor, have a good day."

"I demand to speak to your boss!"

"You are speaking to my boss. Now good day."

Catie messaged Blake about the good Mr. Calderon, "I just interviewed a George Calderon, what were you thinking?"

"John Bradley to see you," Barty said as he let the next interviewee into the room.

"Cer Bradley, have a seat," Catie instructed.

"Thank you, Cer MacGregor."

"Call me Alex."

"If you'll call me John."

"Of course. I see here that you graduated from the U.S. Air Force Academy four years ago, and you've been here in Delphi for eight months; tell me why you were released from your commitment early?" Catie asked.

"Didn't they explain that in my file?" Bradley asked.

"Yes, but I'd like to hear it from you."

"Force cutbacks caught me last year, and I suspect my last fitness report wasn't any help."

"Why was that?"

"I would claim that my boss was not impressed with my diligence when I reported a problem with the weapons system we were evaluating. I found several substantial problems in the software design that set the program back a couple of years. The Air Force took the opportunity to cancel the program."

"Why would he care?"

"He was retiring, and planned to go to work for the company."

"But they didn't have a need for his expertise after the program was canceled?"

"Got it in one."

"Let's move on. You have a masters in computer engineering, spent your career working on program management for weapons systems; what are you looking for here?"

"I want to actually get out there and work on a ship," Bradley said, "preferably a starship. A freighter seems like a good chance to do that, and an opportunity to start out at the beginning of a new business concept."

"Liz, do you want to go get a snack?" Catie asked. It was 1700 and they just had time for a short break before the follow-up interview with Commander Griggs.

"How did your interviews go?" Liz asked Catie.

"Not bad. I only had one ass."

"What did he do?"

"You assume it was a man."

"You said they were an ass," Liz said, giving Catie a chuckle.

"He didn't think I was qualified to interview him," Catie said.

"You have to admit you look pretty young; in fact, sixteen is pretty young."

"True, but he basically refused to be interviewed. I'd have been okay with a little skepticism, like Commander Griggs had."

"Okay, how about the others?"

"I think Commander Griggs will be our chief engineer. She's very impressive. I have a computer electronics guy I like for the electronics officer. And good options for the other positions."

"Sounds good. I assume Commander Griggs is our six o'clock?"

"Yes. How did you do?"

"I've got our first mate, and good candidates for the other positions."

"You *have* our first mate?"

"Yes. Do you remember Hayden Watson? He was the navigator on the Victory."

"Not really," Catie said. "I was only there for a short time."

"We'll interview him tomorrow morning, first thing. I think you'll like him. He's sharp, and a good teacher. He just finished the accelerated Academy training and thinks a cargo ship sounds like fun."

"If you like him, I'm sure he'll be okay."

"Commander Griggs, this is Commander Liz Farmer, she'll be conducting the interview with me," Catie told Commander Griggs when she joined them at 0600.

"It's an honor to meet you," Commander Griggs said as she took Liz's hand.

"Thank you, please have a seat," Liz said.

Commander Griggs looked around the room, she seemed a bit bewildered.

"Were you expecting someone else?" Liz asked.

"I was. You're pretty well known, and I don't recall an advanced degree in your background," Commander Griggs said.

"Oh, I'm just here to make sure you don't have two heads," Liz said. "Alex is going to be asking the hard questions."

"If you'll excuse me, Alex, you seem a bit young to be able to cover this material in detail," Commander Griggs said to Catie.

"I am, but I've had access to the core files on the technology for four years," Catie said.

Commander Griggs' eyes got wide, "That would make you Catie McCormack, wouldn't it?"

"Busted," Liz said.

"Yes, it would," Catie said. "I'm being forced to attend the Academy, so I'm maintaining a disguise."

Commander Griggs nodded her head, "That's smart, you don't want to be a celebrity at the Academy."

"Yeah, being Princess Catie would make it all worse," Catie said.

"You're not happy at the Academy?"

"I'm happy, but it means I'm missing out on a lot of stuff," Catie said.

"You're young, you'll have plenty of time," Commander Griggs said. "And your experience at the Academy will be with you forever."

"She's young, but she's a greedy girl," Liz said.

"Hayden, thanks for coming in early," Liz said as she met Hayden Watson at the door to their rented office.

"No problem, Commander. I'd do just about anything to get this job, coming in early doesn't seem like that much."

"I'm glad you feel that way. Let's go in and get this started," Liz said as she led Hayden through the outer office and into the one she'd used for his interview the day before. "This is Alex MacGregor, one of my partners. She'll be helping with the interview, and this is Commander Griggs, our chief engineer."

"Pleased to meet you," Hayden said as he gave Catie and Commander Griggs a small bow.

"I'm glad to meet you as well," Catie said. "Please have a seat."

"Since I interviewed you yesterday, I'll let Alex start with a few questions," Liz said. "Commander Griggs will jump in when we start asking what you know about the technical stuff."

"Sure," Hayden said, returning the smile he got from Commander Griggs.

"Before I start, do you have any questions?" Catie asked.

"Not now. I'm sure I'll have lots later."

"Okay, then tell me, what is the single most important trait you want to see in your captain?"

"Competence," Hayden replied without hesitation.

"After competence?"

"Trust. I want my captain to trust me, and I want to be able to trust them."

"Now, let's skip competence and trust, what is the most important quality in a first mate?" Catie asked.

"Empathy," Hayden replied.

"Empathy? Please explain."

"Well, the first mate is the buffer between the captain and the crew. A good captain is always demanding, so the first mate has to be able to empathize with the crew in order to see if the captain is being unreasonable, or if the crew is just griping as usual."

"You expect the captain to be unreasonable?"

"No, but they can't keep everything about the ship top of mind. So sometimes the captain asks for something that is unreasonable given the current situation. The first mate has to figure that out so he or she can work with the captain to modify the request to fit with the current situation."

"And if the captain is not being unreasonable?"

"The first mate needs to listen, tell the crewperson that all captains are Tartars, and tell them to get after it before the captain decides to space them. And if that doesn't work, the first mate needs to kick a little ass and take names until the crew figures out that they're expected to pull their weight."

◆ ◆ ◆

"*He's got my vote,*" Catie messaged Liz and Commander Griggs as they approached the end of the two-hour interview. Hayden had shown a solid understanding of the workings of a ship, good people skills, a sense of humor, and the necessary drive.

"He had mine to begin with," Liz messaged back. She had to concentrate to do it, but it only took a second. She envied the way Catie could just zip out a message using those nanites. Liz had them, but it still took concentration for her to type.

"Just give us a ping," Catie messaged to Commander Griggs.

Commander Griggs used her HUD to ping her yes vote.

"Well, Hayden, it looks like you have the job," Liz said. "Do you have time to help us interview for the rest of the officers?"

"Really, just like that?" Hayden gasped.

"Hey, we're a decisive team."

"That's for sure. And I'll certainly stay and help with the interviews. I work for you now, so I'll take it as an order."

"I like a man who can take orders," Catie said.

It took them until late Wednesday to finally finish hiring all the officers. Catie was happy to leave it to Liz, Hayden, and Commander Griggs to hire the other officers and the rest of the crew.

The wedding was a simple affair. Paul acted as best man and Natalie was the matron of honor. Captain Desjardins conducted the ceremony. The wedding was held in the first greenhouse that Blake had built at the site of Orion, their new capital. About a third of the colony showed up to witness the ceremony. Others had opted to view it on video from the comfort of one of the restaurants or bars.

Samantha wore a simple tea-length, ice-blue silk dress with a sweetheart neck and long sleeves with light blue sandals with 3-inch heels. She carried a bouquet of pink roses from the greenhouse where they were growing plants from Earth. Marc had been lazy like most men and wore the uniform that Blake had invented for the governor.

"Doesn't Sam look beautiful," Liz whispered to Catie. They were watching the ceremony from the boardroom in Delphi City with Fred, Blake, Nikola, Dr. Metra, and Kal. Linda had opted out of the party.

"She'd look more beautiful in a big, white, royal gown," Catie whispered back.

"Let it go!" Liz ordered.

Captain Desjardins conducted a very brief ceremony, it only took him five minutes to pronounce them husband and wife. Marc made a big show of kissing the bride, then everyone applauded and started popping Champagne corks. Samantha had secretly brought along an adequate supply since she'd started planning the wedding long before they left Earth.

Blake popped the Champagne they had on ice and poured a round for everyone. "Here's to the bride and groom, may they enjoy each other's company for years to come." Samantha recognized the toast with her glass of cider.

"Here, here!"

◆ ◆ ◆

"Alex, aren't you ready?" Yvette called out.

"Yes, just getting my shoes," Catie replied. "I'm wearing slippers until we get there."

"Oh, I should do the same," Yvette said as she pulled off her heels and grabbed a pair of slippers from her drawer. The slippers were so thin, that they could be folded and slipped into her purse, but were sturdy enough to walk down the sidewalk. "Ready, Alex?"

"As ready as I'll ever be," Catie replied.

"In that red dress, we might need to make sure there are some EMTs at the party. *Oh là là*," Yvette said.

They walked down to the street where they were met by their taxi, a small electric car. Delphi City had grown enough to warrant a larger taxi than a golf cart, so they'd brought in small electric cars with governors that restricted them to a maximum speed of forty kilometers per hour.

◆ ◆ ◆

"Professor Cooper, this is my roommate, Alex. Alex, Professor Cooper, his family is hosting me," Yvette introduced Catie. Yvette was referring to the fact that Professor Cooper's family was her Academy Family, a source of family living when home was too far away.

"Pleased to meet you," Catie said.

"I'm happy to meet you. I'm glad you could make it, please come on in. We've reserved the entire courtyard for the party," Professor Cooper said. All the condo buildings in Delphi City had an inner courtyard to give the residents a private area for recreation. The professor signaled to a woman standing next to the pool. She came over to join then.

She didn't wait for the professor to introduce her. "Hello, Yvette, I'm glad you could make it." Turning to Catie she held out her hand, "I'm Yolanda Cooper, the professor's wife."

"Hi, I'm Alex MacGregor, Yvette's roommate."

"Go ahead and get a drink. There are several young men here from my husband's class, and, Alex, you're already attracting attention."

"How come the professor only invited men from his class?" Catie asked.

"Because that's what Yolanda and I asked him to do," Yvette said. "I've invited four other women from our class. We don't need any more competition than that."

Catie and Yvette walked up to a group of four men who were chatting by the pool.

"Hi, guys," Yvette said. "Are you in Professor Cooper's class?"

"I am," one of the guys said. "Jerome Walsh." He extended his hand. All of the men were struggling not to stare at Catie in her hot outfit.

"I'm Yvette, and this is Alex. We're both going to Delphi Academy."

"Military women," another guy said. "Jerome, they'll have all your moves figured out before you finish your drink."

"That's Braxton," Jerome said. "I would say he's a friend, but now I'm not so sure."

"Hi," Braxton said. "What are you two studying at the Academy?"

"I'm studying program management," Yvette said. "Alex is studying aerospace engineering."

"Aerospace engineering, that's cool. You should be getting the latest on all the Delphi technology," Braxton said.

"I hope we are," Catie said.

"Do you know anything about the station that Delphi has in the asteroid belt?" Braxton asked.

"You mean Gemini Station?"

"Yes."

"A little."

"How big is it?"

"He's a nerd," Yvette whispered to Catie. "You can have him." Yvette slipped her hand inside of Jerome's arm and walked off with him toward the bar.

Catie had to hand it to Yvette, the woman really knew how to relax. They'd checked into the Four Seasons two days ago and had already had three appointments at the spa. Right now, Yvette was at the nail salon having her nails clipped nice and short. Long fingernails were unlikely to survive on one of the schooners for very long.

"Alex, you always know so much about technology here in Delphi City, don't they have some kind of lotion you can put on that will act like a glove?" Yvette asked when she came back to the room.

"What?!"

"Act like a glove, to protect our hands from the salt grime that will be on those ropes. I hate to think what working that schooner will do to my poor hands. *Très mauvais.*"

"I've never heard of anything like that," Catie said as she messaged the idea to Marcie. Dr. Metra could probably think of something. A glove that you put on like lotion sounded pretty neat.

"Oh, I am going to hate these next two weeks!"

"Hey, it won't be as bad as Guatemala."

"No, to be worse than Guatemala, they would have to kill us."

"You're such a big baby."

"Yes, and don't you forget it. I work hard to make my body beautiful. They should not work so hard to make it horrible."

"You'll survive. It's only two weeks."

"Yes, and it starts tomorrow. We must go to the spa again and get facials. Maybe they have a lotion that will protect our skin from the salt air."

"I thought salt air was good for your skin."

"Only when you wear a bikini and suntan lotion."

"You actually wear a bikini?" Catie joked.

"At least the bottoms."

3 Board Meeting – Jan 3rd

"I call this meeting to order," Marc said. "Is everyone linked in?"

"We're good here," Blake said.

"I'm in," Catie messaged. She was alone in the room at the Four Seasons. Yvette was at the spa having her last treatment.

"Okay, Nikola, you said you had something to discuss."

"Yes, as you all know, we're critically low on quantum relays. We've been skating by with all of the ones we took off the Paraxean ships after the war. But we've used most of them."

"That's not good," Catie said. "Are we going to have to cannibalize them from our Foxes?" One in ten Foxes had the quantum relay to enable continuous contact with the squadrons.

"Only if absolutely necessary. They're critical to our control of the squadrons; I don't want to go below the one-in-ten ratio," Blake said.

"Hasn't Dr. Nakahara figured out how to make them yet?" Catie asked.

"No, and he's not optimistic about solving the problem anytime soon," Marc said.

"But he has solved our problem," Nikola said. "He's come up with a quantum cable."

"A what?"

"A quantum cable, it's like an optical cable, but better," Nikola said. "He can make them up to five kilometers in length, they have zero delay, and are immune to interference. We're going to be replacing all the control lines in our spaceplanes and starships with them."

"How does that solve our problem?" Liz asked.

"Because the Paraxeans would like to have a lot of them."

"I still don't understand."

"Not our Paraxeans, the Paraxeans on Paraxea," Nikola said. "And they're willing to trade quantum relays for them."

"Oh, you have been busy," Marc said.

"You *did* ask me to solve the problem."

"It will solve our problem for now, but won't they just start making their own cables?" Liz asked.

"You can't print them, and Dr. Nakahara says that they'll be difficult to reverse engineer. So we should be able to continue to trade with the Paraxeans, exchanging cables for the relays for a few years," Nikola said. "Hopefully, Doctor Nakahara will figure out how to make the relays before the Paraxeans figure out how to make the cables."

"Do we have enough cables to do a trade?" Marc asked.

"We've been making them for a few months," Fred said. "We were planning to refit the Victory with them right away."

"Can we hold off on that?" Marc asked.

"Yes."

"Then I think we need to rearrange our first cargo mission. We need to get the relays, or we'll have to live with gaps in our satellite coverage here on Artemis. And we are marginal in our bandwidth between here and Earth."

"Okay, so we make a run to Paraxea. That delays our run to Mangkatar by six weeks or so, and pushes you guys out for the same amount of time," Liz said.

"It would, but I want you to make a loop," Marc said. "Go to Paraxea first, then come directly here. Then you can go back to Earth and do a run to Mangkatar."

"That's a long trip," Liz said.

"Not if you can get the Paraxeans to swap cargo containers on the fringe," Catie said.

"That might work," Liz said. "How much cargo are we talking about?"

"For this exchange, one cargo pod of the cables, the relays would fit in a large suitcase," Nikola said.

"Okay, I'll work with Nikola and figure out how to handle the exchange with the Paraxeans. I'll let you know the timing," Liz said.

"I want you to leave as soon as possible," Marc said.

"You're expecting us to bring colonists out?"

"Yes."

"Well, this is asking them to be ready to leave six weeks early. I guess we're set with cabins since we were expecting to ferry a bunch of Paraxean colonists."

"Hey, they're all on Delphi Station training," Samantha said. "I would think they could be ready to leave in a few days."

"And I get the joy of telling them," Liz said.

"I can send the message," Samantha said.

"Please, that might divert some of their frustration," Liz said.

"Okay. Keep us updated, Liz. Next item," Marc said. "Fred, how is production?"

"Our standard production is doing fine. Orders are solid, and profits are obscene, but I suspect you want to know about the cabin production?"

"*Yes,*" Marc said, feeling a bit exasperated.

"We're keeping up. We completed putting cabins in the last passenger pod yesterday. It's a good thing that Paraxeans and humans are about the same size since you're going to be getting their cabins," Fred said. "We've had to hire another two thousand workers to keep up, so that's another five thousand residents here on the station. Besides building cabins for the pods, we had to rush to complete a lot of the build-out in ring four."

"You mean you finished ring four?" Catie asked incredulously.

"Only about half of it, but that was enough to get everyone housed," Fred said. "We hope to have it completely built out by March."

"That sounds like good news. Hopefully we'll get more services and small businesses going on Delphi Station."

"You do know we're having a mini population explosion in Delphi City?" Fred said.

"I've heard," Marc said. "The prime minister is attributing it to the colonists."

"Yes, who would have thought that attracting colonists for Artemis would result in a big growth in our permanent population," Blake said.

"How is that happening?" Catie asked.

"It seems that about twenty percent of the people who come here to volunteer as colonists, decide to just become Delphi City residents instead," Blake explained. "And then, there are the relatives of the colonists who decide to move to Delphi City because they think it will keep them in closer contact with their family on Artemis."

"Are we able to accommodate all the extra people?" Samantha asked.

"Yes, we're well ahead in finishing out the condos we've already built. There are four more buildings going up, and we're going to add another line of quads on the south side of the city."

"Good, good. Blake, how's your recruitment and training going?" Marc asked.

"We've pushed eight hundred through the short Academy course," Blake said. "Most of them were already part of Delphi Forces, but we got about two hundred new candidates through. Of course, that left us exposed, so Catie and Liz could poach eight of our best graduates."

"You were the ones who said all of our line officers had to be Academy grads."

"But you've even poached a few engineering officers," Blake added.

"Hey, who else understands our systems, and they were right here," Catie said.

"Yeah, if we didn't need that ship of yours to be sailing by next week, I'd yank a few of them back."

Catie stuck her tongue out at Blake.

"Liz, that brings up the question, will you have sufficient time to train the new crew?"

"They're training now," Liz said. "We hired them just before Christmas, gave them two days of orientation, then had them back to training the next week. We're paying a bonus for the inconvenience."

"That's nice of you," Samantha said.

"It's all part of our expedited delivery charge," Liz said.

"How did you know you would be having an expedited cargo to deliver?"

"Fred and Nikola may have mentioned something," Liz said.

About thirty minutes later Marc moved to close the meeting. "Okay, so production and sales are good. We're growing. We're establishing trade with the Paraxeans, Catie's poaching our trained officers and crew; anything else we need to discuss?"

"I think we've covered everything."

"Good, have fun everyone. Meeting's over."

4 The Dutchman and The Princess

Catie and two hundred first- and second-class cadets stood on the dock looking at the four clipper ships. Even though they were clipper ships, only the foremast had square sails, the other three masts were set up so they could mimic square sails by going wing on wing with the two gaff sails on their mast. Catie was studying the layout of the sails when a foghorn blew to get everyone's attention.

"Your Comms have your ship and cabin assignment; get aboard your ship, stow your gear and be on deck in five minutes!" yelled the big sailor who seemed to be in charge. The previous week, each cadet had been told what to bring for gear, and what time to show up at the dock. That was it, no other hints about what to prepare for.

Catie scrambled onto the Delphi Princess. *"I wonder if Uncle Blake thought it would be funny to put me on the Princess,"* Catie thought. She saw that she was in a cabin with four bunks, meaning three roommates, *"Wonderful!"*

Once she made it back on deck, she moved over to the group that was standing around the wheel. She assumed they were there because the four sailors standing there looked like they knew what they were doing.

Cadet Colonel Miranda Cordova came up from below and walked over to the group. "What are we supposed to do next?" she asked.

"Wait," the sailor with the hat said.

Miranda rolled her eyes; she wasn't used to being told to wait.

The foghorn blasted across the dock again.

"Listen up," the sailor with the hat shouted. "The race starts now. You have two weeks to sail the course, first ship back wins." He crossed his arms and gave everyone a smug look.

"How do we sail her?" Miranda asked.

"Don't look at us. We're just here to make sure you don't sink her and that nobody gets hurt . . . too badly."

All the cadets looked at each other in shock. "We're supposed to just figure it out," someone gasped.

"Alright, who's sailed before?!" Miranda shouted.

Cadet Mayhew, a small second-class cadet, looked around and eventually raised his hand when no one else did.

"What did you sail? And how much?" Miranda demanded.

"My grandparents own a forty-six-foot Oceanis; I've been sailing since I was five."

"Anyone else?!"

"No? Then, Mayhew, you're our sailing master, get over here!" Miranda ordered. "Anyone else have some experience sailing a ship like this?"

Cadet Bradley raised his hand. "Ma'am, I've never sailed, but I've read a lot of books about sailing in the eighteenth century."

Miranda looked at Cadet Mayhew.

"How do you tell how fast the ship is sailing?" Mayhew asked.

"You toss a line over the side after you flip the thirty-second glass, then count knots until the sand runs out," Bradley replied.

"We can use him," Mayhew said.

"Okay, Bradley, you're the assistant sailing master. Anyone know how to navigate?"

Cadet Mayhew raised his hand again. Catie looked around, and since no one else was raising their hand, she raised hers.

"MacGregor, what's your experience?"

"I've navigated a yacht around the ocean," Catie said. "I learned to take sightings with a sextant to figure out our position for fun, and I'm good at math."

Cadet Mayhew nodded his head.

"MacGregor, you're our navigator. Get to the navigation cabin and start charting a course. Now, come on, some of you have to have been on a sailboat before!"

Several other cadets raised their hands.

"Okay, you, you've got the foremast, first watch; you," she yelled, pointing to another, "you've got it for second watch," Miranda continued to yell out commands as she selected each of the eight cadets, dividing them between shifts for each of the masts.

"Okay, we need a cook!"

"I can cook, I've done a lot of camping," one of the cadets offered.

"Good, you're our cook. Go to the galley and make sure we have enough food for two weeks!" In short order, Miranda had all forty-nine cadets assigned to the various jobs that she had decided they needed to fill. Everyone just assumed she would be the captain.

Miranda turned to the older sailor, "Will you guys answer direct questions?"

"Generally," he answered.

"Thanks. Mayhew, start training the crews for each mast. Take one of these guys with you and ask questions on anything you don't understand."

"Yes, ma'am."

Catie was in the navigation cabin. She had found the charts and was trying to figure out which ones she needed. There was a note that said that the race course ran from Delphi City to the Pitcairn Islands and back to Delphi City. It also noted that they were supposed to make the circuit within two weeks. Catie measured the distances on the chart. In order to sail the route in two weeks, they needed to average over ten knots or better for the entire two weeks. *"But that assumes we're sailing in a straight line, which sailing ships don't do,"* Catie thought. She checked the wind charts and plotted a course that took best advantage of the wind; it meant they were traveling farther, but she hoped that the wind would allow them to make at least twelve knots instead of ten.

Catie made her way back on deck to consult with Mayhew and Miranda about their course. She could see two of the schooners already starting to pull away from the dock.

"What do you need, MacGregor?" Miranda asked.

"I've got a few questions about navigation."

"Talk to Mayhew."

"Ma'am," the cook said, coming back on deck right behind Catie.

"Yes, Aquino, what do you want?"

"We have enough water, but there's only a few days' food," Cadet Aquino said.

"Where do we get our food from?" Miranda asked the sailor with the hat.

He smiled and pointed to the warehouse on the dock.

"Bradley, form up a team and go get our provisions, take the cook with you!"

"Catie, can you talk?" Liz messaged.

"Yes," Catie replied. She was alone in the navigation cabin.

"How are we supposed to lift all this freight up to the Dutchman? Do you realize that one of those cargo pods carries as much as most cargo ships?"

"Of course I do. You have to maximize the cargo if you're going to make any money. To answer your question, I had Ajda build a special Skylifter to take the pods into orbit. It's basically four big grav drives, four fusion reactors, one for each drive, and a cockpit," Catie said.

"So?" Liz quizzed.

"It will lift one of the cargo pods, even if it were full of iron," Catie said.

"Must be some big grav drives."

"Yeah, the biggest," Catie said.

"How much did that cost us?" Liz asked. She knew they'd already spent the four hundred million they'd started with and were now borrowing money to get their company going; of course, they were borrowing the money from Catie. Samantha had asked to invest, and Liz wondered when Catie would suggest they take her up on it.

"It didn't cost us anything."

"How's that?" Liz asked.

"Daddy had to pay for it."

"That doesn't seem fair," Liz said. "We can't be taking charity from your father."

"It's not charity. He needs a Skylifter on Artemis; it's our design, so he has to buy it from us and pay us to deliver it. We're giving him a break on it since we'll be using it to load up," Catie said.

"And the next trip?"

"The Paraxeans will need one, too. After that, we'll have enough money to pay for one of our own."

"Where do we put it?"

"It takes the place of one of the cargo pods and stays within the Dutchman's profile. You can put it in any of the pod slots."

"Clever."

"Damn that Miranda, where did she come up with the idea that everyone should have to work the sails?!" Catie thought as she struggled to pull the foresail up. She was one hundred feet above the deck with her feet balanced on a rope with her stomach lying across the crossbeam. The old sailors had conveniently removed the lines and winches that managed the canvas from the deck, forcing the cadets to climb up and claw it up into a bundle whenever they had to reef the sails.

"About time," she thought as she was finally able to tie the canvas. *"Damn, I broke another nail."* Catie worked her way along the rope until she reached the mast. She had to wait while the three cadets in front of her made their way down the rigging. *"I would wind up being on the team that has to manage the top sail."*

Catie thought about how she would get even with Miranda for her brilliant idea, but then figured that since Miranda had actually been up on that rope with her, it might be a bit petty; she'd already paid the price for her idea.

"Exhilarating, wasn't it," Miranda said as she and Catie met at the ladder that led to the crew quarters.

"More like terrifying, and cold," Catie said, rethinking her idea about getting even.

"But it does teach you to coordinate your efforts with your fellow crew. You pull too early and you're lifting the entire canvas by yourself, too late and your neighbor might kick you off the beam."

"So that's what it was. I thought we all fell into a robotic stupor and just let our bodies be controlled by the sail master."

"Like you would ever fall into a robotic stupor," Miranda said, giving Catie a big smile. "See you at breakfast."

"ADI, can you connect me to the Paraxean minister who's coordinating our trades?" Liz asked.

"Yes, Cer Liz, . . . he is on your Comm now."

"Hello, Minister Hastara," Liz said, allowing her Comm to do the translation to Paraxean.

"Hello, Cer Farmer," Minister Hastara replied.

"I would like to confirm the cargo we are delivering to you and ask if there is anything else you wish to trade," Liz said.

"Thank you. We have agreed to trade ten thousand quantum relays for ten thousand kilometers of your quantum cables," the minister said.

"That's my understanding," Liz said. "We also want to exchange the container while at your fringe, which would be 60AU from your sun; we will be traveling at 0.16 times the speed of light. Can you accommodate that?"

"Of course," the minister said. "We will have our ship there as soon as you give us the coordinates and the vector for your ship."

"Good. Now is there anything else you would like to trade?" Liz asked.

"We have been talking with Dr. Teltar, and he informs us that you have several grains and bean varieties that are very compatible with the Paraxean diet, as well as being good stock for our meat vats."

Liz pursed her lips as she thought about that, "Which ones?"

"We like your wheat, corn, and soybeans," Minister Hastara said. "We would be interested in acquiring as much as you can deliver to us."

"Our ship can carry thirty-two of those pods we sent you the spec for. Are you sure you want as much as we can carry?"

The minister laughed a bit. "Yes, we are quite sure."

"What would you have to trade for them? More quantum relays?" Liz asked.

"No, we would prefer to trade other goods. Based on the experience of our previous colony missions, one of the things that the colonists find most frustrating is how long it takes to make the larger fixtures they're used to having. By that, I mean sinks, toilets, and bathtubs, as well as the fixtures that go with them. Also, the appliances used for cooking; I understand we use similar ones. We could provide those in exchange."

"I would have to check on that," Liz said. "I actually would be surprised if that were a problem since we're providing them the cabins they travel in, so they are getting those fixtures."

"I would be surprised if you were providing enough to make a comfortable living unit," the minister said, "but by all means, check."

"What else would you have to trade?"

"We can provide electronics, copper wire, and stainless-steel sheets that they could use to manufacture other fixtures."

"Okay, let me check on what matches their needs, and I'll get back to you. Why don't we plan on talking again in twenty-four hours?"

"That works with my schedule. I look forward to talking with you again."

Liz closed the call and quickly messaged Catie.

"Catie, can we talk?"

"I'm free in twenty," Catie messaged back.

"What's up?" Catie asked when she and Liz connected again.

"The Paraxeans are asking us to ship them a bunch of grain," Liz said.

"How much?"

"They're saying as much as we can carry," Liz said.

"Wow, that's a lot of grain."

"How are we going to pay for it?"

"How much would it cost to fill all the pods we need to fill?" Catie asked.

"I calculated that it would be almost 200 million dollars," Liz gulped.

"Oh, that much," Catie said. "That should impact the grain markets; which grains?"

"Wheat, corn, and soybeans; they want as much as we can deliver," Liz said.

"Nice. ADI, we need to buy futures," Catie said.

"Yes, Cer Catie," ADI said. "I'll spread one hundred million across them."

"One hundred million," Liz gulped.

"Hey, we're playing in the big leagues now," Catie said. "If the Paraxeans want that much, we'll put a big dent in the world's stockpiles. Prices will start to go up. We'll lock in big profits for the next few deliveries."

"What do you mean by we? We don't have that kind of money."

"I'll split the profits with our company since the information came from us," Catie said.

"That's nice. When did you become such a big trader?" Liz asked.

"Artie taught me," Catie said. "He's always talking about trading in futures. I thought he was just blowing smoke until he showed me his portfolio."

"I didn't realize he had that much money."

"He doesn't have that much yet, it's his return on investment that's impressive, you can just slide the decimal place to fit your needs."

"Okay, I'm impressed. Back to how we're going to pay for the grain?" Liz said.

"I'll put five hundred million into the company," Catie said.

"Hey, it's not fair for you to have to pay."

"Don't worry, the company will pay me U.S. T-bill rate," Catie said. "We'll buy T-bills with what we don't use, but we have to charge our customers for the use of our money. I suggest we add one percent per month to the shipping bill."

"Okay, that makes it easy, and you'll make a good profit on your money. What's the price premium for the freight?"

"The crew will cost about five hundred K per week and we have to cover the amortization for the ship. I'm figuring one billion over fifteen years."

"Why one billion, I thought we only paid four hundred million?" Liz asked.

"We owned the designs, but if someone else wanted to build one, it'd be close to one billion. Especially since we got great deals on labor and material. Anyway, that's 1.2 million per week. We should figure one million for operating expenses per week; fuel, food, wear and tear on the ship."

"I thought with fusion and antimatter we didn't have to pay for fuel," Liz said.

"Hey, it might just be water, but we have to get it into space, or mine an asteroid. Nothing's free."'

"Okay. Wait, why is it just water?" Liz asked. "I thought we needed hydrogen and deuterium."

"When we load water, point zero two percent of it will be heavy water that will take care of the deuterium for the fusion reactors. We separate the water into hydrogen and oxygen, we use the oxygen for air, pull the deuterium out and save it for the fusion reactors, and save the hydrogen for use in the antimatter reactor. Excess hydrogen and CO_2 we'll use for the thrusters. That way, we are the most efficient. If we have a problem in the middle of nowhere, it'll be nice to have plenty of water."

"Okay, that's smart," Liz said. "I can figure out the cost based on that."

"Don't forget about profit."

"How much?"

"As much as you can get, but at least ten percent of the freight cost," Catie said. "Since we're actually trading the goods, we should be able to do better."

"Do you want to negotiate this deal?" Liz asked, feeling a bit overwhelmed.

"No, you're going to have to do it sometimes, might as well start now. Besides, I've had lots of time to think about all this, you've been busy. Once you're in the middle of it, it won't feel so complex."

"But I might not get as much as I should."

"Cost of learning," Catie said. "Aren't you the one who always says the painful lessons are the ones you remember best?"

"Marc, the Paraxeans are offering to trade plumbing fixtures and stuff like that," Liz said.

"Oh, that would be great, the colonists are all complaining about only having the one bathroom," Marc said. "We haven't been able to set up any manufacturing yet. Those are on our list."

"So, you're willing to buy them?" Liz asked.

"Buy them? Oh, I guess you two are in business," Marc said. "How much are you asking?"

"Cost plus twenty-five percent," Liz replied.

"Plus twenty-five percent!"

"Interstellar freight, and we have to use our money to buy the goods."

"How are you going to figure cost?"

"We'll use the equivalent cost here on Earth."

"Okay, I guess we can stand that," Marc said. "While we're on the subject, what are you going to charge for transporting colonists?"

"Since you're keeping the cabins, the cost of the cabin plus thirty percent," Liz suggested.

"What?!"

"We have to feed them and put up with them for the whole trip," Liz countered.

"I guess I should be glad that Catie is busy," Marc said. "I'll run some numbers, but I think we've got a deal."

The entire crew on the Princess cheered as they made the final turn, finally rounding Pitcairn Island. They couldn't see any of the other three schooners on the horizon and everyone was feeling pretty good. That was until someone asked Mayhew how they were doing.

"I'm not happy," Mayhew said.

"Why not? Two schooners had to turn back and get their supplies. We beat the third out of port by at least an hour."

"But the number one rule of yacht racing is to stay in sight of your competition," Mayhew said.

"Why?"

"The wind."

"Mayhew, I'm going to come over there and throttle you if you don't elaborate!" Miranda threatened.

"You always want to be sailing the same wind as your competition. If they hit a pocket of stiff breeze, you can get into the same pocket. If you are bestilled, so are they. The fact that we cannot see them makes me worried that they have found better wind. That can change the race by days, not just hours."

"Oh, you sure know how to spoil a party," Julie said.

"There's nothing we can do but sail our best," Miranda said. "We've had good winds so far, now we have to see if our navigator has selected the right course for our return leg."

"Thanks for putting it all on me," Catie muttered as she headed to the navigation shack to recheck their course.

◆ ◆ ◆

"Arrr!" Liz growled.

"May I help, Cer Liz?" ADI asked.

"Probably; I'm running the numbers on the freight, and we need to come up with some more freight to take to Paraxea, or we'll have to leave there with half the cargo pods empty. It's not like we can pay dollars for their stuff."

"And because the fixtures are so much more valuable than grain, you can't bring enough to Paraxea to pay for a full load out?" ADI asked.

"Yes, especially when you measure it by volume. We need to add some high value, low volume cargo to the Paraxean leg so we can trade for a full load of cargo for the Artemis leg."

"What have you offered them?" ADI asked.

"Nothing yet, they only expressed interest in the quantum cables and the grains."

"Have you considered offering them some of the new Comms?" ADI asked.

"That's a good idea, but how many do we have?"

"We have fifty thousand in stock," ADI said.

"Why so many?"

"Cer Kal and Cer Blake want their people to carry two. And we have been building ahead in anticipation of the colonists needing them as well."

"Are we talking about Catie's Comms?"

"Yes."

"Okay. Warn Marcie that we're taking them so she can schedule more production," Liz said. "What else?"

"The Paraxeans here on Earth are really enjoying watching Earth movies, especially the old ones. And books, perhaps you should set up a service in Paraxea to give access to digital content from Earth."

"How would we do that, use the quantum relays?"

"No, they do not have enough bandwidth to be able to afford to stream entertainment."

"I thought the quantum relays had infinite bandwidth."

"They have zero delay, but finite bandwidth. One pair can only support a data rate of 250 megabytes per second."

"Okay, I get it. So we would have to copy the database. How would we stop them from just stealing the data?"

"We have to trust them a little, but we can install a server that mirrors those here on Earth. We would bring database updates when we fly there. They would just need to have the appropriate apps on their Comms."

"Where would we host the database?" Liz asked.

"We could make a satellite with a large computer in it. Mostly it would be data storage. If you had the Paraxeans put it in orbit around Paraxea, we could set up the service."

"How much would that cost?"

"Approximately forty-two million dollars," ADI said.

Liz gulped, "Forty-two million?"

"Yes, plus you would have to pay for the licenses you need from the various Earth services."

"But wouldn't that be a pay as you go deal?"

"They would want upfront money," ADI said.

"Can you go over it with Catie to see if she's interested? She's got the money to make the deal, and she might want to form a separate company instead of bringing it under our umbrella."

"I will work on that for you," ADI said.

"Thanks."

After another day of research and two hours of negotiation, Liz finally had a balanced load for the trip. Coming back from Artemis, they would be full of the new grain Samantha was promoting and a lot of ore from the platinum metals group. Catie had decided to form a separate company for the data service, and was going to include Liz, Samantha, and Kal. She offered it to the other members of the inner board, but they turned her down.

"Mr. Morton, I'm Elizabeth Farmer. We talked earlier about my company purchasing your corn."

"Glad to meet you, Ms. Farmer. Call me John."

"Okay, John. You said you wanted to meet to discuss the price," Liz said.

"Yep, I like to meet the people I deal with," John said. "You said you'd pick it up here on my farm. I don't think you're going to get much into that there Tahoe."

"We have a cargo lifter," Liz said. "It's flying overhead and can set down whenever we reach a deal."

"Well, why don't you bring it in and then we'll talk."

"It's pretty big. About the same footprint as a football field, thirty-four by eighty yards, and it's heavy, especially when loaded."

"There's plenty of room in front of those silos. And that ground can use some compacting."

Liz had the Skylifter set itself and the cargo pod down where John told her.

"That sure is a funny looking ship," John said.

"It's a cargo pod with the ship, a Skylifter, on top of it. The pod is placed on our big ship. Then Skylifter takes a place next to it," Liz explained.

"How do you fill it up?"

"You can see the access panels here on the side. We can start at the top and fill from there, or we can work our way up. Depends on what you have for lifting the grain. It's about sixty yards to the top access."

"Them silos over yonder are full. We can pull from the bottom and fill her right up. We've got a portable conveyor system we use. How do we weigh the grain?"

"The Skylifter can weigh the pod to within ten kilos," Liz said.

"Do you mind if I test that?"

"Not at all."

The farmer pulled out his phone and made a quick call. "Jamie, you still have that feed in your truck?"

"I'm just getting ready to unload it."

"Well, don't. I want you to drive over here by the silos."

"It's your dollar," Jamie said.

"Darn right it is, now get on over here," John said. He smiled at Liz. "My nephew, he can be a bit slow at times."

Liz and John chatted about the ship while they waited for Jamie to show up. It took him five minutes to get there.

John pointed to the lower door of the cargo pod. He'd had Liz open it while they waited on Jamie. "Put a few sacks of that feed into this here thing."

"What the hell is that thing?" Jamie asked. "I was ready to turn around and call the Sheriff, but then I saw you and figured it must be okay."

"It's the cargo pod we'll be loading our grain in; that thing on top is the spaceship they'll be using to lift it up. Now get to moving that feed."

Jamie hefted a bag of feed onto his shoulder and started toward the cargo pod. "You helping?"

"No, I'm an old man, I can't afford to strain myself on minor tasks like this."

Jamie rolled his eyes, but didn't make a comment. "How many bags?"

"Four."

Jamie dropped the bag he was carrying into the pod, then he quickly shifted three more bags.

"Okay, how much does your ship say that weighs?" John asked.

"Paul, what weight are you reading?" Liz asked the Skylifter pilot.

"Ninety kilos."

"Just under two hundred pounds," Liz said.

"That's pretty good. Ask him how much it weighs now," John said as he stepped into the pod.

"Somebody just added another one hundred and ten kilos," Paul said.

"He says you weigh two hundred forty-four pounds," Liz said.

"Yep, with my boots on," John said. "You want to start filling 'er up?"

"We should agree on a price first," Liz said.

"Oh, you think so?" John said with a smile. "Okay, come on up to the house and I'll give you a cup of coffee, and we can talk turkey."

Liz followed John up to his house. He led her to the kitchen, where he poured them both a cup of coffee. He grabbed the newspaper and looked up the prices being offered for corn at the various silos and mills.

"Damn electric cars!" John said. "It's really hurting the price of corn. I put those silos in so I could hold onto some and try to catch a better price. But the price keeps going down. Chinese have been buying some, but it's not helping the price much."

"Well, we're hoping to open a new market," Liz said. "How much corn do you have in those silos?"

"More'n you're going to be able to put in that there pod."

"We have more pods."

"Oh, interesting. Well, let's talk price. Right now, corn is selling at one hundred ten dollars a ton. But I was hoping to get more, that's why I've still got it."

Liz knew that corn was actually trading at one hundred five dollars a ton at this time, but she didn't bring it up. "Well, we save you the cost of having to ship it to the railroad or the mill."

"Yep, you would at that," John said. "How much corn are you looking for?"

"We could use anywhere between five hundred and six hundred thousand tons."

"Yee howdy! That's a lot of corn. I've got about one hundred fifty thousand tons, but there are some other farmers around here that are holding some."

"The price?" Liz prompted.

"Well, if'n you're buying that much, the price will go up."

"Maybe."

"Sure it will."

"Tell you what, I'll pay you one twenty per ton," Liz said. "And if things go well, I'll be back next year to buy that much again. What do you say?"

"I say you've got a deal."

"Let's go and start loading it up," Liz said.

"Sure." John led Liz back outside. He was on his phone, calling Jamie. "Jamie, get some boys over here and set up our conveyor. We're going to be loading all our corn into that there pod."

"It won't all fit."

"I know! They'll bring another pod when that one's full. Now get to it." John paused and looked at Liz. "You know, that lifter thing of yours should be able to help my friend Harry out. He's got some corn he would be selling. But right now, he's got his new tractor stuck in a bog. We've been trying to pull it out, but it's stuck real good."

"I'm sure we wouldn't have any problem lifting it out," Liz said.

John pulled out an iPhone and called his friend. "Hey, Harry, that tractor of yours still stuck?"

"Yes, are you calling to laugh at me some more?" Harry snapped back.

"No! I'm over at my place selling my corn. They brought a cargo hauler that can lift that tractor out of that bog."

"No semi-truck is going to be strong enough to pull it out. Yours and Jake's tractors couldn't, and they're both stronger than any semi-truck."

"It's not a semi-truck, it's some kind of spaceship. Just meet us over by the bog, and we'll get your tractor out."

"A spaceship?!"

"Just be there!" John yelled into his phone. "Now, can you give me a ride in that thing? I never even seen a spaceship, much less rode in one."

"No problem," Liz said. "Paul, can you land Popeye? We've got a short errand to run." They'd named the Skylifter Popeye, since it was over-muscled like the comic character.

"Copy, I'll be landing it in just a minute. Where are we going?"

"Just about five miles to the west," John said.

◆ ◆ ◆

Harry was staring at the Skylifter when they landed next to his truck. "You weren't lying when you said it was a spaceship."

"Yep, and this thing carries a cargo box that's bigger than it is. Quite a sight to see the two connected. Now let's get that tractor of yours out of this bog."

It only took twenty minutes to hook the chains that were already secured around the tractor onto the Skylifter. Then Paul eased the Skylifter up and slowly pulled the tractor out of the bog. Once they had disconnected the tractor, he set the Skylifter back down.

"Oh, looky there, it's sinking," John said, pointing out the fact that the Skylifter had sunk in about two feet.

"Yep, this ground is useless. I've been draining it for two years, ever since my Pa left it to me," Harry said. "It still holds water. I dug a well to help drain it, but it's so boggy that I'm not sure it'll ever finish draining."

"How much does that ship weigh?" John asked.

"About twenty thousand tons," Liz answered.

"Couldn't you use it to compress that bog? It wouldn't get stuck, would it?"

"Now hold up a minute. I haven't even paid her for getting the tractor out. I can't afford to pay for that big ship to do that."

"There's no charge for getting the tractor out," Liz said. "And I'd be interested in seeing what it would do to the bog. If you're game, we'll see."

"You sure it won't get stuck?"

"Absolutely."

"Then I'm a might curious too," Harry said.

"Paul, can you work the Skylifter around that bog and see if you can compress it, so the water is easier to drain?"

"It's your ship. Who's going to clean it?" Paul asked.

"I've got a big steam cleaner I use on my tractors," John said. "We'll take care of the cleaning."

"Paul, go for it, let's see how good your piloting skills are."

The three of them leaned up against Harry's pickup while they watched Paul work his way around the bog. Within an hour, he'd compressed the ground so much that he had turned the bog into a pond. It was about a meter deep and five hundred meters on a side.

"We can compress it even more if you like," Liz said.

"We don't want to keep you," Harry said. "And I don't think having that thing just sit there will do much more."

"Oh, but it can push downward," Liz said. "The same way it pushes down to fly up, it can push up to go down."

"I don't understand none of that, but if you're willing, let's see it."

"Paul."

"I heard, I'll take care of it," Paul answered.

It only took him another thirty minutes to make the pond another half meter deep.

"Now that's nice," Harry said.

"Hey, you going to drain it, or are you going to keep it like that?" John asked.

"I'm thinking I should get some trout and release them. It'll make a nice fishing hole," Harry said.

Liz sent Marc a video of them compressing the swampy land, figuring he might want to do the same on Artemis.

Liz had Marta join her when she went to Ukraine to buy wheat. Marta was the Russian mercenary who had joined the Delphi Defense Forces after she had been injured and captured when she and her team had tried to seize Delphi City just after they had declared independence. She spoke Ukrainian as well as Russian and English.

Between Marta and ADI, they had identified the best region to shop for wheat, now Liz just needed to make a deal.

"I know you, you were here during war," Mr. Kolisnyk, the head of the local farmers said. He was pointing at Liz.

"Yes, I was here during that incident," Liz said.

"Why you call it incident, it was war," Mr. Kolisnyk said.

"Yes, it was a war," Liz agreed.

"So why you bring Russian with you? We no like Russians in Ukraine."

"Marta is a friend and she helped us during the fighting," Liz said.

"If you say, then I not spit on her."

"Please don't," Liz said. She was pretty sure Marta would gut him if he spat on her.

"Okey dokey. Now we have much wheat. So how much do you want to buy?"

"We need six or seven hundred thousand tons," Liz said.

Mr. Kolisnyk gulped, then he started to laugh. "You make joke."

"No, that's how much we need."

"Then you are Uri's best friend. We have much wheat; Uri make you special deal. Come."

Liz followed Uri Kolisnyk over to his truck. "Come ride with me to my office, your Russian friend, she can ride too."

"This is a nice truck."

"Yes, new hybrid," Uri said. "I buy so I not use much gas. Price go down, stick it to the Russians."

Liz laughed, "Do you think you're making that much of a difference?"

"Not me, all farmers changing to new fuel cells with plug-in technology, for tractors too. Now Ukraine has more oil than it needs. Good for our economy, bad for Russian economy."

"You sure hold a grudge."

"My son, he say look forward not back. But I lose friends in war, so you forgive me if I look to side and find way to stick it to Russia."

Liz spent three days in Ukraine with Uri, getting the wheat they needed. With his help, not only did they get a good price, but he coordinated with all the farmers so that a group of them would bring it to a central location, eliminating the need to move a partially filled pod.

But when it came to soybeans, it was a different story. Since it was before the harvest in the southern hemisphere and well after it in the northern hemisphere, there were hardly any soybeans to be found.

"Catie, I'm going nuts trying to find enough soybeans. We're having to ferry a cargo pod all over the country and get a little here, a little there," Liz said.

"They did say as much as we could get, just get what you can and make up the difference with corn," Catie said.

Three days later, the Dutchman was ready to head out to Paraxea.

"Sail ho!"

"Where away?!" Miranda demanded.

"Off the starboard bow!" the lookout replied.

"Mayhew, what do you think?"

"We're on opposing tacks, heading toward the same patch of water," Mayhew said.

"And?"

"I don't know. We're still twenty miles from the city, it'll come down to the wind."

"Then we had better find the best wind!"

"Sally has the best eyesight," Mayhew said. "Send her up, tell her we need to know where the dark patches of water are."

"Sally!"

They had just tacked away from the other schooner when Catie came up on deck.

"So we have a real competition now," Catie said to Miranda and Mayhew.

"Yes," Mayhew said. "We sent Sally up to look for better wind."

"We're only about fifteen miles from Delphi City, will the wind make that much difference?" Catie asked.

"It will make all the difference," Mayhew said. "If we only knew which direction it was blowing over by the city."

"How would that help?"

"We can set up our tacks so that we have the best wind and the longest reach to the city. We'll be screwed if we have to tack an extra time to make it into port."

"Oh, then tell Sally to look for an Oryx. They always land into the wind if they can."

"But that's not always true," Miranda said.

"Sure, they avoid flying over the city, but if we get the angle of their landings, we can figure out the wind direction, or at least narrow down the range," Catie said.

"Sally! Give us the direction of the next Oryx that's heading into Delphi City!"

"Aye-aye!"

◆ ◆ ◆

It was ten minutes before Sally spotted an Oryx lined up for a landing. She called down the direction.

Catie sketched out a map, "See, here's the city. The airport rotates around this island that's out about a kilometer. So, if it's oriented like this, that means the plane is landing directly into the wind. There's plenty of room to adjust for the wind at this angle, so it must be head on."

"Are you sure?" Mayhew asked. "That's twenty degrees off of the normal wind direction."

"Absolutely," Catie said.

"Then that will give us an advantage; if the other schooner doesn't know about the wind change, they'll come in on the wrong tack."

"Keep your fingers crossed and set us up," Miranda ordered.

"Yes, ma'am."

◆ ◆ ◆

The Delphi Princess had already established herself in the best position before the other schooner figured out that the wind by Delphi City was shifted from normal. The Princess was beating up toward the city's pier on a straight line, and they would be able to cross the finish line without tacking.

"Yay!" the cry went up as everyone realized they had the other schooner beat.

"Sail ho!" Sally yelled.

"Where away?"

"At the dock!"

"Shit, someone beat us back," Mayhew cursed.

"Keep your wits about you! All we can do now is keep going," Miranda yelled. "We're racing that schooner over there, nothing we can do about the one in port already."

Miranda went about the ship keeping everyone focused on the task at hand. The crew was depressed, but with her encouragement they refocused on their immediate competition and rallied.

"Alright!" Miranda exclaimed as they crossed the finish line. "I'm proud of all of you. Now, let's bring the Princess into port like the proud lady she is."

"How did that ship beat us back?" Catie messaged ADI.

"It circled Oeno Island, instead of Duice," ADI said.

"What? You had to go around all four islands!" Catie said.

"They thought Oeno was Duice, so they thought they had made it around all four. The navigator was confused."

"So they're disqualified?"

"I believe so," ADI said.

"Who was the navigator?"

"Cadet Jamison."

5 Back to School

"Land, I thought we'd never make it back," Julie yelled as she knelt down and kissed the dock.

"Cadet Delacroix, mind your decorum," Miranda hissed.

"Sorry, ma'am. Kind of forgot about the Academy and all that."

"It's okay, I'm pretty happy to be off that ship and onto something more solid, even if it is floating."

Commandant Lewis was waiting to greet the Princess and her crew.

"Congratulations," Commandant Lewis said as Miranda walked up and saluted her.

"Thank you, ma'am. We're happy to be back, just wish we could have won," Miranda said. "But we did our best. I had a great crew."

"Oh, but you did win," Commandant Lewis said.

"How?" Miranda asked, pointing to the other schooner.

"They messed up their navigation and cut the course short."

"Did you hear that! We won!" Miranda yelled.

"Cadet, mind your decorum," Commandant Lewis whispered.

"Sorry, ma'am."

"You have two days to celebrate before classes start. Have fun."

"Thank you, ma'am."

"Yvette, what ship were you on?" Catie asked when they finally met up in their dorm room.

"The first one back," Yvette said.

"Oh, I'm so sorry, what happened?"

"That idiot Jamison screwed up the navigation. Several of us tried to tell him and the captain that he was wrong, but, No! they couldn't be wrong. And because they both went to the Citadel, they wouldn't listen to anyone else."

"You're lucky that they didn't make you go back and actually circle the Pitcairn Islands."

"Oh, gawd, don't say such a thing, someone might hear you and think it's a good idea. It was bad enough having to spend two weeks on the schooner."

"But you survived."

"Yes, after breaking four fingernails, getting a rash on my *derrière*, and ruining my hands."

"What did Jamison say afterward?"

"Nothing, but most of the guys have started calling him Hasty Pudding."

"Hasty Pudding?"

"A euphemism for a guy who always finishes early," Yvette said with a wink.

"Oh, I'm sure he loves that."

"Definitely. And now, I've heard he's saying something about female navigators and suggesting that you cheated."

"How could he say that?! There was another schooner that we just barely beat past the finish line."

"It doesn't have to be true for him to say it. He's just trying to distract from his failure."

"He is such an ass!"

"Hey guys," Catie said as she joined Yvette and Joanie for lunch. The discipline at the Academy was a lot more relaxed this semester so it was possible to have lunch off-campus. They were meeting at Giorgio's for pizza.

"Hey, Alex," Joanie said. "I've hardly seen you since Guatemala."

"I know. Everyone has been so busy. I'm glad they're finally letting us off-campus. What have you two been talking about?" Catie asked.

"We're comparing notes on roommates," Yvette said.

"Oh, please!"

"Do you know that after ten minutes, I know more about Joanie and her family than I know about you and yours," Yvette scolded.

"That's because Joanie is a blabbermouth, and my life is boring," Catie said.

"Yvette just told me you went to a New Year's Eve party and met a guy."

"There were lots of guys at the party," Catie said.

"But only one of them kissed you goodbye."

"Apparently, Yvette is also a blabbermouth."

"What would you ladies like to have today?" Giorgio asked as he handed Catie a menu.

"I'm going to have the Hawaiian pizza and a glass of your house lager," Catie said, handing the menu back.

"And you ladies?"

"We're going to share a pepperoni pizza and I'll have a glass of the lager as well," Joanie said.

"A glass of the Pinot Noir," Yvette said.

"Coming right up."

"So, have you gone out with him again?" Joanie asked.

"When could I? We were out on those schooners for the first two weeks of the year," Catie said.

"Yeah, I'm still washing the salt out of my hair," Yvette said.

"We've been back two and a half weeks," Joanie said. "What about tonight?"

"He's out at the asteroid belt," Catie said.

"What?"

"His class is doing a design project on a new smelter design that will separate the platinum metals from each other while they're being smelted. They're out there working on it."

"Only Alex would pick up a guy who was leaving the planet," Yvette said.

"I didn't pick him up."

"Keep telling yourself that. When is he supposed to be back?" Yvette asked.

"They're supposed to be back in February."

"That's only three or four more weeks," Joanie said. "Maybe we can double date."

"He probably won't even call me," Catie said.

Yvette was nodding her head and rolling her eyes, letting Joanie know that Catie would probably be getting a call.

"Alex, did you get your results from the combat strategy test?" Yvette asked.

"Yes," Catie said.

"Well!"

"I made the space fleet ops class," Catie said. "How about you?"

"I didn't make it; but Miranda did," Yvette said.

"Miranda?" Joanie asked.

"Miranda Cordova."

"You mean *Cadet Colonel* Miranda Cordova?"

"Yes."

"How do you know she made it?" Joanie asked.

"She told me," Yvette said.

"You're friends with her?"

"Yes, we were in the same class. Alex tutored us some. Miranda got an A, and she says it was because of Alex's help."

"You tutored Miranda. On *what*?" Joanie asked incredulously.

"Basic Structure of Starships," Catie said. "I studied up on it when I was at UCSD."

"You are full of surprises. So, you're going to be in the same class as Miranda."

"I don't know. I think there are going to be three different classes," Catie said. "They didn't say how they were structuring it. There were over three hundred in the first two weeks of the lecture."

"What?!"

"Let me explain," Yvette said. "Alex skips over too much. The lecture was for all the First- and Second-Class Cadets as well as one hundred line-officers. Only the ones who got a good grade on the combat test last semester and scored well on the fleet strategy test that we just took, get to take the space fleet ops class, the rest of us will be taking a more basic class."

"Oh."

"Here are your drinks," a waitress said as she set them on the table. "Your pizzas should be ready in five minutes."

"Did Baker make it into the advanced class?" Joanie asked. Cadet Major Baker had been Joanie's and Catie's squadron commander during basic training.

"I don't know, but I would think so," Catie said.

"The most important thing is that there will be older officers from the active fleet in the class," Yvette said. "And our friend Alex will need to have them over to study."

"Oh, and I will probably need you to help me with one of my classes as well," Joanie said. "I'll have to come to your dorm room so you can help me study."

"But of course. Now, Chérie," Yvette put her hand on Catie's shoulder, "please, only the cute ones."

◆ ◆ ◆

"First Mate, are we ready to jump?" Liz asked. They had finally crawled out of Sol's gravity well and were now at the fringe. It had taken just under two weeks. This would be the first jump with the ship fully loaded, and Liz wondered if the extra mass would make a difference. *"Well, the Sakira was really loaded, and she made it,"* Liz thought.

"Yes, Captain, jump is laid in, waiting for your order," First Mate, Hayden Watson, replied.

Liz checked her board; engineering and navigation showed green lights; they were ready.

"Then engage," Liz ordered.

The stars went out, then winked back in. The transition took longer than Liz remembered from her experience on the Roebuck. *"Well, this is a bigger ship,"* she thought as she blew out a sigh of relief.

"The next jump is a small one," Hayden said. "We can make it now if you like."

"Are we ready to jump?" Liz asked.

"Yes, Captain."

Liz checked her board, again it showed green for engineering and navigation. "Then launch probe," Liz ordered.

"The probe shows clear space on the other side of the wormhole," the sensor operator reported.

"Then, Hayden, take us through."

"Pilot, increase speed by ten MPS," Hayden ordered.

"Ten MPS, aye."

"Wormhole is closing," the sensor operator reported.

"Eight-hour recharge," Hayden informed Liz.

"Then give us some gravity, Cer Watson," Liz ordered. "I'll be in engineering."

Liz messaged Engineer Chief Griggs that she would meet her in the engine room, then she made her way off the bridge and took the elevator down to it.

"Hello, Captain," Arlean Griggs said as Liz made her way into the engine room.

"Hey, call me Liz. How did the engines do?" Liz asked.

"If you call me Arlean."

"Sure."

"The engines groaned a bit, but that's to be expected," Arlean said. "I was a bit surprised that we had enough in the capacitors to do a second jump."

"Me, too. How did they handle the acceleration profile?"

"Not bad. We could have done a bit more, but then we wouldn't have been able to keep the capacitors charged. And I'm sure the children wouldn't have liked it. The 1.25Gs wasn't too hard on them. Probably got everyone into a little better shape."

"I'm sure it did. It definitely didn't stop them from complaining about it," Liz said. "I have to have lunch with a different group of colonists a few times a week. Their constant complaining does get old."

"Well, it is a bit boring being stuck inside a ship. At 1.25Gs, you're not inclined to do much, and you're not really set up for entertainment."

"Yeah, we should have added a few comics and music acts for the bars, maybe a magic show for the kids. Set ourselves up more like a cruise ship."

"That would have been expensive," Arlean said.

"Maybe, but I bet Marc would have paid."

"Come into my office, and we'll have a drink to celebrate the first jumps."

When they got to Arlean's office, she grabbed a bottle of scotch from her desk drawer and poured each of them a glass.

"Scotch, you're going to fit in just fine with the MacKenzie crowd. The McCormacks pretty much keep Glenlivet in business," Liz said.

"Oh, I didn't know. Here's to our first loaded jumps," Arlean offered up the toast.

"Hear, hear."

"Liz, tell me what you thought of the first outbound trip for the Dutchman?"

"It wasn't too bad. I was busy most of the time. Amazing how much paperwork there is."

"Paperwork. Why do we still use that term when it's all e-documents?"

"We still say hang up the phone instead of close the call," Liz said.

"But back to my questions: how is your significant other going to deal with you being out in space for six to eight weeks every couple of months?"

"I don't have a significant other," Liz said. "So nobody complains. Well, except for Catie."

61

"Don't you date?"

"Well I swore off men for a while. Recently, I've been seeing an ad executive so you know how that is. Between his road trips and my cargo runs, we don't see each other much. It's just as well since I haven't figured out what I want."

"What do you mean?"

"Well, if these Paraxean treatments do what we think they will, I've got well over one hundred years left, maybe two hundred," Liz said. "I'm not sure I want to spend that with one person."

"Hmm, I love my husband, but I'm not sure I'm interested in another hundred years with him. What do the Paraxeans do?"

"That's interesting. Apparently, some of them don't bother to extend their lives, and a lot of them can't afford it. Dr. Metra says Paraxean youths are just like human ones, they have a hard time imagining being over thirty. Then when they get there, they get bored and figure why bother. Others, like Dr. Metra, have been around for hundreds of years."

"Hundreds?!"

"Well, that's because they go into stasis when they do interstellar travel. Or at least they used to. So she's outlived a few husbands and is still only about ninety years old."

"Children?"

"Yes, she's got two sets, about eighty years apart."

"Interesting. I guess with long lives, we might wind up staying married just long enough to get the children raised," Arlean said. "Then, we might just decide to separate and do something different, become a colonist."

"Or a starship engineer," Liz said, raising her glass to Arlean.

Arlean laughed. "I'm not doing this to get away from the family. But I didn't think about multi-legged voyages. You could easily have a trip that takes eighteen to thirty weeks."

"Yes, we didn't think about multi-legged voyages either. We'll have to find another engineer so you can do every other trip," Liz said. "I'm glad we're doing a flyby cargo exchange with Paraxea."

"Yes, not having to go into their system is saving us four weeks, but I don't think they'll want to do that very often."

"Probably not. They must really want those quantum cables to agree to the extra hassle," Liz said.

Catie entered the simulation room. This would be her first combat simulation for the strategy class. She would be acting as the commander of a convoy. She was a bit nervous, there would be a lot of moving pieces to keep track of.

She moved to her assigned simulation table and began to set up the simulation. There were six tables in the room, which allowed the instructor to observe each student. There was another room with six identical tables, which allowed the simulation to be carried out between the two rooms.

Captain Clark got everyone's attention; he'd been their instructor for the past week. "Set up your convoy," he ordered. "You've had a day to analyze your convoy and weapons."

Catie set her two carriers up forward with the four cargo ships behind them. Behind the cargo ships, she placed her two frigates. She put out the standard fighter pickets to provide early warning of any attacking force. She added another set of pickets, one at 45 degrees above their vector and another at 45 degrees below. She set her Comm up to manage the display via voice commands; she didn't want to use her nanites since Captain Clark would be expecting to hear her talking.

"Myrtle, verify all settings," Catie ordered her Comm. She'd named it Myrtle the Turtle when she first got it, but almost never talked to it preferring to communicate to ADI who was always listening to her Comm.

"Do you mind if I play?" ADI asked.

"What are you doing?!" Catie messaged back.

"I like these one-on-one simulations. They're very interesting," ADI said.

"You can't just watch?"

"It's more fun to be involved. Can't I just be Myrtle for you?"

"Okay. You're so spoiled."

"I like it that way," ADI said.

"The simulation is going to run at one hundred times speed. We don't want to be here all week," Captain Clark announced. "It will slow down to 10X when you're in sensor range, and four X during any engagements."

The simulation table provided Catie a three-D view of the space around her convoy. She quickly set up regions in the display to show her sensors, the position and speed of any fighter squadrons she sent out, the position of any missiles, and positions of any mines. The missiles were designed to operate either as a missile or a mine, so that simplified the logistics of arming the fighters.

Captain Clark paused at her table and observed all of her preparations. After a few minutes, he moved on to another table.

Ten minutes later, ADI announced, "Contact!" The simulation switched to 10X speed.

"Where?"

"Thirty thousand kilometers off our starboard. They're approaching at sixty kilometers per second, accelerating with a 10G stutter profile," ADI announced.

"What's their attitude?"

"They're aligned with our forward vector."

"Omega Squadron, drop missiles, use your fighters to give them a vertical velocity of 30 kps, do not engage their engines. Alfa Squadron, same maneuver but with opposite vector," Catie ordered. The two squadrons of fighters that were out toward the enemy but up 45 degrees accelerated directly toward the enemy flight path, dropped their missiles, then accelerated back away. This left the missiles coasting along, coming in from above and below the enemy's horizon.

"Give me five squadrons to match the enemy fighters. I want them to accelerate at 8Gs. Go below the horizon for five minutes, then accelerate for point Charlie," Catie ordered. She marked the point where she expected the two squadrons to intersect.

"Aye-aye," ADI answered as she sent fighters out from the two carriers. Soon forty fighters were racing toward the enemy formation. "So you are planning to have your coasting missiles intersect their fighters five minutes before our fighters arrive?"

"Exactly."

"But our fighters will be going slower than theirs when they engage."

"It's relative velocity, so it doesn't matter."

"You don't think they'll adjust their vector to take our fighters head-on?" ADI asked.

"No, their target is the convoy, the fighters are just a distraction to them."

Six minutes later, the simulation alerted Catie that it had switched to 4X speed as the engagement approached.

Catie watched as the two icons showing her the positions of her silent missiles approached the enemy fighters. They were almost on top of the fighter location when she ordered, "Weapons, take the missiles live!"

The enemy fighter formation was decimated as it was hit from the top and bottom by the now active missiles. Within seconds, the screen showed only twenty enemy fighters still active while eighty were marked as burning hulks.

Now the enemy's velocity was against them as they tried to slow and turn back toward their fleet. Catie's fighters accelerated and tore into them. Only five enemy fighters escaped.

"Impressive," Captain Clark said. "You should give Jason a call. He thinks you're mad at him."

"Wha . . ."

"Female, right height and weight, three-dimensional thinker, it's not hard to guess who you really are," Captain Clark whispered. "Exceptional job, MacGregor!"

"Busted," ADI messaged.

◆ ◆ ◆

"Hi, Jason, I saw your father the other day, and it reminded me that we haven't talked for quite some time," Catie said.

"Hey, Catie. Yeah, it's been a while. I was wondering if I'd pissed you off somehow."

"What would make you think that?"

"I don't know, I bailed on your mission to build the Gemini station."

"You didn't bail, Uncle Blake pulled you," Catie said. "He pulled Kasper as well."

"But then you guys didn't take me on the Roebuck."

"Uncle Blake and Liz made that call. I think it had to do with balancing out the experience they had here at Delphi City while we were away."

"Anyway, I just wondered."

"Well, I'm not mad at you. How are you and Annie doing?"

"We're doing fine. Still dating, if you can believe it. She's in college now, going to Delphi University."

"How does she like it?"

"She loves it. She likes that they let her do a lot of the classes virtually. She just has to go in for the tough ones. And they have a bunch of study groups that she can go to."

"Why does she care about taking classes virtually, it's not like Delphi University is very far from her condo?"

"It still saves her a lot of time, and she's at home between classes, so it's easier to get things done."

"That sounds pretty cool. What are you doing?"

"I'm taking classes too. I'm hoping I'll get accepted into the Academy as a junior, instead of having to start at the beginning," Jason said.

"I'm sure you will, you've already got two years of service. That should count for something."

"What about you?"

"Taking classes, working on projects. I'm sure you've heard that Liz and I started a shipping company."

"Everyone has heard that. We're all jealous."

"Well, you should talk to Liz. She's been complaining about all the work she's been doing to buy the cargo."

"I'll bet, but how come you've dropped out of sight?"

"I've just been busy."

"I'm betting you're at the Academy in disguise."

"What would give you that idea?"

"It just makes sense. Otherwise, I'd be seeing you around. There's no way you gave up flying for anything less than the Academy."

"Well, I wouldn't recommend spreading that conjecture around. Uncle Blake would get really mad."

"Don't worry, mum's the word, *Cadet*."

"First Mate, are we ready to jump?"

"Aye-aye, Captain. Jump is laid in, engineering and navigation are green," First Mate Hayden Wilson replied.

"Send the probe through."

"Probe shows clear space," the second mate reported from his station on the sensors.

"Then take us through," Liz ordered.

The Dutchman moved through its wormhole, emerging in Paraxea's system. There was a large cargo ship two thousand kilometers off their port side. It hailed them immediately.

"Dutchman, this is Parmira One, welcome to Paraxea Prime. I am Captain Talgor. Do you require assistance? Over."

"Open the channel," Liz ordered. "This is Captain Farmer. We are happy to be here. It will take a few moments for us to release your cargo pods, then we will be happy to accept assistance in attaching the new ones. Please hold steady while we match course and speed. Over."

"Please let us know when we should approach. Over" Captain Talgor said.

"Copy," Liz replied. "Helm, match their course and speed."

"Matching course and speed," Helm replied. "We will be matched in ten minutes."

"Excellent."

Ten minutes later, Helm announced, "Course and speed matched."

"Release the upper pods," Liz ordered. Liz had placed all the cabin pods in the front of the Dutchman and the cargo pods behind them. That allowed the colonists and crew easier access between the various occupied spaces.

"Upper pods released."

"Helm, give us 0.1G akeel for ten seconds."

"0.1G akeel . . . 0G," Helm responded.

"Pods are clear," the sensor operator announced.

"Helm, move us to starboard of the pods, one kilometer, and rematch course and speed," Liz ordered.

"Aye, one kilometer to starboard, rematch course and speed."

A moment later, Helm reported they had reached their new position.

"Release the lower pods," Liz ordered.

"Lower pods released."

"0.1G atop for thirty seconds," Liz ordered.

"0.1G atop . . . 0G," Helm responded.

"Pods are clear," the sensor operator announced.

"Rematch course and speed."

"Aye, rematch course and speed."

"Captain Talgor, your pods are free. We should be matched to your course in a moment; would you join me in our shuttle bay?" Liz requested.

"We'll be right over with your relays," Captain Talgor replied.

◆ ◆ ◆

Once the shuttle bay had recompressed, Liz met Captain Talgor at the hatch to his shuttle. She had sent three Lynxes out to oversee the pod movements and provide protection if necessary, leaving plenty of room for Captain Talgor's shuttle.

"Welcome aboard the Dutchman," Liz said as she bowed to Captain Talgor.

Captain Talgor floated to the deck, using the magnetic couplings in his boots to firmly attach himself to the deck. "This is an interesting ship. I was trying to imagine what it would look like from the containers you had us make."

"Thank you, my partner designed it. It was the most efficient means she could come up with to move such large quantities of cargo."

"It does seem efficient. And your unloading process is quite impressive. I'm curious to see how you load the new pods."

"We will just use some thruster modules. They'll attach to the cargo pods and steer them to their place, then the crew will lock them down."

"What do you do when you have to bring them up from the surface?"

"We have a special ship to do that. It is capable of dropping them to the surface of a planet or lifting them from the surface," Liz said. "It can do two to three pods per day. Now, if you'll follow me through the airlock, we can complete our exchange."

"Certainly," Captain Talgor said as he followed Liz through the airlock.

Liz led him to the conference room right next to the flight bay. He handed her the package he was carrying. Liz opened it to reveal the quantum relays. She selected a few pairs randomly and put them in the tester she'd placed on the table earlier.

"They all test out," ADI confirmed as Liz cycled through the pairs she had selected.

"Thank you, ADI," Liz said. "Captain, we'll push the satellite out of our cargo bay. Once you put it into orbit, your people will be able to start viewing the entertainment files. It has registered your credit for the money we still owe you."

"I am looking forward to watching a few of the programs. Governor Paratar has told me quite a bit about your planet. I hope you plan on making more trips out here."

"I'm sure we will," Liz said. "Will you be wanting more grain?"

"Possibly. But we are interested in these solar panels that Governor Paratar has told me about. They sound very efficient, and they would help to alleviate our overcrowding."

"You're overcrowded?"

"Yes. As our standard of living has increased, it has also increased the power consumption that people deem necessary to maintain that standard. That has led to the concentration of people close to the power plants. Distribution of power is very expensive. Those solar panels would allow people to live farther from the power stations without having to give up their standard of living."

"Don't you have solar panels?"

"Yes, but they are only about thirty percent efficient. That makes them cost-prohibitive. We have better uses for the resources."

"We could deliver some on our next trip," Liz said. "We'd need to settle on a price."

"We understand. It would be better if we could manufacture them ourselves. Of course, Governor Paratar did not provide the design or manufacturing process. I wonder if you would be willing to license the process?"

"ADI, is Marc available?" Liz asked.

"Hello, Liz. Hello Captain Talgor," Marc said as he joined them on their Comms. The captain and Liz had been using their Comms to communicate so that they would provide the translations.

"Hello, Your Excellency," the captain said.

"Marc is fine," Marc said. "Now, how can I help?"

"Captain Talgor has inquired about licensing the technology for the solar panels so that they could manufacture them here," Liz explained.

"We could do that," Marc said. "But how would we be able to track how many you made?"

"Captain," ADI interjected, "the main DI here could be instructed to track them. It would then provide a reliable count."

"Okay, that works for me. And how would you pay for them?"

"We would provide credit for the ones we manufacture, which you could use to purchase trade goods on your next mission," Captain Talgor said. "Similar to the credit we have with Cer Liz. You would just need to tell us how much to pay for each unit."

"I have been discussing with Governor Paratar about setting up a Galactic Currency so that we can manage trades like this," Marc said. "We've agreed to call it an "aurora" and have set its value at one gram of platinum."

"You would pick platinum since you've got such nice reserves," Liz said. *"Didn't you just make yourself the richest man in the galaxy?"* she messaged.

"You have a ready source of platinum?" Captain Talgor asked.

"We do, as well as the other platinum metals," Marc said.

"We would be very interested in acquiring more of those metals. We've exhausted most of our supply and have to rely extensively on recycling to maintain our manufacturing capability."

"You don't just go out and mine your asteroids?" Marc asked.

"Of course we do. But there are a finite number of them, and we have consumed the richest ones. It is very expensive to mine the ones with marginal deposits."

"Well, we certainly can export some of the metals," Marc said. "I'll work with Liz to set up a time when she can deliver some to you."

"That would be a great help to us," Captain Talgor said as he rubbed his hands together, which to Marc indicated that the captain would be raking in quite a profit on the exchange. "Now, about licensing the solar panels."

"We are charging Governor Paratar two auroras for each panel. They would be for internal consumption only. We would extend the same license deal to you," Marc said.

The captain closed his eyes as he did some mental arithmetic. "That is acceptable. What about the polyglass and polysteel processes?"

"One hundred auroras for every cubic meter of polyglass. We would prefer to license the polysteel process with a one-time fee."

"That would be excellent, what would that fee be?" Captain Talgor asked.

"One hundred million auroras," Marc said.

The captain gulped. "Would it be possible to pay it over time?" he asked.

"Yes, we would accept a five-year payout."

"Year?"

"A galactic standard year. Your DI will have the details, but it is about as long as your year, the time it takes Paraxea to travel around Paraxea Prime."

"That is acceptable. Should I work out the details with Cer Liz?"

"No, I'll have our lawyer call you and work out the details of the contract as well as cover issues related to interstellar trade," Marc said.

"Excellent. This has been a very beneficial conversation," Captain Talgor said.

"You mean profitable," Liz said.

"That too," the captain conceded.

It took the rest of the day to exchange the cargo pods and prepare the Dutchman for its jump out of Paraxea's system.

"How are things going?" Marc asked Tim Garity, his assistant. Garity was responsible for coordinating all the work in Orion City.

"We're doing okay, but we're not getting enough diesel to run the digger and the tractors."

"Are you serious?"

"Yes."

"What are you doing about it?"

"You mean, besides yelling at Natalia?"

"Yes, and let me tell you, yelling at Natalia could be hazardous to your health," Marc said.

"Yeah, I know that. If she doesn't kick your ass, that husband of hers will bury it."

Marc laughed. "As if she needs Paul to help her deal with loudmouths."

"Yeah, I know. Anyway, we've added extra batteries to the tractors and that digger. That way we can plug them in overnight, that saves us quite a bit of fuel. But if we don't start getting more, we're going to either stop digging or abandon some of that grain you've planted. Those tractors really drink the diesel."

"Okay, I'll see what I can do."

"Natalia, how's it going?" Marc asked as he met Natalia at the diesel panels. The panels were filled with algae and were arrayed like solar collectors. The algae produced the diesel that they were using to fuel their equipment.

"Are you here to complain about the diesel production?" Natalia asked.

"I'm here to understand what our options are," Marc said. "I know better than to complain."

"Good!"

"So what's our problem?"

"I've made some adjustments that I think will improve production by about ten percent, but nothing like the forty percent that Garity is asking for."

"Ten is better than zero. What can I do?"

"We just don't have enough nutrients for them."

"Not enough nutrients?"

"Not sewage coming in."

"You're not serious. We don't have enough waste to produce the fuel we need?"

"That's exactly it. I've tuned the system so that it aerates the tank more often and circulates the water through the collectors faster. But there's just only so much you can do without more input."

"So you're saying we need to ask everyone to eat more?"

"That would help. I blame the problem on all the men and boys that take a whiz in the field or behind the barn instead of using the facilities."

Marc burst out laughing. He laughed so hard that he cried.

"It wasn't that funny," Natalia said.

"No, but it does put the problem in perspective," Marc said. "I'll talk to Doctor Mallock and see if he can put together a small refinery to convert some of our oil into diesel until our population expands enough to supply your needs. We'll also look at putting in some algae panels to produce diesel, it can't hurt and they capture most of their own fertilizer from the air."

"Doctor Mallock, is he Paraxean?"

"No, he's human, just has a weird name."

"Doctor Mallock, do you have some time?" Marc asked.

"Of course, Governor," Dr. Mallock said. "What can I do for you?"

"Our diesel production isn't keeping up with demand. I was wondering if you could put together a small refinery to produce diesel from the petroleum we're using for the polysteel?"

"What's the problem with the algae converters?"

"Not enough nutrients," Marc said.

"You don't want to just pump fertilizer through them?"

"We don't have fertilizer."

"How are you growing plants?"

"We have a clover derivative that puts nitrogen into the soil. We plant it in the field along with the crops."

"Oh, I remember something about that. Anyway, how much diesel do you need?"

"Five thousand gallons per day," Marc said.

"That much?"

"Yes, is that too much?"

"No, but it will take a little bigger refinery than I was thinking about. Maybe I'll just make two of them."

"How long?"

"What's my priority?"

"Pretty high."

"Then three weeks," Doctor Mallock said.

6 Board Meeting – Feb 7th

"I believe everyone's here," Marc said, checking his Comm to verify.

"We're all here, the question is are we all awake," Blake said. "It's pretty late for the admiral."

"I know, trying to sync up all these time zones is problematic," Marc said.

"It is. And just what time zone are you in?" Blake asked.

"We're in Orion Mean Time," Marc said with a laugh. "But that brings up our first agenda item, Galactic Standards. I call this meeting to order."

"Galactic Standards?"

"We need to set some frame of reference as we deal with the various colonies and worlds. We just defined the aurora as the value of one gram of platinum. I'd like to set some standards for time and schedules."

"You're just like Napoleon and his metric systems," Blake said.

"Uncle Blake, he did make some lasting standards."

"Okay, tell us," Blake said, giving Catie a dirty look.

"We are going to set the Galactic Second to be the same as Earth's cesium definition. We'll also keep the definition of minute and hour consistent with Earth. However, a Galactic Day will be twenty-five hours and a Galactic Year will be four hundred days."

"Hey!" Blake yelped.

"Artemis has a 26.1-hour day and a 330-day year; Mangkatar has a 27.3-hour day and a 402-day year; Paraxea has a 23.2-hour day and a 410-day year, so we thought we'd pick round numbers that divide easily into one hundred," Marc said. "Local time will still be measured locally, but this allows everyone to make one transformation to the standard from which everyone else only has to do one transformation back to their local time."

"Hey, at least we don't have to learn new constants for gravity and mass," Catie said.

"Umm," Marc interjected. "We didn't use Earth Standard for gravity. One gravity is ten meters per second squared. We did keep Earth's definition of a meter and a kilogram, but that still means a Galactic Newton isn't the same as an Earth Newton."

"It's a good thing we have our Comms to do all those conversions," Liz said.

"Okay, okay, enough of the boring Galactic politics," Blake said. "Let's get on with the meeting."

"Fred, I hear you've scheduled a press conference to announce our new airline," Marc said.

"Yes, it's noon on Friday, Earth Standard Time," Fred said. "We have eight jets ready to start flying. Crews are trained and ready."

"Excellent. I wish you the best of luck at the press conference," Marc said.

"Daddy, you could do the press conference remotely," Catie suggested with a big smile.

"Fortunately, we're keeping quantum relays a secret, so that is not actually possible," Marc replied. "Liz, where are you?"

"We're just over a week out," Liz said. "The Dutchman is scheduled to make orbit of Artemis by February 16th."

"We look forward to having you over for dinner and showing you around," Samantha said.

"I'll be happy to have some of your cooking."

"Fred, how is the company doing?" Marc asked, cutting off any further planning between Liz and Samantha.

"It's doing well. We got some great positive press after Liz bought all that grain. Farmers are actually upbeat for once."

"How come you got all the good press?" Catie asked. "We're the ones buying the grain."

"Yes, but MacKenzies is the one that opened trade with Paraxea," Fred said. "We did throw you a bone."

Catie immediately started whining. "Not much of one . . ."

"Moving on!" Marc interjected.

"The platinum metals market has stabilized," Fred continued. "We've built our stockpile back up, so we have a reserve. We're scaling back the mining on the asteroids to two shifts. That should match our consumption and still leave plenty for Liz and Catie to export."

"That brings up a point," Liz said. "Where should we buy our platinum metals from, Earth or Artemis?"

"I think we should buy them from whichever one we're making a direct flight from to the consumer," Catie said. "That will change depending on how we arrange our flights."

"I agree," Marc said. "We'll endeavor to have a sufficient stockpile in both locations to take care of demand. Of course, you should focus on Artemis if you're doing exclusive deliveries. Go on Fred."

"We've released our batteries into the open market," Fred said. "Demand immediately outstripped our supply, but we're ramping it up."

"Did that make President Novak happy?" Marc asked.

"It made everyone happy except Herr Johansson," Fred said. "But he was mollified by the fact that we will meet his requirement first."

"What about Tata?"

"They weren't happy, but they've pretty much owned the truck market before the batteries, so they think they have a big enough edge that they'll continue to maintain their market share."

"Solar panels?" Marc asked.

"Eighty percent share," Fred said. "We're still scaling up production, the second hub is getting full."

"Speaking of the second hub, what are the Russians doing up there?"

"Right now, they're focusing on chemicals. They've developed a few drugs that can only be manufactured in microgravity. They say they have some promising chemicals that will be announced soon."

"Good for them. Fuel cells?"

"We're getting the recycling and recharging thing figured out. We'll be opening that process up to the market soon."

"And how do you like being president?" Samantha asked.

"Pretty well. Especially all those golf games I have to play with our clients and suppliers," Fred said.

"How do you like the golf course?" Catie asked.

"Everyone loves it," Fred said. "But eighteen holes goes by too fast. I'm back in the office too early."

"Fred barely manages one game a week," Blake said. "And it's usually on Sunday."

"But I have aspirations."

"Yeah, and getting a score below par should be one of them," Blake shot back.

"What, I thought high score won," Fred chuckled. "I'll let Sam cover the license agreements."

"Yeah, are we rich after licensing the polysteel process?" Catie asked.

"You're already rich, but the license deal didn't help all that much," Samantha said. "And before you cry foul, let me explain. First, we owed Paraxea for our unlicensed copying of their space carriers. We have also been freely using their designs for the Foxes and Lynxes."

"Boo!" Catie said. "What about the fact that those designs are like one hundred years old?"

"That worked in our favor," Samantha continued. "We agreed to cross-license the polysteel for all the Paraxean designs we're using. I got them to agree to cross-license our use of their Comm design in exchange for a cross-license of your mini-Comm for Paraxean use only. I'll send you the paperwork. Our guys made enough improvements to the fusion reactors that we did a cross-license for them as well."

"What about the antimatter reactor?" Catie asked.

"Same thing, we've improved it enough that they agreed to a cross-license."

"But didn't they get that design from someone else?"

"Yes, but they did a broad technology exchange. No limits were placed," Samantha said. "And, we've cross-licensed the Oryx design as compensation for the Foxes and Lynxes. They still don't know how to scale the sonic suppressors."

"Yay, Dr. McDowell," Catie cheered. "By the way, is he rich now?"

"He's got more money than he knows what to do with, and that's before the two of you get your shares in the new jump drive company."

"Catie's getting part of the jump drive?!" Blake asked, crossing his arms and giving everyone a childish pout.

"Dr. McDowell said she was instrumental in his figuring it all out. He's the one who insisted that he split it with her. We're forming a separate company to keep things simpler. You'll get a percentage based on your MacKenzie stock."

"Wow!" Catie said.

"So where did we end up?" Kal asked.

"We ended up even, except for the license for the solar panels," Samantha said.

"And that was a brilliant deal," Fred said. "That license will make us a ton of money."

"Thank you," Samantha said.

"Anything else on the licensing?" Marc asked.

"Just that it assumes licensing from one system to the next. So our solar license will be recorded via the U.N. We'll need them to set up a process for managing the licenses cross-system."

"Blake, you get to handle that," Marc said.

"No!" Blake howled, grabbing his head with both hands as though he were in pain.

"Next! Catie, what's the status of our jump drives?" Marc asked, ignoring Blake's antics.

"Dr. McDowell has finalized the design of the ships," Catie said. "Ajda already has them built, they just need some minor changes then we'll be ready to run some tests."

"Good, I'm looking forward to the results. Kal, anything on security we need to know?"

"Nope, we've got the people we need, training is moving along," Kal said.

"Are you staying busy?" Marc asked.

"Hey, I'm the one here without a college degree," Kal said. "It's harder for me to keep up. I didn't even get to go surfing last week."

"Poor Baby," Liz said. She had no sympathy for Kal using the no-college card.

"Hey, you're not even doing much for MacKenzies," Kal shot back.

"Yes, and you should see what Fred did to my paycheck," Liz said. "It looks like someone took an axe to it."

"I'm sure Catie is making up the difference," Fred said. "We only pay for what we get."

"Catie . . .," Liz said.

"We'll talk," Catie said. Catie earned enough money from her investments that she'd completely forgotten that Liz would need income when they set up StarMerchants.

"Last thing," Marc said. "I've sent you all a copy of the script for our reply to the aliens; review it and send your feedback before the end of the month. Fred, good luck with the press conference. Bye everyone."

"Thank you for joining us. I'm here to report that MacKenzie Discoveries is launching its newest venture, Peregrine Airlines," Fred said to open the press conference. "The airline will use the new jetliners we've designed. They are being manufactured in Guatemala at a new factory we've built south of Guatemala City. The design has just been certified, and we have four jets that we will be putting into service today. The jets are rated for Mach 3.5 and will carry four hundred passengers."

Fred waited for the reporters to settle down before continuing. "We will merge our current small luxury airline under its umbrella. The new jetliners will be based in four cities: Los Angeles, New York City, London, and Frankfurt. Each base will serve four different cities, the network will extend to service Paris, Singapore, Tokyo, and Bangalore, India, as well as flights between the four hubs. You'll find a list of flights in your brochure. I'll now take questions."

"Aren't you worried about hurting the existing airline business?"

"The airline business is very competitive. We feel we have a unique offering to make and expect the existing airlines to adjust. We don't offer any unique value for flights under four hours, so we will not be competing there," Fred answered.

"Why don't you feel that you offer value for shorter flights?"

"The travel time is based on boarding, takeoff, landing, and the actual at-altitude flight time. It takes approximately thirty minutes to take off and reach altitude and approximately the same amount of time to land. We cannot improve on that. So, unless the flight is over four hours, we're only cutting two hours out of the total time. We feel that is at the margin of the value for our service."

"Why are you manufacturing the jets in Guatemala?"

"We have a special relationship with Guatemala, and we hope to stimulate their economy and improve the economy of its neighboring countries."

"Aren't you hurting other businesses like Boeing?"

"We only expect to manufacture twelve planes per year. Most of the components come from the existing supply chain used by Boeing and Airbus, so the disruption shouldn't be too severe."

"Will you sell your planes to other airlines?"

"Not at this time," Fred replied. "In the future, we do expect to sell to other airlines."

"Why aren't you offering a coast-to-coast flight in the U.S.?"

"Because the FAA has restricted airspeed to below Mach 1 for flights that originate and terminate within the U.S. They are protecting the market for the existing airlines." Fred didn't mention that they were considering a touch-and-go airport in Mexico and Canada to get around that restriction.

"Hello, Samantha," Dr. Metra said, after answering her Comm. "I hear congratulations are in order."

"Are you talking about my marriage or the baby?"

"Marriages are neither here nor there, the baby of course."

"I'll be sure to let Marc know."

"Good, he needs to know where he stands. Now, what can I do for you?"

"I wanted to talk about the pregnancy. I'd like to know what to expect."

"You do know where babies come from," Dr. Metra teased.

"Of course. But with the nanites, what's changed?"

"You do know that you have a perfectly good doctor on Artemis, don't you?"

"Yes, but she's not my friend," Samantha said.

"Okay. We've had quite a number of births here in Delphi City, so we have lots of data. The good news is that the first three months are a breeze, you'll hardly know you're pregnant," Dr. Metra said. "The nanites will control your hormones so you won't have morning sickness or anything like that. You'll gain about three pounds."

"Really, that's a relief," Samantha said.

"Now, for the next trimester you have to decide how much weight you want to gain."

"Why do I have to decide?"

"Well, evolution has programmed your body to gain a lot of weight to protect against a sudden loss of food. Since that shouldn't be a problem, you don't need to gain a bunch of fat as a reserve. But some women like to anyway, they say it makes them feel more comfortable."

"Oh, well I only want to do what's best for the baby."

"Then your Comm will make sure the nanites are set to manage your weight. You'll gain about one pound per week, and it will all be part of the baby, placenta, amniotic fluid, and extra blood. Generally, women say they love the second trimester."

"Oh, so now the bad news?"

"It's not bad, you're having a baby. But in the third trimester, which is really about fourteen weeks, you'll really notice the weight gain. You won't be gaining it any faster, but your body will have to start stretching to fit it all in. We've found that the women here in Delphi

City tend to reach term at thirty-eight or thirty-nine weeks instead of forty. I think it's because the baby develops so well with our health care that it wants to get out sooner."

"You guys never developed an artificial womb?"

"Oh, we did. But that was a bad idea," Dr. Metra said.

"Why?"

"Bonding between the baby and mother. After twenty weeks, your baby starts to hear your voice and sense your movements. The next twenty weeks are critical to its mental development. It needs to hear and feel you. We actually recommend that even after birth, you carry the baby in a sling for the next three months, so it's close to you. The sling will support its head and allow you and baby to continue bonding."

"Oh, what happened with the artificial wombs?"

"The children born that way had severe mental health problems. We could treat them, but they were never completely normal."

"What do you do with premature babies?" Samantha asked.

"We don't have many of those, but in the rare cases when we do, we put a sound pad in the incubator and use the mother's Comm to transmit the sounds to the baby. It makes a huge difference, and we've found that the children develop almost normally."

"That's amazing."

"It shouldn't be. Do you know that when a baby is born, it can already understand the structure of your language? Multiple languages if you speak them. Although we recommend you stay to one or two languages when talking to your baby."

"You mean after birth?"

"No, before birth. Your baby knows when you're talking to it."

"What about the birth itself?"

"Oh, it's not too bad. We block the pain receptors so it's not overly painful. We're able to give localized muscle relaxers to minimize the problems. But you will need to push, and most women do display a colorful command of the language."

"You don't do cesarean sections?"

"Not if we can avoid it. It's best if the mother is fully mobile after the birth; it's easier on her and the baby."

"I can't tell you what a relief this is," Samantha said.

"Good. Now don't tell Marc, you still want to make him run around to take care of you. After all, he does have the easy part in all this."

"I'll keep that in mind."

7 Artemis

The Dutchman made orbit half a day early. She slid into orbit right behind the Sakira, which was in geosync orbit above Orion City. Liz had them dump the cargo pods as soon as they matched speed with the Sakira. They immediately pulled the Oryxes out of their container and started ferrying colonists down to the planet. Although they were moving the pods with cabins down with the colonists still in them, they still had over five hundred colonists crowded into the passenger section of the Dutchman. Using the Oryxes as well as their Lynxes would significantly speed up the process.

Once that was running smoothly, she allowed half the crew to go on shore leave. The remainder stayed on to oversee the continued migration of colonists to the surface as well as support the Artemis pilots who were now using the Skylifter to take the cargo pods to the surface. Each trip would be one cargo pod down and one up. Working 25 hours per day, they would be able to make four trips per day; that meant it would take four days to exchange all the pods. They would use the Oryxes to unload the cargo bays once the colonists were all down.

"Sam, will dinner be ready?" Liz asked as she prepared to leave her cabin.

"When have you ever known me to be late with dinner?" Samantha replied.

"Never, but that was when you had hot and cold running help," Liz said.

"We have warm and cold running help here," Samantha said with a chuckle. "Maybe by next year, we'll have hot and cold. I've got a couple of young ladies helping me out."

"Good, I'll see you in two hours."

"Hi, Marc. I'm supposed to catch a ride home with you," Liz said as she leaned against the door jamb of Marc's office.

"I'll be just a minute," Marc said as he turned back to his desktop to finish up what he was doing.

"Let's go," Marc said as he stood up. "We don't want to be late or Sam will kill us both."

"Hey, I was on time. Besides, we've still got twenty minutes."

"Yeah, like that will matter to Sam. And we have a twenty-minute drive."

"You're not in the city?"

"No. We had to build that place that Blake dreamt up for the aliens. We just moved in last month."

"Oh, as I remember, that's a really nice location. Why don't you work there?"

"Because it's twenty minutes away. People here do not like to have their time wasted. They find it distasteful enough to have to deal with the governor."

"They don't like you?"

"Government, they don't like government."

"Ah, I see. Anyway, you've got a boatload more of them coming down."

"Don't I know. That's what I was dealing with, making sure they all have accommodations for the night."

"Didn't you have plenty of notice?"

"Your early arrival messed that up," Marc said. "We were expecting to be able to slide their cabins into the new building before they needed to go to bed. Everything is ready, and with a twelve-hour head start we thought we could keep up. Your arrival at nightfall instead of right at daybreak blew that plan out of the water. The guys will be working all night to get ahead of them."

"They could have spent the night on the Dutchman."

"They're stubborn. I notice you didn't try to dissuade them from coming down as soon as they could."

"Well, the ones coming down now knew they'd be staying in temporary accommodations."

"Doesn't stop them from bitching," Marc said. "Here's our jeep, jump in."

◆ ◆ ◆

"Hello, Liz," Samantha said. She was standing outside to greet them when the jeep arrived.

"Hi, Sam. You're looking good."

"Did you expect otherwise?"

"Well you're pregnant, so I thought you might be having a hard time. You know, morning sickness."

"Oh, well, there's no morning sickness with the nanites on my ovaries," Samantha said.

"That must have been a relief."

"It was and is. Now, come in and have a drink and we'll chat before I serve dinner."

"Don't let me interfere with your cooking."

"Don't worry, Macie has everything under control."

"Macie?"

"One of the young ladies I hired to help for the evening," Samantha said. "She'll clean up while we're having dinner, then she'll head home."

"Convenient," Liz said as she followed Samantha into the house.

"Do you want a glass of wine or some scotch?"

"Scotch, please," Liz said.

"I'll put your bag in your room," Marc said, carrying in Liz's luggage from the jeep.

"Oh, sorry, I forgot," Liz said. "Just point me and I'll take it."

"No problem, I've got it. You and Sam chat."

"He's probably on a call," Samantha said. "Carrying your bags serves him right."

Samantha handed Liz a glass of scotch and carried a glass of wine for herself.

"Don't tell me the nanites let you drink alcohol?"

"No such luck. Alcohol-free wine. It's not bad and lets me feel part of the group."

"Oh, that's good. Hey what is she, like twelve?" Liz asked, pointing to the young girl in the kitchen.

"Thirteen, I think. It's just like Delphi City; the young children all have small businesses that let them earn money when they're not tied up with school or chores."

"Impressive. What do they spend it on?"

"Sweets and extra snacks, but you'd be surprised how many are saving up so they can buy a house or some land."

"Industrious of them."

Marc, Liz, and Samantha enjoyed a nice quiet meal, catching up on the activities on Artemis as well as Delphi City. Liz went to bed early, since ship time was shifted from the time in Orion City. She'd been awake for over twenty hours.

"How do you like our new chopper?" Marc asked as he, Liz, and Samantha prepared to go on their tour.

"Why do you call it a chopper, it doesn't have a rotor?" Liz asked.

"Hey, big bubble in the front, engines in the back, and it hovers, so people just started calling it that."

"I assume it has gravity drives."

"Yes."

"Where's the fusion plant?"

"Doesn't have one. We use a diesel fuel cell and capacitors," Marc explained.

"And capacitors, are you serious? Without a rotor you don't have autorotation, if you have to make a fast maneuver, won't it just fall out of the sky?"

"The fuel cell can keep it in a hover," Marc said. "The capacitors are used when you want to have a lot of lift, quickly."

"I guess that sounds okay. I still think autorotation would be nice."

"I'll talk to our engineers about it. Now are you going to get in?"

"Do you really know how to fly it?"

"Of course he does," Samantha said. "Trust me, I made sure the pilots gave him a grueling test before I'd fly with him."

"That's our great lake, Lake Diana," Marc said as he flew the chopper over a small body of water. He set it down next to the lake and they got out.

"I hate to tell you this," Liz said, "but that's not a great lake."

"It will be," Samantha chided. "It just needs some time to grow up."

Marc laughed. "We're putting about three or four ice asteroids into it each day. See that big island out there?" Marc pointed to the big hill rising up in the middle of the lake.

"Sure."

"When the lake is full, it'll reach that tree line. We've removed all the foliage below the lake's final level."

Liz looked around eyeing the depression to get a measure of how big the lake would finally be. She couldn't see the other side of the depression and had to remember how it looked before they landed.

"I guess that might be a great lake. How big will it be?"

"Almost the size of Lake Huron," Marc said.

"Wow, that is big. How long will it take you to fill it up?"

"We're losing about half the water to seepage and evaporation, but that will start to stabilize. With the Skylifter, we'll be able to direct about half the ice asteroids we're bringing in to the lake. Right now, we're only managing one per day, but we'll take that up to three or four a day."

"So how long?"

"Another year," Marc said.

"What's going to keep it full?"

"The lake will create a local microclimate. It should help to increase the rainfall in those mountains. Plus, we expect the climate to moderate as we increase the foliage here and at the equator."

"What formed the basin?" Liz asked.

"A glacier," Samantha answered.

"If a glacier formed this, then where did all the water go?"

"Dr. Qamar thinks that Artemis had a close brush with a big asteroid and it stripped off about half of its atmosphere. That led to excessive evaporation and very high temperatures, so a lot of water vapor leaked out into space," Marc explained.

"Well, at least it didn't hit the planet."

"That might have been less destructive, but you'd have to ask Dr. Qamar. Now back to the chopper and we'll go look at the canal."

Marc flew to the river where the canal started. It cut east through the higher plain where the city was built. It didn't have any water in it yet. They followed along its path, passing the huge excavator that was digging it.

"Wow, that's a big digging machine," Liz said.

"Yep, we've kept it busy since we landed. First it had to dig the channels for all the roads in the city, but since then it's been digging the canal. We should break back through to the river in another month."

"Why not build the city closer to the river?"

"We want the city out of the flood plain. This gives us the best of both worlds, no risk of flooding, and easy access to the river. The city is twenty-six meters above the river; we've built locks about a mile from the city on both sides, so we can raise the ships up to the city's height. It gives us easy access to the ocean. We'll expand the fork that comes from the great lake once we finish filling it, that'll make it easy to take a barge up there. We'll be expanding our farming there next. We'll probably even build a small city by the lake."

"That sounds like a nice place to live. Hey, what's that small lake for?" Liz asked as she pointed to the lake just on the outskirts of the city.

"We have fish there. Lots of the locals like to go fishing, but mainly it's the water reservoir we'll use for the lock. We will pump water up to it continuously, then when we need to raise a ship, we'll grab the water from the lake. That will save energy and time."

"Let's go to the fishing village," Samantha said. "I'm looking forward to some fish and chips."

"Yes, *Dear*," Marc said, ducking as Samantha tried to slap him on the back of his head.

"This village is eighty kilometers from the city. The fishermen like it because they can get right to work, avoiding the two to three hours of downriver sailing. It makes a nice place for a short vacation. We have several cottages on the beach that people from the city can use," Samantha explained.

"It also houses our salt production plant," Marc said. "You can see the marsh area north of the river. We've got a five-acre section at the edge that we use to trap the water and let it evaporate."

"How much salt do you need?" Liz asked.

"Not as much as we can produce. The plant only runs long enough to generate one load a month right now. We won't exceed its capacity for a few years."

"Enough about salt, I'm hungry and I want to go to Felicity's for lunch," Samantha declared.

"This is our mining town," Marc said.

"Isn't that where your friend, O'Brian is?" Liz asked.

"He's not a bad guy, just a slow learner," Marc joked. "Anyway, you can see we've set quite a few cargo pods next to it. Hopefully we'll have all of them full for your next trip to Paraxea. Right now, we've only got six ready for you."

"Are you able to mine that much already?"

"Yes, O'Brian is pretty efficient when he sets his mind to it. There are five large mines within a few miles of here and the big gold mine is here. The smelter runs twenty-six hours a day, seven days a week."

"Pretty impressive," Liz said.

"You can see the stockpiles of ore waiting on the smelter."

"Do you have problems with pilferage?"

"Not really, we're the only buyer, so what would you do with it? Security is tight; with cameras and Comms, we know where everyone is."

"How do the miners keep their Comms from getting knocked off?"

"Most of them have the mini Comm from Catie. They wear it right above their boot when they're working, and as a watch when they're not."

"Catie's gotta love that."

"Yes, she was pleased about the order you're bringing in."

"Hey, I'm heading back to the Dutchman today," Liz said as she carried her bag from her room.

"Why so soon?" Samantha asked. "Your guys won't finish loading until tomorrow."

"Right, but I've been down here while the rest of the bridge staff has been rotating their shore leave so we always have someone on watch. It's time for me to take my turn."

"You've had your head buried in that HUD half the time you've been here. I'm sure you've done your share of work."

"But everyone needs to get a break on the surface. I've got to go up, so Ms. Griggs can come down and have a day off to explore the city."

"Okay," Samantha acquiesced. "Let me give you a hug to take to Catie for me."

"First Mate, are we ready to break orbit?" Liz asked.

"Yes, Captain. Cargo pods are locked in, engineering and navigation are showing green," First Mate Hayden Watson announced.

"Then let's head home," Liz ordered.

The Dutchman broke orbit and started its two-week climb out of Artemis Prime's gravity well.

"Hey, Cer Marc, how are you doing?" a young girl and her friend asked as they caught Marc on the sidewalk in front of City Hall. Marc figured them for about ten or eleven years old.

"I'm doing fine, what can I do for you young ladies?"

"We want to open a business. I'm Katya, and this is Sebrina."

"Very enterprising of you; how can I help?"

"Cer Sam told us we need a permit."

"Yes, you do, but that should be easy to take care of. Come on in," Marc said as he held the door open for them. He led them over to his office and indicated they should have a seat. He pulled his chair around from behind his desk and sat with them.

"Okay, let's talk about what you need."

"First, we need that permit," Katya said.

"What kind of business are you going to open?"

"A delivery and errand service like they have on Delphi Station."

"I see, just a minute," Marc said. He messaged his assistant. "Melinda, can you set up the two ladies I have in my office with a permit?"

"What about the fee?" Melinda asked.

"Charge it to me."

"Yes, sir, I've got their names from their Comms, so I should have the permits ready in a couple of minutes."

"Okay, will that take care of your needs?" Marc asked.

"Well, we are hoping for more," Katya said.

"And what would that be?"

"Some kind of exclusive license deal, like a franchise."

"Oh, I have two budding titans of industry here. I don't see how we could give you a franchise on delivery services, you'll just have to come up with a way to make your service unique."

"But the big boys can run faster than we can, and they have bigger backpacks," Sebrina cried. "Cer Sam suggested that you'd be able to help us get an edge."

Marc nodded his head. "Oh, I see, you two have important connections. I guess you need a way to level the playing field."

Katya shook her head violently, "No, we want to tilt it in our favor."

Marc laughed. "Okay, so your problem is, you need to deliver the goods fast and in volume."

"Right!"

Marc leaned back in his chair, thinking. "I've got it, why don't you use bicycles?"

"We would if we had them. Can we get them, and can we be the only ones with them?"

"I can get you the bicycles, but everyone will be able to get them," Marc said.

"Well, then we need more!" Katya demanded.

"Okay, give me a minute. . . . I think I have something for you. What if you were the only ones with a trailer for your bicycles? Something you could load up with groceries or meals."

"That sounds good. When can we have it?" Katya asked.

"Just a moment. Call Chief O'Donnell," Marc told his Comm.

"What can I do for you, Governor?" Chief O'Donnell asked, when he answered his Comm.

"I've been told that it is high time we had bicycles down here," Marc said.

"Oh, have you now? Are we getting so big that people can't walk from place to place?"

"It's more of a speed thing."

"Aye, well we can make up a few. What kind are you thinking?"

"Let's start with two three-speed bikes. Stand up," Marc motioned to the two girls.

"I am standing," the chief said.

"Not you," Marc said. "I need to measure your clients." Marc had his Specs take pictures and measurements of the girls. "And I want to add an exclusive feature."

"And what might that be?"

"You know those trailers they make for hauling your kid around behind you?"

"I've seen something like that."

"Well, these ladies want a trailer similar to that that they can use to ferry cargo," Marc explained.

"The bikes are not for off-roading, then?"

"Correct. They want them for local deliveries."

"I can have them made, no problem; are we going to set up a manufacturing process for them?"

"Let's call these two prototypes. You can set up a process to make more later."

"That will take at least a month."

"Oh, it'll be a month before anyone else can get a bicycle," Marc repeated out loud so the girls could hear.

"Alright!" Katya said.

"Where do I deliver these bicycles and wagons?"

"My office will be fine. How long will it take?"

"I'll have them to ya in two days."

"Thank you, Chief," Marc said as he held up two fingers.

"Two days?" Katya asked.

"Yes. I assume I'll see you then."

"For sure. How much do we have to pay for the bikes and trailers?"

"Why don't we say ten percent of your earnings for two months," Marc said.

"Deal," Katya said, putting out her hand to shake.

Marc showed the two girls out of the office. As he watched them run down the street, Melinda came up behind him.

"Ten percent for two months; you big softie," she said.

"Hey those two will be running this place in ten years."

"You think it'll take that long?"

Marc looked up and rocked his head, "Maybe not."

8 Hello Again

"Hello, I'm Governor Marc McCormack. My brother had some personal business to attend to on our homeworld, so I've taken over as governor here on Artemis." Marc was in the now real office that Blake had mocked up for the first communication.

"We see that you are still approaching Artemis. However, I have to tell you that we are not willing to share the system. We've found that that just leads to problems. We are, however, willing to institute trade between our various worlds. In fact, we have just sent a shipment of grains and metal ores back to the homeworld."

Marc got up and walked around the desk. "I thought I'd show you a bit of our colony and indicate some things that might interest you." Marc walked outside where they'd arranged for a busy group of people in the front yard. "Most of the colonists are still living in our capital city. Some of them will be moving to their farms or ranches later this year, but now we're still focused on getting the colony off to a strong start."

Marc got into the jeep and had the driver head toward the city. "I'm a little remote out here, so I have an office in the city. That makes it more efficient for the colonists to set up appointments and such. It is a lot of work to manage such a busy colony."

As they approached the city, Marc had them keep the camera angle tight so that it didn't show the edge of the city. They'd declared the day a holiday, so there were the maximum number of people on the street, shopping, dining, or just strolling around.

"We've followed the convention of our homeworld, setting things up so that people live close to where they work. That minimizes vehicle traffic, which cuts down on noise and traffic hazards. The people of Artemis like to stroll the streets and dine at our sidewalk cafés."

Marc walked into a building that housed their manufacturing facility for the housing units. The units were constructed as a module, similar to the cabins that they'd brought down from the Sakira and that the

Dutchman had brought. It showed them adding the appliances and fixtures that Liz had delivered from Paraxea.

"We build our habitats as modules," Marc said. "It's more efficient that way. Once they're installed in the building, they're expanded and customized based on the size of the family, but they all have this core of two rooms and a bathroom. We have quite a few colonists who are impatient to move into their own lodgings; they're having to double up right now since they are the second group to arrive.

"As you can see, we have some nice appliances and fixtures that we manufacture. We would be happy to trade those with you once we catch up with our internal demand. Of course, we have the grain and raw platinum metal ores that we could trade as well. Maybe you can provide us with some idea of what you would have to offer in exchange."

Marc then drove the jeep to the lake. "We made quite a bit of progress terraforming this planet. We've been able to increase atmospheric moisture substantially. We hope that by the end of the year, the climate will start to adapt, allowing for a greater range of vegetation, and eventually make the planet a little cooler and more to our taste."

Marc ended the presentation at the airport where he had arranged for one of the spaceplanes to take off. "We just put in our new airport. We're very proud of our new spaceplanes. They can even make orbit, which allows us to easily ferry supplies to and from our spaceship.

"Well, that's all we have for now. Please let us know what you're interested in trading. I look forward to meeting you. Until later."

"Cut!" Samantha yelled.

"What do you think?" Marc asked.

"We'll have to see. I wonder what our friend, the captain, will do to counter your Oryx."

"What do you mean?"

"What will he show you or tell you so that you know his is bigger," Samantha said with a snigger. "ADI and I will review and edit it. It should be ready for your final review by tomorrow."

"Thank you, and thank you too, ADI."

"You're welcome, Captain," ADI said.

"Who are those people?" the alien captain yelled. He had just finished watching the reply from Marc. "How arrogant. What kind of fool does he think I am? His brother had a personal matter that required him to return to the homeworld. BAH!"

"Why else would they have changed governors?" the lieutenant asked.

"Who knows. Maybe they have elections. But a personal matter that is worth traveling two to three years to resolve; that is ridiculous."

"What do you think of their spaceplane?"

"I don't believe him. That thing cannot make orbit. He is just trying to intimidate us."

"Even if it cannot make orbit, it is still impressive," the lieutenant said.

"Have that footage analyzed. I want to know everything about it. Especially if it is doctored. I find it hard to believe they have that many colonists on that planet."

"Hello, Governor McCormack. We are happy to see that you're making such good progress on your colony. We see that there are some things that we can learn from you," the alien captain started out. He was resplendent in his uniform and ribbons as he had been on his first reply.

"I can envision some trade between our two civilizations. I think you'll find that we have much to offer. We have very advanced technologies we would be willing to trade. It is unusual to see different star systems trade among themselves since they're usually separated by such vast distance. We are fortunate that our homeworld is a relatively short distance from, Zagawani, Artemis as you call it.

"Possibly we should create a mutual defense agreement between our civilizations. We have a strong military system and have developed many advances in space weaponry. Possibly the weapons systems would be of interest to you. We look forward to meeting you and sharing the stories of our homeworlds."

9 Murder Most Foul

"Good morning, Sam," Marc said as he joined Samantha for breakfast.

"Good morning to you. Did you have a nice run?"

"Yes."

"Are you going in to the office today?"

"No, I think I'll take the day off. I don't believe there are any problems that require my attention. ADI?" Marc prompted ADI to inform him if there were any issues he wasn't aware of.

"Captain, there are no issues requiring your immediate attention," ADI said.

"*ADI*, that sounds like there is an issue," Marc said.

"I'm sorry to inform you, but there has been a murder in Delphi City," ADI said.

"A murder?!" Marc asked.

"How can that be?" Samantha asked.

"Chief Nawal is investigating," ADI said.

"Well, I'm sure she'll let us know if there is any issue," Marc said as he watched Samantha shudder.

◆ ◆ ◆

"Give me the details," Chief Nawal requested as she arrived on the scene.

"Ma'am, the body was discovered at one twenty this morning," Constable Gamon said. "He has been identified as William Markham. He came home and entered the building through the service entrance."

"Why would he do that?"

"Saves him having to walk around the building. According to his Comm, he died at 1:05 a.m."

"He was wearing his earwig?"

"Yes, ma'am."

"I don't suppose his Comm picked up who killed him?"

"No, ma'am, he had the video and audio recording turned off."

"Interesting. What next?"

"He entered the building and was murdered almost immediately, maybe twenty seconds. The outside camera didn't record anyone entering with him."

"Did anyone leave the building after he was murdered?"

"Several people exited via the main entrance around one fifteen. They probably are second shift people heading out for the night after getting off from work."

"Any record of people entering just before he did?"

"Several people entered via the main entrance between thirty minutes after midnight and one fifteen."

"Okay, and just how was he murdered?" Chief Nawal asked.

"Carotid artery was sliced open. Lot of blood, but if the killer was behind him, they probably avoided it."

"Did he struggle?"

"No sign of it. You can get a whiff of alcohol, if you can get past the blood. His Comm has him coming from a bar."

Chief Nawal surveyed the scene. The body was in the hallway that paralleled the loading bay. "So the killer likely hid here inside the doorway to the loading dock. The victim walks by, the killer steps out of the doorway and what? Grabs him and then stabs him or did they just stab him as he walked by?"

"It could have happened either way. He obviously wasn't very attentive."

"Or he knew his killer," Chief Nawal suggested.

"Might have, but this is an odd place to meet someone. There are lots of cameras in the loading area, just nothing in this hallway, so it wasn't for privacy."

"No alarms, so the killer either got in via their Comm, or they tailgated someone else entering the building."

"Or they live here."

"If only it were that easy."

"Chief Nawal, can you provide any details on the murder last night?" Sophia asked. She had been lying in wait for the chief to come back to the station ever since she'd been notified of the killing.

"A body was found at one twenty this morning. We are withholding the name pending notification of next of kin. I cannot provide any more information since it is an ongoing case," Chief Nawal said.

"Come on, even I know it was William Markham, he lives in the building where his body was discovered by one of the other residents!" Sophia shouted.

"I'm glad to see that the press is so well informed. But we have protocols to follow and one of them is we don't go shouting the victim's name until next of kin is notified." Chief Nawal pushed her way past Sophia and into the police building.

Chief Nawal went down to the coroner's office to get the details on the autopsy.

"What can you tell me, doctor?"

"And hello to you as well," Doctor Kramer said.

"Sorry, hello, how's your day been?"

"Fine. You know this is the first autopsy I've had to do since those Russian Commandos. It's been months since I've been down here myself."

"I know how you feel. Our first murder. I hope it's not an omen of things to come."

"I'm sure it's not. Okay, your victim was a healthy, well-nourished male in extremely good condition. He died of exsanguination due to a single knife wound in his throat. The weapon had a double-edged blade, approximately four inches long and two and a half inches wide. It was very sharp."

"Anything you can tell me about the assailant?"

"Cold blooded bastard, right-handed. There are no hesitation marks, the blade went in and was immediately withdrawn with a backward pull, the pull was angled down. Due to the width of the blade, it severed the carotid artery and sliced open the trachea as well. There are no defensive wounds. There is a slight bruise on the victim's forehead, consistent with hitting the floor or the wall."

"That matches our findings," Chief Nawal said. "We believe the victim was stabbed from behind, then pushed. He fell and hit his head against the wall. Between the blow and the knife wound, he was dazed enough that he just lay there until he bled out. Would the assailant have gotten blood on them?"

"Possibly; there certainly would have been arterial spray, but if they remained behind the victim, it is possible that they avoided the blood spatter."

Chief Nawal frowned. "The knife was wiped clean on the victim's shirt. All of the blood we found was in front of the area where we believe the victim was standing when stabbed. What about the assailant's height, strength?"

"It wouldn't have taken much strength. As to height, I would say at least 160 centimeters, five-three, probably not over 180 centimeters. Other than that, I can't say."

◆ ◆ ◆

"Oh my God," Catie exclaimed.

"What, *Chérie*?" Yvette asked.

"Someone was murdered last night."

"Here in Delphi City?"

"Yes. I can't believe it."

"Do they know who did it?"

"It says the police aren't saying anything."

Catie messaged ADI, "ADI, what happened?"

"Chief Nawal is investigating," ADI said. "I cannot say any more about an ongoing investigation."

"What?"

"I have to follow the police protocol," ADI said.

"So you cannot tell me anything? Are you helping to find the killer?"

"I am helping, and no you are not on the list of people I am authorized to share information with," ADI replied.

"ADI, come on, it's me."

"I know, but there are rules," ADI said. "I'll inform you of any new information as it is released."

"Thanks, but I bet I can count on Sophia to do more than that."

"She is not bound by the same rules I am."

"Alex, what else does it say?" Yvette asked.

"Not much. Where it happened, the victim was a male, stabbed just inside the service entrance to his condo building after midnight," Catie read off the information listed in Sophia's column.

"How could someone get away with murder here? There are cameras everywhere," Yvette said.

"Apparently not everywhere. I'll be very interested to learn how they pulled it off," Catie said.

"As will the police."

Chief Nawal approached the podium to begin her official announcement to the press.

"It's with great sadness that I announce that Delphi City had its first murder last night. The victim was found by another resident in his building. The victim was William Markham, the director of sales at Vancouver Integrated Circuits. His family has been notified. He was killed at one fifteen Sunday morning just inside the service entrance of his condo building. We believe this was not a random act, but a well-planned execution. We are continuing our investigation. Anything the public can tell us about the victim or his movements during the last week would be helpful."

"Can you tell us how the victim was murdered?" Leslie Walters asked. Sophia was mad that the Chief had called on Leslie instead of her, just because Leslie was an internationally known reporter. Sophia was after all the resident Delphi reporter.

"He was stabbed in the neck from behind and bled out."

"How could that have happened without being caught on camera?"

"The stabbing occurred inside the building's service entrance. There is a camera watching the entrance, but there is not one inside the building in that location."

"So you have no clues?"

"None that we're willing to discuss with the press."

"Do you think this was a paid hit?" another reporter asked after the Chief pointed to him.

"We are considering that possibility. We know of no reason for the victim to be targeted, but we have just begun our investigation."

"I cannot believe that the chief ignored me," Sophia thought. "She must be mad about me ambushing her outside police headquarters."

10   Board Meeting – March 7th

"I call this meeting to order," Marc said. "I assume everyone has been following the murder investigation."

"I have a hard time believing someone pulled off a murder in Delphi City," Blake said.

"It's hard, but not impossible," Kal said. "Even the best security has holes in it."

"Do we know who the perpetrator is yet?" Liz asked.

"No."

"Do the police have any suspects?" Nikola asked.

"Lots of potential suspects, but nobody that really piques their interest. They're still researching his life to see who would want him dead," Marc said.

"This has many of our residents terrified," Nikola added.

"The prime minister needs to reassure everyone that this is an unusual event," Marc said. "It was a methodical, carefully planned murder, not some drive-by shooting or mugging gone wrong. It's highly unlikely that anyone else will be targeted."

"Easy for you to say," Nikola said. "But how do we get the message out to our citizens?"

"Have Sophia interview the prime minister," Catie suggested. "Then she can make all the points that Daddy just made. Everyone reads the Gazette."

"What I wonder is what we'll do once they catch the bastard," Blake said.

"What do you mean? There will be a trial," Samantha said.

"And if he's convicted, what do we do with him?"

"Throw him in prison!"

"What prison?"

"Oh, I see what you mean," Marc said rolling his eyes. The little things you miss when building a nation.

"We will just have to build one," Blake said. "This is unlikely to be the only violent crime we'll see in Delphi City."

"Where? Do we make a separate quad to house the prison, floating off the city like the airport?" Marc asked.

"Why would we do that?" Kal asked.

"To prevent escape, to make people feel comfortable. Nobody wants to live next to a prison," Marc said.

"I assume we'll just build it on the airport," Kal said. "That's isolated enough. And with the subdermal tracker, we really don't have to worry about escape."

"Those can be removed," Blake said.

"Well maybe for violent criminals we need to place them deeper in the body, a location where it takes a doctor to remove them.

"Wouldn't that violate their rights?" Samantha asked.

"What rights? They're convicted criminals. I think we can make a case that they've given up any right to privacy. Besides, it only tracks their movement, and alerts us if they try to disable it or remove it. I don't see how you could argue against it."

"Sure, that coupled with a Comm attached around their neck like a choker necklace should take care of any issues."

"What's the Comm for?"

"It records what's going on in the area from the local cameras, records any conversation the prisoner is involved in, and it will also stun the prisoner if they become violent, or if a guard triggers it. Avoids having a prison riot," Kal explained.

"Hard to have a prison riot with just one prisoner," Catie said.

"Can't they just take the comm off?"

"It's attached with a band made of that flexible polysteel Dr. Zelbar came up with. They can't cut it off and it's too tight to slip over the head. Besides if it's removed it sets off an alarm and activates the shock paralyzer."

"Oh, nice."

"Let's move on to the business of this meeting," Marc said. "I assume you've all reviewed the alien's reply to our message."

"Yes, it sure didn't take him long to reply," Blake said.

"That surprised me as well," Marc said.

"I would also say that he's inviting you to amass your forces at the point where he enters the system. Now why would he do that?" Admiral Michaels asked.

"That bothers me too," Blake said. "I'd like to put it down to arrogance and stupidity, but I don't think that's what it is."

"He looked angry," Catie said.

"Yes he did, didn't he," Samantha agreed.

"We've got eight weeks to figure out how we want to respond," Marc said.

"We could just ignore him and see what he does," Samantha suggested.

"I'd rather keep poking him to see how he responds, but I'll consider that," Marc said. "Now, moving on. Fred, I loved your press conference."

"Thanks. Peregrine Airlines started flying last week. All their flights are booked solid."

"That's excellent news. How's our cash reserve doing?"

"What cash reserve?" Fred joked. "We've used up a lot of it. We need to take a breather or find another source of income."

"We could sell more platinum metals," Kal suggested.

"Liz is bringing you a load, along with about five million tons of our new wheat," Marc said.

"That should help a lot. But what's next?"

"You could borrow money from Catie," Blake quipped.

"We're overcommitted," Catie said.

"How can that be?!" Marc gasped.

"I want to build another StarMerchant," Catie said.

"Another one! We've barely got this one crewed!" Liz groaned.

"I know, but it will take six months to build. We just have to work on the hiring. If we're going to trade with Paraxea, we can use the extra capacity. And don't forget, they have other colonies and those other civilizations they've met; we'll want to start trading with them as soon as we can, so we should be engaging in a lot of trade."

"No one ever accused Catie of thinking small," Blake said.

"You're not asking for a loan, are you?" Marc asked.

"No, we just don't have anything extra. We'll use the profits from this run to build another Skylifter for the Paraxeans, then we have to build one for the Dutchman. That plus laying the keel for the next StarMerchant uses up most of our reserve."

"What about 'your' reserve?" Blake asked, using air quotes to stress 'your'.

"Oh, well I do have some there," Catie said.

"Don't worry, we won't ask you for a loan. I hear you charge exorbitant interest anyway," Fred said. "Besides, we can always borrow from Marc or Blake."

"Don't look at me," Blake said.

"Back to the meeting!" Marc said. "Where are we with the jump ships?"

"We've just finished modifying the ships based on our last test. We should be ready to run another set of tests in a week," Catie said. "After that we should be able to tell you more. I assume you want to get the Victory to Artemis."

"You assume right."

"I would predict by mid-May," Catie said.

"Okay, we can't afford to take much longer than that."

"I understand."

"Now, Dr. Metra, how are our clinics doing?"

"We've now opened one in every major country. That plus the regional clinics seem to be covering most of the demand. We're expanding treatment to cover other diseases besides just childhood ones."

"That sounds good. How about your birth control clinics?"

"Of course, all of the new clinics are offering birth control. We are getting some strong pushback in certain countries, but our underground clinics are managing the distribution there."

"Are the women at risk?" Liz asked.

"There is some risk. There has been an uptick in violence against women who don't get pregnant, but we're doing what we can there," Dr. Metra said.

"What are you doing?" Marc asked.

"I believe the general response has been to give the men the nanites as well. It curbs their testosterone level, which reduces their tendency toward violence."

"All the men?" Liz asked.

"No, they just give the women who have been abused a bandage to apply to their husband," Dr. Metra said.

"I think a 9mm bullet in the head would work better," Kal said.

"We shouldn't have to go that far," Dr. Metra chided Kal.

"Okay. Keep us posted. Is your budget still adequate?" Marc asked.

"Yes, since the clinics are handling most of the need now, the budget is more than sufficient."

"Admiral Michaels, how go things with the alliance?" Marc asked.

"The usual politics. It wouldn't be worth it if we weren't able to live in Nice," the admiral said.

"We all have our crosses to bear," Marc said.

"Thanks. We are making progress on the rules for engagement. We should be ready to start integrating the forces in a couple of months."

"I look forward to hearing how that goes," Marc said. "Blake, how about our discussions with the U.N. on the licensing situation?"

"*Our* discussions," Blake said. "*Our discussions* are a royal pain in the ass."

"*You are royalty,*" Catie messaged Blake.

"*You just wait!*" Blake replied.

"But we are making progress," Blake continued. "I have a conference call with the G8 leaders tomorrow to review the latest proposal. Of course, the biggest sticking point is Russia's and China's complete disregard of the current patent and licensing laws."

"That's to be expected. This should help to garner some more respect from them," Samantha said. "A new market should make the values of the patents and licensing they control more valuable, so the overall respect for the laws protecting them should go up."

"One would hope," Blake said. "I'll keep you informed."

"Kal, are you getting in enough surfing?" Marc asked.

"You bet. And our military force is doing well. We've got all four aircraft carriers in place and crewed. Our Marines are shaping up well, we've built a mock spaceship to practice infiltrations on. It's in orbit just behind Delphi Station."

"Oh, that sounds like fun," Liz said.

"We'll run you through it when you get back," Kal said.

"What about me?" Catie whined.

"I think your Academy class will go through it in May," Kal said. "You stick out too much to try to sneak you through."

"Pooh!"

"Hey, Alex, what are you doing on Saturday?" Yvette asked.

"I don't have specific plans. I thought I might go hang out with my Academy Family," Catie replied.

"Want to go with Miranda and me for a golf lesson?"

"Golf?"

"Yes, all aspiring officers need to play golf."

"Since when?"

"Since they just got a new golf pro, *très beau*."

"You're hopeless."

"Hey, I like to shop," Yvette said. "So, are you in?"

"Sure. But I've never played before."

"That's the best, lots of hands-on instruction."

"So, you ladies want to learn how to play golf," Victor, the golf pro, said. He was a very nice specimen as Yvette had suggested. Tall, broad shoulders, small waist, and a handsome face.

All three of the girls were wearing a mid-thigh skirt and a light cotton blouse. Yvette had taken them shopping the day before so they would be properly attired and attractive.

"Yes."

"Have any of you ever played before?"

"I have," Miranda said. "I only took a few lessons. I never had enough time to spend on it, so I stopped playing."

"Okay, that should help. Let's get each of you a six-iron, that's what we'll be using until you have the basic swing down."

Victor led them into the pro shop where he selected the appropriate club for each of them. Anytime she could get away with it, Yvette took up position behind Victor where she could signal her approval of his various attributes.

Victor led them back onto the driving range. "Today, we're going to focus on the swing; your swing is the single most important aspect of your long game. Once you have that down, we'll move on to putting. After that we'll address things like sand traps and chip shots."

The three girls nodded their heads.

"First let's get the grip right. Each of you hold your club like this, right hand extended, left hand behind."

"Like this?" Yvette asked, prompting Victor to wrap his arms around her from behind and help her adjust her grip.

Once he had all three of them gripping the club correctly, he had them stand back. "Now, let me show you what a proper swing looks like. There are seven parts. First, address the ball." Victor approached the ball that was teed up and described his stance.

"Next, there is the takeaway." Victor described the moves as he brought the club back until it was horizontal to the ground. Yvette pointed to his butt and signed her approval.

"Now the backswing. Your hips need to rotate evenly, keep your arms straight, let your left knee flexed . . ." Yvette pointed out that Victor had very nice legs.

"The top of the swing . . . on the downswing, your hips should start moving first, twisting . . ." Yvette let Miranda and Catie know that she really liked Victor's hips.

"Now impact," Victor said as he hit the ball, "and follow-through. You need to keep the swing going. Your body will anticipate the follow-through, so it has to be right or you'll mess up your downswing."

The ball shot out about one hundred meters before a drone caught it to bring it back. The driving range was on the side of the city, facing the ocean. Similar to the course, a drone caught each ball before it hit the water. However, the player's HUD showed the full flight path giving them the satisfaction of seeing how far their shot went.

The girls all clapped. "Nice."

"Who wants to go first?" Victor asked.

Yvette pushed Catie forward. "Alex is first."

Catie just rolled her eyes as she walked over to Victor.

"Now let's get you set up." Victor took position behind Catie and positioned her in front of the ball. "Bend your legs . . ." Victor used his knee to bump Catie's knee forward until it was bent correctly. "Lean over." Victor held Catie's hips and used his thumbs to indicate when she'd reached the proper angle. "Keep your back straight." He used his forearm to get Catie to straighten her back, prompting her until her spine touched it all the way up and down.

"Now, the take-away . . ." Victor guided Catie through the process; she hit the ball and it traveled about twenty meters before the drone caught it.

"That was very good. Let's look at the replay," Victor said as they all turned to the display to see how Catie had done. Unfortunately, the camera had also caught Yvette's antics of appraising Victor as he wrapped his arms around Catie to guide the swing.

"You should pay more attention to the golf swing," Victor said, giving Yvette a stare. She smiled demurely and ducked her head. Victor just shook his head and turned back to Catie. "Alex, you did a nice job for your first swing. Let's do it again."

Victor worked with each girl on her swing until she had it down. Of course, Miranda got hers down in almost no time and Yvette took the longest, asking for clarification of every minor detail.

"Now, let me set you up here," Victor said, as he led them to three stations that were partially enclosed. "This station has cameras and sensors; it will check your swing and give corrections to you via your HUD. They also have several large electromagnets which will correct minor errors in your swing as you're practicing. The head of the clubs you're using has a magnet in it that allows it to couple with the electromagnets so they can make the necessary corrections. The more your body makes the correct swing motion, the more ingrained the muscle memory will be."

Victor got each of them set up at their station, worked them through a few swings, then left them to practice. "Try to hit two dozen balls. If you'll come every day and hit two dozen, you'll have your swing down within a few weeks. I'll leave you to practice. The computer will alert me if you're having trouble."

"Alex," Miranda said, "I just realized you're driving right-handed. Aren't you left-handed?"

"Yeah, but I thought it would be easier on Victor if we all played right-handed."

"You should have said something," Victor said. "We should go and change clubs."

"Don't worry, I'm ambidextrous. I do lots of things right-handed. I shoot right-handed and I play pool right-handed."

"Why?"

"My teacher was right-handed, so that's how I learned." Catie's Uncle Blake had taught her to shoot pool and shoot a handgun, and Kal had taught her how to shoot a rifle. Both of them were right-handed.

"If that's how you want it," Victor said, "but I can teach both ways."

"No, this will make it easier for us to help each other."

Victor shook his head as he started back to the office.

Catie focused hard on her swing, and after a dozen balls she was able to hit it about seventy meters. Since she was the first to set up, she finished first and turned to watched Yvette and Miranda. Miranda was getting her balls to travel about ninety meters, but Yvette was nailing hers. Each ball traveled at least one hundred ten meters.

"Yvette, your golf swing has improved remarkedly since Victor left," Catie said.

"*Maudit*, these computers, they take all the fun out of a golf lesson," Yvette said. She hit her next ball over one hundred twenty meters.

"What's your handicap?" Miranda asked.

"Six!" Yvette said, sounding very unhappy. "Well, there's always putting."

◆ ◆ ◆

"Paul," Marc greeted his friend.

"Hey, Marc, you wanted to talk?"

"Yes. You've seen the Skylifter?"

"Oh yeah. It sure makes short work of bringing an asteroid down to the surface," Paul said.

"Yes, *so*?" Marc prompted.

"I'm guessing you'd like to have more asteroids coming in."

"Right. I knew you were the man for the job," Marc said. "We should be able to handle at least ten per day."

Paul shook his head. "You're not asking for much are you?"

"There has to be a way to speed up delivery."

"I'm sure there is. I'll look into it."

"Thanks, let me know if you need anything."

"Don't worry, you're on my speed dial."

"Nattie."

"Yes, Paul."

"Marc has asked me to figure out how to get more ice asteroids delivered here."

"I assume you mean he wants them to show up faster," Natalia said.

"I knew there was a reason I married you."

"How are they delivering them now?"

"Using the tried-and-true method you and Catie developed."

"And Liz," Natalia added.

"Sure, and Liz. But it takes half a day to rig one up. We fly them here where we have to break them up before we can lower them to the surface. Now the Skylifter can bring them down in one piece."

"So they don't need the grav drives on this end."

"Right, but we have to use them to fly them here."

"ADI."

"Yes, Cer Natalia," ADI replied.

"Can we accurately plot a course that will send an asteroid to Artemis without grav drives on it?"

"If you can accelerate it onto a prescribed trajectory, I can calculate one which will bring them into Artemis's orbit," ADI answered.

"So we just need to push them," Paul said. "You thinking of using an Oryx?"

"No, too much fuel," Natalia said. "But we don't have to go through all that effort to mount the gravity drives and everything. Maybe we can just make a framework with them on it, then grab the asteroid and push it."

"Grab it with what?"

"We just need to make sure it doesn't slip off. Let's go out there and check it out."

◆ ◆ ◆

Natalia and Paul took the Sakira to the asteroid belt. With the Sakira they had a manufacturing facility to prototype whatever they needed to push the asteroids around. Captain Desjardins was happy to get out of orbit and give his crew something to do. Training opportunities were never to be taken lightly.

"So, are you going to share your idea?" Paul asked.

Natalia brought up the image of the last asteroid they'd sent toward Artemis on the display in their cabin. "What do you see?"

"The asteroid, the grav drives, the reactor with the control module," Paul said.

"Now what?" Natalia used her HUD to erase the asteroid from the image.

"Just the grid of all that equipment."

"So?"

"So, you want to make a frame and mount them all on it. But the asteroids are all different shapes. How are you going to make it fit any of them?"

"Three points define a . . .?"

"Plane," Paul answered.

"So if we mount the reactor and control module on top of one of the drives, then we should be able to find a section of the asteroid where the three points can anchor without causing a problem. Four points, would make it likely that one of them wasn't anchored. But with three . . ."

"Oh, yes. Unless it were a really wonky asteroid, you'd find one side that would let you do that. But how do you keep the frame from slipping off?"

"Just put some points on the end of each leg. Use the grav drives to drive them in. Then you can start to maneuver it."

"And to pull them out?"

"Newton's first law."

"Newton's first law? You've gotten pretty damn smart with all those classes you've been taking."

"Thanks, I think. Anyway, Newton's first law says that what's moving, keeps moving."

"You could have just said inertia. So that means you just reverse the gravity drives and let the asteroid pull itself free."

"ADI, will that work?"

"I am certain of it, Cer Natalia," ADI replied.

"So, we just need to make up a few of these," Natalia said.

"You know we could have done all this on Artemis?"

"Yes, but then you and I wouldn't have this nice cabin to stay in with a steward running around to bring us stuff and a nice wardroom to eat in." They were staying in the owner's cabin on the Sakira. Once they had started using the Sakira for missions, they had divided the huge captain's cabin into two separate cabins. The captain still had room for two guests, but the owner's cabin also had three separated sleeping cabins as well as a large day cabin.

Paul smiled at Natalia, "I knew . . ."

"There was a reason you married me," Natalia finished.

When they reached the asteroid belt, it only took a day to prototype the first asteroid pusher.

"It looks like a tripod," Paul said.

"It does. ADI and I decided that we'd just make hard links between the drives so we could route power. It's double-hinged so that it'll be easier to find a good spot to anchor it down."

"Doesn't that make it harder to fly?"

"Cer Paul, I assure you that it will not be a problem for me to fly," ADI said.

"But what about a miner flying it?"

"That's the best part. With this thing, ADI says that she or ANDI can pick the asteroids out, attach the pusher, and send them toward Artemis. We won't have to have the miners stay out here."

"Don't tell them that yet," Paul said.

"Are they going to be upset?"

"No, they hate this assignment. I just want to make sure they adequately recognize what you're doing for them."

"Sure, whatever. Now let's see if we can move a few asteroids."

Natalia, with ADI's help, flew the pusher to the next asteroid the miners had identified. She easily maneuvered it into position then had the grav drives anchor it.

"Okay, ADI, push it," Natalia said as she released the controls.

"Pushing," ADI said.

"How long to put it on course?" Paul asked.

"It is on course now," ADI said.

"Great, so we can bring the pusher back and get another asteroid?"

"Yes," ADI said.

"ADI, how long will the asteroid take to reach Artemis?" Natalia asked.

"Seven point three years," ADI replied.

"Oh, I guess we need to push it a little longer," Paul said.

"How long do we need to push it if we want it to arrive in one week?" Natalia asked.

"Approximately forty-eight hours."

"Oh, that's a bit long. What if we want it to get there in three weeks?"

"Approximately sixteen hours."

"How hard are we pushing?" Natalia asked.

"I am pushing it at one gravity."

"Can we push it any harder?"

"With this mass, I can have the gravity drives push it at 2.1 gravities."

"Okay, so do that. How long will it take to get the module back here?"

"Six hours," ADI replied.

"So, one asteroid every twenty-two hours or so depending on their size. So how many pushers do we need to make?"

"They can handle about ten a day," Paul said. "Let's make ten, Marc can figure out how to handle an extra one every now and then."

"Okay, how many drives do we have?"

"Oops, just six more," Paul said. "The rest are on the way to Artemis."

"Are there at least twenty-one gravity drives in route?"

"I think so."

"Cer Paul, there are twenty-four drives on asteroids between here and Artemis," ADI said.

"Okay, we have plenty. So, do we leave a crew here to assemble the pushers as the drives come back?"

"No, we can do that at Artemis and let ADI fly them back."

"Great, I'll get the boys to make up two more, then we can all head home."

"Men and ladies, I have some bad news," Paul said.

"Oh, what now?" the crowd groaned.

"Well, these asteroid pushers that Natalia designed are going to change things out here. They take special handling and maintenance."

"Damn, and I was hoping it would take fewer of us to manage them. That Oryx we're living on is crowded."

"I guess it is. And we need that Oryx back at Artemis," Paul added.

"Where the hell do you expect us to live and work from?"

"That's the point. With all the special care, we've decided to let the DIs manage pushing the asteroids. All you guys are out of a job."

"Hallelujah!"

"You know you'll have to go to work in the mines now."

"Hell, that will seem like a vacation after this. Where's Natalia? I want to buy that wife of yours a drink."

"Ms. Michaels," Chief Nawal said as Sophia joined her in her office. Sophia was hoping she was getting an exclusive interview. She'd been asking the police for one for days.

"Call me Sophia."

"Ms. Michaels, we've been informed by the last two witnesses we've interviewed that they had just been interviewed by you."

"So?"

"So, you know that it is against the law to interfere in a police investigation."

"I'm a reporter, I'm investigating the news," Sophia said.

"That may be, but you are interfering with our investigation. Your questioning of the witnesses is contaminating their interviews with the police. They have been able to prepare answers, and know more about the investigation than they should."

"It's not my fault that the police are too slow," Sophia said.

"Nonetheless, you are interfering."

"What do you expect me to do?"

"I expect you to clear your interviews with me first."

"No! We have freedom of the press. I don't have to do that."

"If you continue to interfere in the investigations, I'll have to arrest you."

"You can't do that!"

"I can. But before I do that, I will have a constable follow you everywhere. Whenever you approach a witness, the constable will be there to restrain your enthusiasm."

"You don't have enough constables to do that to all the reporters."

"We don't, but all the reporters are not causing us a problem."

"So what do you mean by clear my interviews?" Sophia asked.

"Call the office, tell us who you're going to interview, and we'll let you know when we've finished interviewing them."

"What if I come up with someone you didn't know about?"

"Then we'll consider whether we should offer you a job as a police detective, and then we'll let you know if we want you to wait before we interview them."

"Will you tell me who else you're interviewing?"

"No, this is a one-way street."

11 Jump Ships

"Hey, how did you two score a private cabin on Delphi Station?" Miranda asked as they boarded the Lynx that would take them to Delphi Station.

"Alex has a friend who keeps a cabin up here. She's on a starship heading out to one of the colonies and said we could use the cabin," Yvette answered.

"Who's this friend?" Miranda asked.

"Liz Farmer," Yvette answered.

"*The* Liz Farmer?" Miranda asked, completely shocked. Catie just rolled her eyes as she kept them moving toward their seats.

"What do you mean by '*The* Liz Farmer'?"

"She's one of the founders of Delphi City. Famous for her part in the Paraxean war and the Ukraine incident."

"*Oh là là,*" Yvette said. "That is why she looks familiar. Alex why didn't you tell me who she was?" Yvette smacked Catie on the arm.

"I did," Catie said. "Not my problem if you're not up on your Delphi history."

"But you didn't tell me she was famous."

"Apparently, she's not famous enough if you didn't connect the name to the fame."

"Alex, how do you know her?" Miranda asked.

"Yes, you never told me," Yvette asked.

"We were on the same flight from Hawaii when I flew here last winter," Catie said. "We chatted and hit it off. We kept running into each other last spring."

"That's all? You just met her and became friends. Next, you'll be telling us you have dinner with Princess Catie once a month," Yvette said.

"Oh, I have dinner with the Princess all the time," Catie said mockingly.

"You're so full of it," Miranda said.

Catie got them settled in the third row and just sat down when she was shocked by the sight of the Khanna twins coming down the Aisle.

"Hi, Alex," they said as they stopped next to her.

"What are you guys doing here?"

"We're going to Delphi Station, silly," the twins said.

"I figured that. But why?"

"We're going to teach some cadets how to run the microgravity obstacle course. Isn't that why you're going to Delphi Station, Cadet MacGregor?"

"I guess I'll be one of those cadets. Yvette, Miranda, these are Prisha and Aisha Khanna. They're my Academy Family. Prisha and Aisha, this is Yvette and Miranda."

"Hi," the twins said.

"Where are you staying while you're on the station?"

"We get to stay in the *president's* cabin," the twins said, making it sound very important and mysterious.

"Well, la di dah," Catie said. "Who's going to stay with you?"

"Nikola."

"Sounds nice. I'm sure you guys will have fun, you always do," Catie said.

"We will. See you later," the twins said as they moved to the back of the Lynx.

"Which one is which?" Miranda asked.

"I never know," Catie said.

"And they're going to teach the class on maneuvering in microgravity?"

"Apparently they're the best," Catie said. "I've been in the obstacle course with them and they're really good. You should see them on film when they're going against someone who's good; it's amazing."

"You certainly have interesting friends," Miranda said.

125

Catie led Miranda and Yvette to the lift after they deplaned on Delphi Station. Neither of them had any microgravity experience, so Catie had to help them maneuver.

"Where did you learn to maneuver in microgravity?" Yvette asked.

"When I came up with those twins. You pick it up pretty fast," Catie said.

"Just get me to the gravity section," Miranda said. "My brain is really confused."

It took them ten minutes to make it to the elevator, down to the gravity section, and to the lift. Then it was a short ride out to the third ring and Earth standard gravity.

"How do you know where we're going?" Miranda asked Catie as she led them out of the lift and turned right without a pause.

"I've set our destination in my HUD; it's highlighting the path for me," Catie replied.

"Oh, I guess we all should have done that," Yvette said.

"No worries. Now, it says the cabin is just down the corridor on this level."

"On this level?"

"Yes, there are five residential levels. The main elevator only stops at level three. You have to take a different lift or the stairs to get to the other levels."

"It makes sense that Commander Farmer would have a prime location," Yvette said.

"Especially since she was one of the first one hundred people to get a cabin on Delphi Station," Catie said. "Here it is. Liz told me that she registered our Comms so we should be able to go right in."

Of course, the door to Catie's and Liz's cabin opened right up for Catie. "Liz's room is the one on the left, I've got the roommate's room," Catie said as she carried her bag into her room. Since it was Yvette who had invited Miranda to bunk with them, they were sharing Liz's room.

◆ ◆ ◆

"Hi, Alex," the twins said as Catie was exiting the cabin with Yvette and Miranda.

"Oh, hi girls. This must be Nikola," Catie said as she extended her hand to Nikola. "Alex MacGregor; the girls mentioned you would be keeping an eye on them."

"Hi, Alex," Nikola said, giving Catie a hard look. Then she smiled as she realized who Alex was. "Are you girls heading to dinner?"

"Yes, we're going to The Four Seasons, I've been told their restaurant is excellent."

"You can rest assured that it is," Nikola said, giving Catie a wink. Catie immediately realized she'd been made. "Have fun."

"Busted," ADI whispered into Catie's Comm.

"I thought they said they were staying in the president's cabin," Miranda said.

"They are. I think it's just down the corridor," Catie said, knowing full well that her father's cabin was two doors down.

"Really?!" Yvette asked.

"Sure, where did you think it would be?"

"In someplace secure. I thought it might even have its own floor."

"The McCormacks aren't into all that," Catie said. "Haven't you read anything about Delphi?"

"Of course I have, but you can only believe so much of what you read."

At 0600, Catie exited her bedroom and met Yvette and Miranda in the common room. They were on their way to the orientation for the week's training. It was being held in the hub, right after the arrival of the Lynx carrying the other cadets. The girls had come up the night before since they had such special accommodations.

"Are you ready for this?" Catie asked.

"I hope my brain is happier with the microgravity today," Miranda said. "It took me most of last night to convince it that up was up."

Catie laughed. "At least you didn't vomit."

"And you'd better not vomit today," Yvette said. "It would totally undermine that hard-ass cadet commander thing you've got going."

"I'll try not to," Miranda said. "Now lead on MacDuff, we don't want to be late. That wouldn't be good for my image either."

"Okay, does everyone have a toehold or their boots locked to the deck?" Lieutenant Fiore asked. He was to be their host during the week. He would oversee their training and be available for questions or other help as needed.

Getting no responses, he continued. "The most important thing about microgravity is maintaining an awareness of where you are and your orientation to the surroundings. Without gravity to tell you which way is up, it's easy to get confused. Keep cues in sight at all times. The wall pattern is top white, bottom blue. The location of chairs or furniture is a dead giveaway." He got chuckles with that.

"Now if your boots are connected to the floor, you're good. But if you want to move about quickly, walking in microgravity is slow and tedious. You want to push off and glide to where you want to get to." As he said that one of the twins pushed off the floor from the back of the crowd; she flipped over, bounced off the ceiling, flipped over again, and landed next to him.

"As you can see, with a little training you can get about quite quickly, as Ms. Aalia has just demonstrated. If you find yourself in microgravity with the need to defend yourself, your maneuverability is your best weapon. A flying body is quite effective at knocking an opponent loose from their foothold. And if you can outmaneuver them, you can catch them, but they cannot catch you. Now Aalia and her sister Prisha will show you how to take advantage of the walls, various fixtures, and such to maneuver in microgravity. Later they'll take you into the obstacle course and play some tag with you to give you a chance to practice what they teach. I'll buy dinner for anyone who manages to tag one of them."

The twins took the cadets through a series of exercises, showing them how to push off at an angle so they could aim themselves. They showed them the proper way to flip or rotate so that they could land on the wall or ceiling feet first.

Once everyone was familiar with the techniques, one of the twins led each person through the course. The cadet was supposed to mimic the twin's move and try to keep up with her. By the fourth wall, almost every cadet was so focused on copying the last move, that they lost track of the twin they were supposed to be following.

"MacGregor, that was pretty impressive," Lieutenant Fiore said. "You made it all the way through the course."

"I've had a little practice; but I never got close to the little witch," Catie responded. Prisha stuck her tongue out at her.

"This next exercise is to teach you how to push off quickly at different angles. One of the twins will take up position in the corner of the course, essentially trapped. Or one might think so, but with three dimensions, you'll be amazed at how hard it is to corner someone."

"Does the dinner bet still stand?" one of the cadets asked.

"Sure," Lieutenant Fiore said.

The twins had worn different shipsuits, so they were easy to tell apart. Aalia went first, moving to the corner of the room and taking a position against the wall. She waited until the cadet being tutored made it to the marked spot, then she bounced up and planted her feet on the wall. She juked back and forth, dancing around the wall, toward the ceiling, the floor, the other walls. She did this for about a minute, then she pushed off and sailed right by the cadet, far out of reach. His lunging grasp fell far short.

Catie watched as half the class went through the drill. *"Oh, Prisha has a tell,"* Catie realized. She watched a few more cadets go through the training. Each time, Prisha gave away the direction she planned to leap with just a small twist of her head. Aalia didn't have a tell that Catie could spot, but Prisha did. Catie waited her turn, adjusting her place in line so that she would go against Prisha.

"Hi, Alex," Prisha said as she set up in the corner.

"Hi, Prisha. You're mine," Catie said.

"As if," Prisha said. "You ready?"

"Always!"

Prisha started her dance. Catie danced back, waiting for her tell. Then there it was, her head tilted left and up. Catie shifted the other way and Prisha kicked off. Catie bounced off the wall, pushing as hard as she could. She saw Prisha zooming by as she reached out toward her, stretching as far as she could. Catie's hand brushed Prisha's boot just before Catie slammed into the wall.

Prisha hit the ceiling, flipped, and bounced back to the floor. "No way!"

"Yes, way!"

"How?!"

"You have a tell," Catie whispered.

"Nah uh!"

Catie flicked her eyes back and forth like Prisha did then tilted her head, mimicking the move Prisha had made that gave away her intended direction.

"Ohhhh!" Prisha whispered as she mentally reviewed her actions.

"Hey, that didn't count!" Cadet Jamison shouted.

"Yes it did," Lieutenant Fiore said. "A touch of any kind is a tag, and that's the first one ever against one of these two."

Prisha stuck her tongue out at Catie as she moved back into position. She was clearly not happy about being tagged.

"So, any touch?" the cadet asked.

"If you can land one, I'll buy you dinner all week," Lieutenant Fiore said.

"I won't collect," Catie said. "I've had a previous round with these two, they're my Academy Family."

"I don't care if they're your sisters, I'll pay. I'll be able to win a few bets on that. Do you mind sharing how you did it?"

"It's a secret," Catie said.

"She let her!" Cadet Jamison yelled.

"No I didn't," Prisha yelled back. "And I'll take him!"

"How did you do it?" Miranda asked in a whisper.

"She had a tell."

"Had?"

"She won't have it anymore," Catie said. "Let's watch her leave big mouth in the dust."

Jamison set up in front of Prisha. She danced twice then shot by him so fast he never even made a try for her.

"I guess I won't have to suffer your company at dinner," Lieutenant Fiore said. "Next!"

"Dr. McDowell," Catie knocked at his lab door. She was ostensibly on duty in the Delphi Station control room but had arranged with Captain Clark to have someone cover for her.

"Oh hi, Catie, are you ready for our experiments?" Dr. McDowell asked, hardly giving Catie a second glance.

Catie was amazed at how oblivious Dr. McDowell could be. It was like a superpower. He had seen her both as Keala and Alex, and had yet to notice anything different. He'd made one comment about her hair, that was it. Captain Oblivious.

"Yes, I am. I've got eight hours," Catie replied.

"Good, the jump ships are in place; they've got a nice small asteroid out there that we can use, so everything is set."

"I assume you've already confirmed that we can open a wormhole."

"Yes, sent a small probe through. It made it to the other side and we closed the wormhole. The ships stayed on this side."

"Oh, that's good. I guess we could have dealt with them jumping through, but it's better this way."

"Of course they didn't jump through," Dr. McDowell scoffed. "They were outside the radius of the wormhole."

"*Sorry*," Catie said. "I see that for today, we're going to see how close to the asteroid the ships can be and still open up a wormhole. How big did you say it was?"

"I didn't, but it masses the same as that Dutchman of yours when it's fully loaded."

"Perfect. Are we ready?"

"As soon as you sit down and start reviewing the readings."

"Of course." Catie sat at the second control console and set the display up the way she liked it. She was glad that Dr. McDowell liked to have her next to him when he conducted the big experiments. He called her his lucky charm, but she suspected that he was afraid that he'd miss something and was used to her being there to point it out.

"I'm ready," Catie announced. "The asteroid's position is matched to the jump ships at one kilometer. Probe is ready."

"I'll open the wormhole on three," Dr. McDowell said. "One . . . two . . . three, engage."

"I've got a wormhole, probe went through. Sending back a positive signature."

"Okay, closing the wormhole."

"Wait! Let's see if we can bring the probe back."

"Good idea, do you have control over it?"

"Sure, here it comes, . . . and there it is."

"Excellent, closing the wormhole. Now next we want to see what happens if the asteroid is moving relative to the jump ships. Who's going to give it a push?"

"Can't we just have the jump ships moving?"

"Oh, that would be easier, all velocity is relative, so sure. Do you want to do the honors?"

"Hmm, . . . I'll have them move at one meter per second relative to the asteroid; it's one thousand kilometers from them. They are at the correct speed, and now they're in lockstep with each other."

"Okay, on three, one . . . two . . . three, engage. Wormhole didn't open."

"Why?"

"Local gravity is changing too fast to compensate I suspect. I'll know more when I review all the data," Dr. McDowell said.

"Okay, let's try ten thousand kilometers."

"Tell me when you're ready."

"Just five minutes," Catie said. . . . "Okay, we're ready. One meter per second from ten thousand kilometers."

On three, one . . . two . . . three, engage. No wormhole."

"Twenty thousand or one hundred thousand?" Catie asked.

"One hundred, we want to find the other side then iterate back to determine the exact distance," Dr. McDowell said.

"That'll take twenty minutes," Catie said. "Would you like some coffee?"

"That would be nice."

Catie went down the hall to the small café and got them each a cup of coffee. By the time she got back the ships were almost in place. Once the ships were at the right distance from the asteroid, Catie took another minute to get their speed back down to one meter per second, then she nodded to Dr. McDowell.

"One more time, on three. One . . . two . . . three, engage. No wormhole."

"Boo, one million?"

"Yes."

"That will be an hour. What should we do while we wait?"

Dr. McDowell was already at one of his display boards working on an equation. Catie shook her head and went back to her console. She thought she might as well work on her paper for her fusion reactor class.

Catie's Comm pinged when the jump ships were at the correct range. "Ready!"

"Oh, good," Dr. McDowell said. Catie was surprised he was attentive enough to have heard her, he must be really interested in these experiments.

It took her another minute to get the ships stabilized for opening a wormhole. "They're ready."

"One more time, on three. One . . . two . . . three, engage. We have a wormhole."

"Whew," Catie gasped. "So do we want to back off to five hundred thousand?"

"No, let's go back the way we came up, subtracting incrementing powers of ten."

"So, back off ten thousand?"

"Yes."

"Just a minute and I'll have them in place. . . . ready."

"Once again on three. One . . . two . . . three, engage. We have a wormhole."

"Probe's through," Catie announced. "Hit the target again. . . . And it's back. Down one hundred thousand?"

It took another hour before they iterated to 817 thousand kilometers as the limiting distance. Then another two hours to determine that that distance was related to the square of the velocity differential.

"Now let's see if the ships can hold the wormhole open while the asteroid continues to approach it. Do we give it a nudge this time?" Dr. McDowell asked.

"I don't see why," Catie said. "Everything is in motion, so the ships are still the easiest things to move."

"Of course. But this time if the asteroid goes through, we can't bring it back."

"We can figure out other experiments, or we can jump the ships through the wormhole and then send it back."

"Oh, yes. Just reverse the process. These jump ships are a wonderful invention if I do say so myself," Dr. McDowell said. Catie smiled at the backhanded praise.

Since everything was already in place, it only took a moment to resync the ships and the asteroid.

"Well, we're ready; do we want to try to accelerate before the jump?"

"Let's."

"I'll go to one-G of acceleration, once the wormhole is open. We're ready."

"On three. One . . . two . . . three, engage. We have a wormhole."

"Probe says the other side is clear. Accelerating!"

"Wormhole is holding steady."

"We're going to have to sit here for an hour while the ships catch up with the asteroid," Catie said.

"Yes, but we want to watch the systems and all the sensors, so no running off to work on equations."

"Did I ever tell you we almost hit an asteroid once?" Catie asked.

"No, when was this?"

"Back when we were going to Artemis the first time. We came through the wormhole and the proximity alarm started blaring. Uncle Blake had the plasma cannons firing within seconds and they obliterated it. That's why we send a probe through when the wormhole is still small."

"Clever," Dr. McDowell said. "It must have been a small asteroid."

"Yes it was. The sensor log showed that it was only about one meter in diameter."

"Lucky."

"Yes. It makes me wonder what would happen if two ships tried to open a wormhole in the same system at the same time."

"Umm, that might not be a good thing."

"My thinking exactly. Of course, just opening a small one and sending the probe through first will help minimize the odds, but what if the other ship comes in a few seconds later."

"We definitely should look into that. Not too much risk since there are only three ships with jump drives, plus these jump ships."

"Since the jump ships can each open their own wormhole, we should be able to run some experiments," Catie said.

"Yes, let me think about it."

. . . "And there it goes," Catie said as the asteroid moved through the wormhole.

"Everything looks steady," Dr. McDowell said. "Closing the wormhole."

"Let's go to lunch."

After lunch, Catie moved the jump ships to the system with the asteroid. Since each of them was capable of making a jump on its own, she moved them one at a time to simplify the coordination effort.

"Okay, they're in the other system," Catie said. "You wanted to open a wormhole with one, then try to open another wormhole with the other one. To different systems, I assume?"

"Correct," Dr. McDowell said.

"I'll manage the Beta ship; you manage the Alpha ship."

"Agreed, let me open the first wormhole. I'll open it to system D-3, you open yours to system F-4 when I tell you."

"Ready," Catie said.

"Opening wormhole . . . it's open. Now open yours."

"Opening it now."

"Mine collapsed."

"No wormhole, it looked like it was forming, then it didn't," Catie said. "The power dropped to the hold level, but there wasn't a wormhole."

"Let's try that again; this time force your power level to stay up."

"Okay, ready."

"Opening wormhole . . . it's open. Now open yours."

"Opening."

"Mine has collapsed."

"Mine did that jumpy thing, then it opened," Catie said.

"Interesting. Jumpy thing, huh?"

"You know, where the power spikes."

"Okay, I'll have to spend some time studying the data. Move your ship to D-3 and I'll put mine in F-4. We'll both try to open a wormhole to C-7." Dr. McDowell sighed as he brought up the control panel so he could fly the ship.

"Doctor, I can move your ship for you if you wish," ADI said.

"Oh, thank you. I hate flying the infernal things," Dr. McDowell said.

"Would you like me to operate it while you study the sensors?"

"Yes, thank you."

"Mine is ready," Catie said.

"Alpha is ready also," ADI added.

"ADI, open your wormhole first."

"Opening . . . wormhole established."

"Now Catie."

"Opening, wormhole established, but there was a power spike."

"The Alpha wormhole is now connected to D-3," ADI reported.

"Oh, mine is connected to F-4," Catie said. "Does that mean they merged?"

"It appears so," Dr. McDowell said.

"Should we send a probe through?" Catie asked.

"Yes, send one, then send it back."

"Sending," ADI said. "Probe transit was successful. . . . I'm now returning the probe, . . . Return successful."

"That opens up some interesting possibilities," Dr. McDowell said.

"So, do you think the first ones merged and that's why they collapsed?" Catie asked.

"Possibly. If they merged, then they would no longer be connected to the jump drive, so it makes sense that they would collapse."

"Let's see what happens if we open one using a jump drive on each end," Catie suggested. "Then I have to head back, I'm expected in a class."

"What class do you have to take?" Dr. McDowell asked. He sounded like he thought she was just trying to duck out of working for the rest of the day.

"It's on the station's environmental systems. What a waste of time, but it'll look bad if I don't attend," Catie said. "ADI, you can stay and help Doctor McDowell, can't you?"

"It will be my pleasure."

"Thank you," Dr. McDowell said. "I have a whole list of experiments to do to determine the max size and mass. They're going to be boring, which is probably why you're not skipping that class."

"Believe me, they will not be as boring as the class."

Catie and her friends stayed over an extra day on Delphi station, while the rest of the class headed back on Saturday morning.

"I'll have the huevos rancheros," Catie said, handing her menu to the server. They were meeting for breakfast at Betty's Diner since none of them wanted to cook.

"So, we're really staying an extra day because Braxton's class is coming back from the asteroid belt, right?" Yvette asked Catie, giving her a knowing smile.

"That might have something to do with it."

"Oh, be honest. You're hoping he'll have dinner with you."

"Not hoping."

"So you already have a date?" Miranda asked.

"Yes. They're stopping here at Delphi Station so they can do that environmental class we just did."

"Oh, too bad for him," Yvette said. "But I'm sure having dinner with you will compensate for it."

"So you found the class boring as well?" Catie asked.

"Not boring, gross," Yvette said. *"Merde* this, *merde* that."

Miranda was laughing, "How did you survive Guatemala if you're so squeamish?"

"It was *très difficile*, but it was only mud."'

"So you won't be joining the Marines?" Miranda asked.

"Non, too much dirt," Yvette said. "Although they are *beaux garçons*, so I might date one."

"You're too much. But Alex, when does he arrive, and do we need to get lost?" Miranda asked.

"They arrive at 1400. We're just meeting for dinner at 1800, so you don't have to get lost."

"What about after dinner?" Yvette asked.

"Expect me back at the cabin around 2300, *alone*."

"Alex, nice dress," Miranda said as she saw Catie exit her room wearing an evergreen party dress. It hit just above her knees, a snug fit that flared from the waist.

"Oh, hi, Miranda, I didn't know you were still here."

"I wasn't letting you go out without getting to see what you would decide to wear."

"Oh là là," Yvette said as she came out of her room. "I thought your red dress was the only pretty one you owned."

"Hey, I have a few dresses," Catie said. She didn't want to let them know that she hadn't packed this dress. She'd just gotten it from the closet in her room.

"Not that I've seen," Yvette continued. "You'll have to let me borrow that one, it looks very nice."

"Sure, now I have to go or I'll be late," Catie said, making a note to take the dress back to Delphi City with her.

"It's good to keep a man waiting," Yvette said. "You must let them know you're worth it."

"Go ahead, Alex, I'll keep this French Poodle at bay while you escape," Miranda said as she moved to block Yvette.

"Bye," Catie said over her shoulder.

"Hello, Braxton, I hope you haven't been waiting too long," Catie said as she met Braxton Graham at the Four Seasons restaurant.

"I've only been here a couple of minutes," Braxton said. He'd been seated in the reception area waiting for Catie. He stood up when she walked in. "You look nice, a lot nicer than in that Academy uniform."

"Thank you."

He walked over and gave her a light kiss on the cheek. Then he took her hand and led her to the receptionist. "Reservations for MacGregor."

The receptionist had a server show them to their table. The server seated them and handed them their menus. "Would you like something to drink?"

"I'll have a glass of water now," Catie said.

"Me too, and a glass of Jack Daniels," Braxton said.

"How did your project go?" Catie asked once the waiter had brought their drinks.

"Great, we got the smelter installed and running. It is really amazing."

"How does it work?"

"Of course, you know it melts all the ore down, but without gravity you have to do things differently. They spin the vat around on a dryer type of drum, so the centrifugal force will give everything a direction. The light, non-metallic material mostly burns off, what doesn't, floats to the surface and can be skimmed off. It does all that at a low spin rate. Then it increases the spin so the metals will separate into different layers."

"Why would they separate?" Catie asked. "The centrifugal force on them would be the same."

"That's right, but buoyancy isn't."

"Buoyancy?"

"Yes, everything's liquid, so the denser metals force the lighter ones upward where there is less pressure. Brilliant, isn't it?"

"Then what do they do?"

"They cool it all down. That's really the secret. The metals each have a very distinct melting point so as they cool it down, the metals cool and precipitate to the bottom. They draw them out, feeding the liquid back in. That was my part of the design."

"That was very clever."

"Yeah, I think so. Of course, osmium mucked it all up a bit. We had to raise the pressure of the vat quite a bit because of it."

"Why?"

"Because its melting point is higher than the boiling point of most of the other metals. I'm the one who cottoned to the fact that melting point isn't affected by pressure."

"That was clever."

"I thought so."

Braxton walked Catie to the park that was just spinward of the Four Seasons. It took up two levels and was sixty by two hundred meters, with small trees and grass. It even had a small pond with fish.

"Wow, this is amazing," Braxton said. "A park on a space station."

"It is nice," Catie said. "It helps people keep from feeling too cooped up. The kids love it."

"How do you know so much?"

"Oh, I read up on it," Catie lied. She kept forgetting she was supposed to be a newbie like everyone else.

"It is definitely a clever idea. What happens to the fish if the spin stops?"

"The book said there was a cover that would come out and keep the water in. It's just under the edge, rolled up like an automatic pool cover."

They wandered around the park for a while just chatting. It was getting late and Catie had to get back before Yvette came looking. "I have to go. I hope to see you next weekend," Catie said.

"Oh, it is getting late. My roommates will be wondering what I'm up to," Braxton said. He pulled Catie into a hug and gave her a kiss.

Catie melted into his arms, "*A nice warm kiss. He does have nice lips*," she thought. Pulling away she smiled at him and said, "Have a good day tomorrow and call me."

"I will."

"How was your date?" Yvette asked when Catie arrived back at the cabin.

"It was just fine. What are you doing, waiting up for me?"

"I just wanted to be sure you were all right."

"I'm just fine, now go to bed, we have to fly home in the morning."

Three weeks after Natalia and Paul went to the asteroid belt, the ice asteroids starting arriving in big numbers. Marc declared a holiday and arranged for a picnic celebration at the lake.

"Natalia had them make two more asteroid pushers. They use them to catch the asteroids before they enter Artemis's orbit. They slow them down and get them into a low orbit where the Skylifter can grab them and bring them down," Marc explained.

"Why don't the catchers bring them all the way in?" Samantha asked.

"Not enough power, and they can't handle being exposed to the heat of reentry."

"Oh. You said that we're getting ten a day, how can the Skylifter handle that many? It's taking it over two hours to bring each one in."

"It's dumping the smaller ones in the ocean," Marc said. "It drops those from pretty high up in orbit. It's only bringing the big ones down here to the lake."

"Cer Marc! How long will it take to fill the lake up?" one of the girls asked.

142

"About four months," Marc said. "But it will be a nice big lake in just two months."

"Will we be able to sail on it?" the girl asked.

"And go skiing?" a teenager asked.

"Yes, and yes," Marc said. "I guess we'd better order up a few sailboats and a ski boat."

"Yes!"

"Lieutenant Lantaq, adjust our course one pico-arcsecond to starboard," Captain Shakaban ordered.

"Sir, that will use up twenty percent of our reaction mass!"

"I gave you an order; I did not ask you how much mass it would take to carry it out!"

"Yes, sir."

"I am returning to stasis. We will see what these so-called colonists say when I wake up."

"Ms. Bowman, thank you for coming in," Chief Nawal said.

"Call me Mariana," Ms. Bowman said.

"Of course. Now can you tell me about your relationship with the deceased?"

"We were just friends. We've lived across the hall from each other for two years."

"Come, please be honest with me. We have several reports that have the two of you going out to dinner together."

"We did dine together quite often. William would call or text me about a restaurant that he was dying to try. We'd go have dinner and talk."

"What did you talk about?"

"Mostly the food, the latest movie or book, our travels. We were both doing a lot of traveling for our jobs."

"Are you saying there was not a personal relationship?"

"Yes. I sometimes wondered if William wanted it to appear that way, but we were never anything more than friends. We occasionally met at a bar after work, but mostly it was at restaurants."

"Why do you say you wonder if he wanted it to appear that you were dating?"

"I don't know, he would mention someone he was seeing when he traveled to Vancouver or the west coast. But I wondered if maybe he was gay. Not that there is anything wrong with that."

"What makes you think he was gay?"

"He was a good-looking guy. He always flirted with the ladies at the restaurant, but it seemed to be fake. He never flirted with me. I'm not sure why he wouldn't be open about it, but maybe because of his job."

"Why, because of his job?"

"Well, he was the sales director at Vancouver Integrated. That's a high-profile position. Maybe the board would have had a problem with his being gay."

"Do you know that he recently got engaged?"

"No, I hadn't heard about that. Who to?"

"A young lady from Vancouver."

"Oh, the poor thing."

"Yes, she was just informed of his death. She's coming to Delphi City for the funeral. Can you tell me, are you dating somebody?"

"Still wondering about William and me? No I'm not dating anyone right now. I was until about six months ago, but then he got tired of all my traveling and found someone else."

"You don't seem to be broken up about it."

"Why should I be? If he can't handle being by himself for a few weeks, then I don't need him. Anyway, that's one of the things William and I talked about, all the travel."

"You travel a lot for your job?"

"Yes, I was Marcie Sloan's assistant. Marcie left MacKenzies, so now I'm Sharon Bodiker's assistant. She's new, got a huge bonus to join the company, so she's working long hours and traveling a lot. One can't blame her. It's a big company, and she wants to hit the ground running. I'm sure it will slack off."

"And you say Mr. Markham complained about his travel?"

"Yes. He was on the road a lot. Said he was getting tired of it. He asked me if I thought there might be a position for him at MacKenzies. I couldn't see him coming on board. He would never get a position as important as the one he had at Vancouver Integrated."

"Since you lived across the hall from him, did you notice if he had any visitors?"

"Not that I know of. I've never seen him have anyone over. That doesn't mean he didn't; I wasn't spying on him or anything."

"Did he go out with anyone else?"

"I'm sure he did. He went to things with his work mates. And he was out a few nights here and there from what I could tell. He never said anything about it, that's why I thought he might be gay."

"Okay, please call me if you think of anything."

"I will," Ms. Bowman said. She got up and left the chief's office.

"What do you think, Chief?" Constable Gamon asked once Ms. Bowman left.

"I have no idea. He seemed to be a bit of a loner. What did you get from his mates at the office?"

Constable Gamon consulted his notes. "Like you said. He was a loner. Went to the odd office function, stopped by the pub after work occasionally with his office mates, but mostly kept to himself."

"When does the fiancée arrive?"

"Tomorrow at five."

"Okay. Call and tell Ms. Michaels that we're finished with the office crowd."

"Yes, Ma'am."

"*Finally*," Sophia thought when Chief Nawal's office had informed her that she could now freely interview anyone from the Vancouver Integrated office. She'd quickly scheduled an appointment to interview Markham's boss, Dorothea Randall. She was the director of marketing and sales.

"Thank you for allowing me to interview you," Sophia said after Ms. Randall's assistant showed her into the office. It was a large office, which was unusual for MacKenzie businesses, but Vancouver Integrated was independent now. Sophia was seated in a guest chair in front of an enormous wood desk. *"This desk is as big as my bed,"* she thought.

"Not a problem," Ms. Randall said. "We just hope to put this whole mess behind us. William was a valued member of my team; we will all miss him greatly."

"What can you tell me about him?" Sophia asked.

"He was a private individual. Even when we traveled together, he never talked about his personal life. We were all shocked when he announced his engagement. Nobody even had an inkling that he was seeing someone. That poor girl. Three weeks after their engagement and he gets murdered."

"I understand the fiancée is from Vancouver. Did he know her there before he came to Delphi City?"

"Mr. Markham came to us from Apple Computer. He was never posted to Vancouver. He did travel there for work, so I assume that's how he met her."

"I understand he did a lot of traveling."

"He did. He was our sales director. That meant a lot of travel for sales, shows, meetings with the regional staff. He was on the road fifty percent of the time."

"Was there any change in his behavior before the murder?"

"Other than announcing the engagement, no. I'm sure he stopped by the pub a bit more than usual. Everyone was willing to buy him a drink to toast his engagement. But other than that, he stayed diligent to his work."

"Thank you," Sophia said. "Do you mind if I ask a few questions of his colleagues?"

"As long as you do it outside the office, I have no objections."

"Thank you."

Sophia left Ms. Randall's office and surveyed the array of desks in the outer office. William Markham, like Ms. Randall, had a separate office, but everyone else was working in cubicles.

Ms. Randall's assistant had provided her with the list of William's associates, and Sophia had spent some time on the web looking into their backgrounds. Now she was looking for Nora Hale. Nora had just joined the firm six months ago; she was young and, more importantly, very good looking, and single.

"There she is," Sophia had spied Nora in the back corner with her head down, typing away at her computer. Sophia walked to the edge of the row of cubicles so she would walk by Nora on her way out. "Hi, I'm Sophia, I'll buy you dinner if you'll talk to me?"

"Is this about William?"

"Yes."

"I didn't really know him."

"The offer still stands," Sophia said, handing Nora her business card. "Today would be lovely."

"I'll think about it."

"Please," Sophia said as she moved on. She didn't want anyone to notice her talking to Nora.

"Thanks for agreeing to meet me," Sophia told Nora when they met at Giorgio's for dinner that night.

"I'm happy to talk to you, but like I said, I hardly knew him," Nora said.

"Well, you might know more than you think. Anyway, let's get our table and some wine before we talk."

Once they were seated and had agreed on a petite sirah for wine, they started looking at the menu while they chatted.

"Have you been here before?" Sophia asked.

"No, but I'm guessing you have since the maître d' knew you."

"I'm the owner and publisher of the Delphi Gazette," Sophia said. "I review the various restaurants around town, so most of the restaurateurs in Delphi City know me."

"Oh, you're the publisher, and you're interviewing me?"

"I'm the publisher, editor, reporter, and whatever. We only have me and a part time reporter," Sophia said. "But we were the first newspaper in Delphi City."

"That's still pretty cool," Nora said. "So, what's good?"

"I love their osso buco, and the veal parmigiana is divine, and any of the pasta dishes."

"I think I'll have the veal parmigiana. I haven't had that in a while."

"Okay," Sophia said as she closed her menu.

The sommelier came to the table with their wine. Once she had served the wine, the waiter came to take their order.

"Now, tell me about William Markham," Sophia said.

"Like I said, I hardly knew him. He was a nice guy, worked hard, mostly kept to himself."

"I'm sure he was a nice guy. But he was also gorgeous. Don't tell me you didn't flirt with him."

"Not in the office," Nora said. "Ms. Randall is a stickler for decorum."

"What about outside the office?"

"Well, at the year-end party, I did some flirting. He seemed to be a little receptive, but then Ms. Randall walked up and killed the mood."

"Why did she do that?"

"I don't know. He and I were chatting over by the bar. Something about how the Champagne was extra bubbly or something. Ms. Randall walked over to us and smiled at me. Scared the shit out of me."

"Why would a smile scare you?"

"I don't know, it felt like the kind of smile a tiger might make before it ate you. Anyway, I made my excuses and left. I wondered if they had a thing going, but I guess not."

"Why do you say that?"

"Well, she just talked to him for a minute, then walked off. I didn't see them interact after that. And when the engagement was announced, she looked shocked like the rest of us, but she immediately congratulated him. She told him to be sure and let her know where they were registered."

"Is that all?"

"Yes. They traveled on business together about once a quarter, but that's to be expected. I never saw any kind of flirting between them at the office."

"But the smile scared you. Did you feel she was staking her claim?"

"Exactly. You remember the head cheerleader in high school and how she would make sure everyone knew who her boyfriend was, it was like that."

"Okay. Weren't you with him the night he was killed?"

"Sure, most of us were. It was an intro party for the new phone. We were all at McGenty's drinking it up. They even had a live band."

"Was Ms. Randall there?"

"At the beginning. She was all dressed up because she had a big charity event to go to. She gave a speech, then headed out."

"What did Markham do?"

"He partied with the rest of us. Then all of a sudden, he left. I think he got a text message just before he left, but I'm not sure."

"Did anyone else leave?"

"Not then. The party was really going."

"So, it was odd that he left."

"Yeah, I guess so."

"Anything else you remember?"

"Not much. Hey, don't be quoting me about Ms. Randall. I can't afford to piss her off."

"Don't worry, I'll keep your name out of it."

Sophia headed over to Ms. Randall's condo building. She'd been in Delphi City since the McCormacks had acquired the major interest in Vancouver Integrated and had established its satellite office here. Sophia's research showed that she'd never moved from the first condo that she had gotten when she first arrived.

Her first stop was the building supervisor. Each condo building had a supervisor who coordinated repairs and maintenance activities with the residents, managed the common areas, and hired and managed the cleaners who kept the place looking nice. Most of them also offered a concierge service on the side as one-stop shopping for all the services that could be had in Delphi City. They then would call the appropriate service, usually some preteen who was running a business on the side to supplement their allowance.

"Mr. Colling, thanks for seeing me," Sophia said as the supervisor let her into his office.

"No problem. I've got plenty of time," Mr. Colling said. "What do you want to know?"

"I'm curious how much you know about Ms. Randall?"

"Her, I know plenty about her. She's always complaining about something. The hallways are not clean enough, the plants look too cheap, the boy bringing her dinner is too slow. That woman is sure full of herself."

"That's what I've heard," Sophia agreed. "She's been here since she moved to Delphi City. I'm surprise she hasn't moved or at least gotten a double unit."

"Oh, that woman has a triple unit," Mr. Colling said.

"How, the records don't show that?"

"Oh, the records show some other people from Vancouver Integrated live in them units. They even show she has a roommate, but nobody lives there except her. She paid to have them connected together and upgraded her condo the first year. She still keeps them other people on the books."

"Does she have many guests?"

"No. She likes her privacy."

"No male visitors?"

"Oh, I think she has someone. Every once in a while, she opens the door herself. Brings her royal-self down to the service entrance, opens the door, then goes back upstairs. I assume she's letting someone in that she doesn't want registered as a guest."

"How often does she do this?"

"Oh, maybe once a month, sometimes twice."

"Have you ever seen this guest?"

"No, it's always late at night. I can just tell by the records that she came down."

"Come on, you mean to tell me that you've never been tempted to look at the surveillance tape to see who she was letting in, the camera must have caught him outside the entrance while he waited?"

"Oh, sure. But whoever it is, wears a hoodie and is careful to hide his face."

"Well, was he a big person or small?"

"Oh, he's a fine strapping man. Maybe 188 centimeters, real fit looking."

That matched Markham's description, making Sophia sure that he and Randall were having an affair.

"Thank you for speaking with me," Sophia said as she got up and let herself out.

"Chief Nawal, a Sophia Michaels is on the line."

"Please tell her to talk to the communication officer."

"She says she has new evidence."

"Okay, put her through," Chief Nawal said as she shook her head. "Ms. Michaels, this had better not be a ploy to get another interview or ask a question."

"It's not," Sophia said.

"Okay, what evidence do you have?"

"First, I want you to promise me that if it leads to an arrest that I get the exclusive."

"Ms. Michaels, we are not in the habit of making deals with the press!"

"Well, I'm not in the habit of doing the police's job for them. I can assure you that I have information that you will find valuable."

"Fine. If your information leads to an arrest, we'll contact you and do our best to give you an exclusive."

"Thanks," Sophia said. "Are you aware that William Markham was having an affair with Ms. Randall?"

Chief Nawal was totally shocked at the suggestion. "What evidence do you have of that?!"

"The building supervisor has seen a man matching his description being let into the building by Ms. Randall on several occasions. One of the women who worked in the office with Mr. Markham was given a signal by Ms. Randall that Mr. Markham was not available."

"What do you mean, not available?"

"As in not in the market for female company. I've also found records showing that often both of them were out of the office on the same days, and other records that show that they took different flights to Wellington on those same days. Their flights would have arrived in the city the same evening. Both returned on different flights the next morning."

"Interesting. How did you come by the information on the flights?"

"I can't reveal my sources, but I can assure you that they are accurate. You probably would rather verify the information yourself."

"Yes, that would be better. We do have her on our list of suspects, but haven't considered her a very strong candidate."

"Just remember my exclusive."

"I will."

12 Daddy's Little Girl

"Sam, have you talked to Catie lately?" Marc asked.

"No, not since the board meeting, why?" Samantha asked.

"Nothing serious, but she wanted to work on a design mod for the jetliners, and she hasn't done much on it yet. It's so unlike her, I'm worried she might be sick or something."

"Liz is in Delphi City now, ask her to check in on Catie."

"Call Liz," Marc ordered his Comm.

"Hey, what time is it in Delphi City," Samantha scolded.

"It is 2300 hours," ADI said.

"Hey Marc. What's up?" Liz asked.

"I was wondering if you knew how Catie is doing?"

"I think she's fine, why do you ask?"

"She hasn't accomplished much on the design mod for the jetliner. I wondered if there was a problem or if she's just busy."

"She didn't look busy when we met," Liz said. "At least no busier than you would expect at the Academy."

"No problems?"

"Not that she mentioned, but I'll check on her tomorrow and let you know," Liz said.

"Thanks."

"And sorry to call so late," Samantha added, pushing Marc's shoulder.

"It wasn't a problem. I was just doing some reading before bed."

"Hi, Yvette," Liz said as she knocked on the door to Yvette's and Catie's dorm room. "Is Alex around?" Liz knew very well that Alex wasn't around. She was in her space fleet ops class.

"No, you just missed her. She's in class now."

"How are you guys doing? Do you have anything special planned for the break, are you going to anyplace exotic?"

153

"No, we just got back from a rotation on Delphi Station. We got certified for microgravity and got some control room experience."

"Oh, that's right, you guys used my cabin. How many cadets were in the class?"

"*Thirty-two*," Yvette said, sounding pleased with herself. "The rest of them were crowded into four rooms. It was so nice to be able to use your cabin."

"I'm happy I could help. What's going on with Alex? She seemed preoccupied last time I talked with her."

"Oh, probably that guy she's dating. They've been out twice and she thinks he's *très rêveur*."

"Oh, been there, thought that," Liz said.

"Just been there? You should have them following you around like puppies."

"Dreamy guys?"

"Yes."

"Problem is, you have to wake up some time and they're not so dreamy then," Liz said. "Tell Alex I said hi."

"Liz, did you learn anything?" Marc asked as he and Liz connected again.

Liz laughed, "Oh, yes. I learned that your life is going to be hell for the next few years."

"Why?" Marc asked, completely puzzled.

"Catie has decided she likes men."

"So?"

"One man in particular," Liz said.

"She can't be dating that much," Marc said.

"Oh, she's only been out with him twice," Liz said.

"So, I'm confused," Marc said. He looked at Samantha who had just started to listen in on the conversation.

"Well, how much did your productivity go down after you started dating Sam?" Liz asked.

"Why would it go down?"

Samantha glared at Marc. "It *better* have gone down."

"Well, I had a little less time since we spent time together doing things besides work," Marc said.

"I'm going to *kill* you!"

"Cer Sam, Marc's productivity dropped twelve percent when he started dating you. Only six percent of that was due to time you spent together," ADI said.

"ADI just saved your ass," Samantha said.

"Really, six percent on other stuff?" Marc said.

"Well, you did need to think about where to take her to dinner, what presents to buy her, much less all the time you spent thinking about how much you enjoyed your time together," Liz said.

"Oh, it didn't seem like it took that much time," Marc said, as he ducked a slap from Samantha.

"Well, daydreams don't seem like they take much time. How often do you find that when you have free time, all of a sudden, you're working on a problem? How many problems do you solve by daydreaming about them?" Liz asked.

"Quite a few."

"Same thing is true with Catie. But now she daydreams about how hunky that guy of hers is. How nice he kisses, what they're going to do, when will he call," Liz said.

"It can't take that much time," Marc said.

"Oh, but the best dates are the ones in your head," Liz said. "They can take a lot of time and you can have as many of them as you want."

"I guess." Marc shook his head. "I'm not sure I'm ready for her to start dating."

"You don't get a choice there," Liz said. "Better get used to it."

———

"Don't worry, she's almost seventeen, it was bound to happen sooner or later," Samantha said. "I just hope he doesn't break her heart."

Sophia had just been alerted that the arrest was happening the next day. It was going to be made in the lobby of Vancouver Integrated when Ms. Randall arrived for work in the morning. Sophia arranged for her and Chaz, her boyfriend and cameraman, to be present in the lobby the next morning.

Ms. Randall arrived promptly by taxi at eight A.M. The taxi dropped her off right outside the door. When she entered the lobby, Chief Nawal was standing at the reception desk.

"Chief Nawal, I wasn't aware that we had an appointment," Ms. Randall said, sounding slightly perturbed.

"We didn't. Dorothea Randall, I'm placing you under arrest for the murder of William Markham. . . ."

"How preposterous! I won't stand for this; I'll have your job."

"You're welcome to it. Now, you do not have to say anything. But it may harm your defense if you do not mention when questioned something which you later rely on in court. Anything you do say may be given in evidence. Please allow the constable to place you in handcuffs."

"I will not!"

The constable took her refusal as an invitation to grab her, push her against the reception desk, and cuff her. Chief Nawal had brought a female constable to deal with Ms. Randall. It looked like the constable had thoroughly enjoyed the fact that Ms. Randall had refused to be polite about being handcuffed.

"I demand my lawyer!"

"You'll be given a phone call when we reach the station."

"Call Timothy!" Ms. Randall told her Comm.

"Sorry, Ms. Randall, your Comm has been disabled. You may place your call when you reach the station."

The constable escorted Ms. Randall out of the lobby and into the police car that had just pulled up.

Sophia quickly used her specs to check her hair and makeup. Then she moved to the front of the door and nodded to Chaz. "You have just witnessed the arrest of Ms. Dorothea Randall for the murder of William Markham. Ms. Randall is the vice president in charge of marketing and sales for Vancouver Integrated Circuits. It came to the attention of this reporter and the police that Ms. Randall was having an affair with the victim and that possibly the announcement of his engagement to another woman led to his murder."

Sophia added a few more lines about Ms. Randall then gave Chaz the signal to cut. "Great, let's edit it and get it on our site," Sophia said. "Take that, Leslie Walters!"

"Good job," Chaz said. "I can't believe you figured this out and scored an exclusive."

"Excuse me, but would you mind leaving the building," the security guard requested.

"Chief Nawal, we've heard you've made an arrest. Can you tell us about it?" Leslie Walters asked as the chief arrived at the police station.

"We've arrested Ms. Dorothea Randall this morning for the murder of William Markham. We are now in the process of serving search warrants for her home and office. At this point all further communication about the case will be the responsibility of the district attorney."

"Can you tell us why Sophia Michaels of the Delphi Gazette was allowed to be present at the arrest?"

"Ms. Michaels was the one who brought certain information to our attention that allowed us to get warrants for Ms. Randall's Comm and to track her movements. This led to evidence being uncovered that indicated that Ms. Randall had murdered Mr. Markham. This resulted in us going to Ms. Randall's office to make the arrest. Given that Ms. Michaels was privy to our raised interest in Ms. Randall, it was not surprising to me that she followed me to Vancouver Integrated's office when I went there to make the arrest."

13 Board Meeting – April 4th

"Let's bring this meeting to order," Marc said. "I assume everyone has heard about the arrest this morning."

"Yes, can you believe it was his boss?" Blake asked.

"Yeah, usually people want to kill their boss, not the other way around," Kal said.

"I can assure you the feeling goes both ways," Marc said.

"Oh, I think he's threatening us," Blake said, feigning fear.

"No, just stating the facts," Marc said. "ADI assures me that they have the right person. Hopefully the arrest will alleviate people's fears."

"I'm sure it will, but I understand they're going to release her on her own recognizance," Nikola said.

"Sure. They'll put a tracking chip in her. And it's not like she can flee the jurisdiction."

"But, she's a murderer."

"Then I would suggest that nobody date her," Marc said. "Seems a low-risk release. Now, let's get to business. Liz, how are you doing?"

"I'm heading up to the Dutchman right after this meeting. We set sail tomorrow."

"Any problems?"

"Not yet, but with a little over ten thousand Paraxean colonists on board, I'm keeping my fingers crossed."

"So they're really using half their capacity for colonists?" Samantha asked.

"It's only twenty-five percent, eight pods and all of our passenger space," Liz said. "The governor says that with us delivering the grain to them, they'll be able to handle that many. They're in a hurry to get that colony on its feet, and they're anxious to get the asteroid delivered as well."

"What did you do with the stasis pods?" Marc asked.

"They used them to pay for the cargo and cabins," Liz said. "We'll be bringing them to Delphi Station on Oryxes for the next few months."

"What are you going to do with them?" Samantha asked.

"Harvest the electronics and metals from them," Liz said. "They're worth about one hundred thousand dollars each."

"That's one billion dollars," Blake gulped.

"Hey, the grain they're buying is three hundred million and then there are all those cabins."

"Still. And what are you bringing back from there?"

"Mostly platinum metals," Liz said. "We'll be half empty though. They haven't been there long enough to mine that much. Their planet isn't as rich as Artemis."

"Is that all?" Samantha asked.

"We're talking about some exotic foodstuff," Liz added. "We'll see what we come up with while we're on the way."

"How did the Dutchman come through the first trip?" Marc asked, trying to get the meeting back to his agenda.

"Ajda did a full inspection. She and Commander Griggs say things look good. They had to do some work realigning the antimatter reactors, but it was just tweaking," Liz reported.

"Good, so are you going ahead with the second ship?" Marc asked.

"That's Catie's plan. We'll have to see how the money goes. This trip will help a lot."

"I'd say so," Blake said. "I knew I should have invested."

"It might not be too late," Liz said. "Damn ships cost almost one billion."

"What?!" Fred said. "I thought a few hundred million. Did you clear that much on the futures deal?"

"Barely, I had to leverage my shares in MacKenzies to come up with enough."

"Who did you leverage your shares with?"

"Catie."

"Ahem," Catie interrupted as her Comm linked into the meeting. "Sorry I'm late."

"Oh, hi," Blake said. "We were just talking about some shipping tycoon named Catie McCormack."

"They were asking if we're going to build the second StarMerchant," Liz said.

"If we can," Catie said. "I'm working out a deal with Ajda and Fred now."

"Are you looking for investors?" Blake asked.

"Talk about that later!" Marc snapped. "What's the latest from Margaret?"

"Why don't we invite her to these meetings?" Blake asked. "I'm just playing messenger boy."

"And a good messenger boy you are," Marc said. "Now, the update."

"The farmers are very happy, grain prices are way up, especially corn. It's made most of the governments happy."

"You mean the grain exporting countries," Samantha said.

"Of course. Importers aren't too happy, but prices were pretty depressed. So moving on, we've reached a tentative deal on the licensing and patent process between star systems," Blake said. "A few of the ambassadors on the Security Council are starting to wonder whether the colonies are really going to be joining the U.N. instead of some interstellar council."

"Awww, are they finally figuring out that they're not masters of the universe?" Samantha asked.

"That's the impression Maggie gave. Marc, do you have a plan for that?"

"I'm just going to let it play out," Marc said.

"Okay. Maggie also says they're having serious discussions about intervening in Africa to see if they can straighten out some of that mess," Blake continued.

"Is that a good thing?"

"Maggie says it is. We'll see what they come up with later. I'll let Kal tell you about Mexico."

"Kal?" Marc prompted, suddenly very interested in what Kal was going to say.

"Mexico is asking for a little help with one of their cartels," Kal said.

"What kind of help?"

"This cartel has essentially taken over one of the states. They want us to help root them out. Part of their message to the cartels is that they need to start cleaning up their act."

"How is taking out one cartel going to help?" Marc asked.

"Well, we've been helping them get ready. ADI and ANDI have traced a bunch of cartel money, around twenty billion dollars. They're going to seize it right after we take care of the one," Kal explained.

"How are they going to seize it? Will the banks cooperate?" Blake asked.

"We're not planning to ask the banks. ADI has managed to get control of the accounts; she's just going to move the money."

"And just how did she do that?"

"Captain, it is amazing how careless people can be with their passwords," ADI said. "Once I got control of their computers, it was easy to find the passwords."

"And how did you get control of their computers?" Marc asked.

"I used a modified version of the virus we used against Russia."

"Will the world ever be safe again?" Samantha asked.

"Yes," ADI said. "You'll need to use biometric passwords with encryption keys. They should be unbreakable, at least without the help of the owner."

"They would be similar to what we have on our Comms," Catie said. "They won't unlock if you're under stress unless you add a code after you register your fingerprint or face."

"I feel better, *I think*," Samantha said.

"So, why take out the one cartel?" Marc asked.

"The Mexican government is afraid of reprisals against the civilian population. They want to have control of the area before they seize the money," Kal explained.

"That's probably smart," Samantha said.

"And they need your help?" Marc asked.

"They're afraid of leaks. Our team can go in, infiltrate the communities, and take down the main players. It's basically what we train for, so I don't see a problem."

"When are you planning to do this?"

"I've already sent in an advance team. Mostly women. Seems nobody takes notice when a few women start showing up in a town, especially if they act like they're interested in making some money on the side."

"Won't they be surprised when those women start taking them down," Blake said.

"Okay, makes sense. Go ahead," Marc said. "As if you were waiting for my approval. Fred, anything to report from your end?"

"We're making lots of money. Our airline president is demanding another eight airliners."

"Do we have enough cash?"

"We will when Catie starts paying for her new StarMerchant."

"What, I don't get a deal?!" Catie yelped.

"Like the deal we got for the cabins?" Marc asked.

"Hey, you got a good deal. I would have charged thirty-five percent."

"And I would have paid thirty," Marc shot back. "But we can talk about business pricing later. Nikola, how are our scientists doing?"

"Nakahara-san is still trying to reverse engineer the quantum relays. No luck, and he's still not very hopeful of a solution anytime soon."

"*Good,*" Dr. Metra whispered.

"I heard that," Marc said. "But I'm sure the Paraxeans will be happy to keep a corner of that market."

"I'm sure they will," Nikola said. "He's still making improvements to the quantum cables. Leo and some friends are working on making an even smaller superconductor. They hope to be able to make our Comm chips with a production process instead of printing them on the molecular printer."

"That would be nice," Catie said. "Our Comms are expensive to make."

"That would explain the price you gave us on them," Marc said, getting in a jab despite his desire to keep the meeting on track. "Blake how are we doing on a welcoming party for our friends?"

"You mean your friends. We're studying the situation, no clear plan. I am concerned about the course change they've just made."

"What course change?" Catie asked.

"They just spent a huge amount of reaction mass to change their course about one pico-arcsecond. It'll take them out away from the Artemis Prime by a bit. Doesn't make sense why they would do it. We didn't detect anything in their way," Blake explained.

"Yes, that bothers me as well," Marc said. "I assume you're adding that to your scenarios?"

"We are. We'll be getting the strategy class at the Academy to run simulations on it soon. Maybe one of those geniuses will come up with a reason," Blake said.

"Come on, it's time for our golf lesson," Yvette said.

"Why are we doing this, when will we have time to play golf?" Catie asked.

"We can practice here at the Academy; we're on the edge, so we can set up a driving range. With your HUD you can practice putting in your room."

"So, when would we play?"

"Anytime you're on shore. All the big boys and girls play golf. Besides, right now, it's about the lesson, not playing."

"You're a letch."

"Ha, you just wait. Putting lessons are the best."

"You two ready?" Miranda asked as she came into their room.

"I am, Alex is being difficult."

"Come on, Alex, we don't want to be late," Miranda said.

"Alright, just for you," Catie said. She put on her golf outfit and grabbed her golf shoes so they could head out.

"How's your driving going?" Victor asked.

"Getting better," Miranda said. "We've managed to practice three days. We're setting up a little driving range at the edge of the Academy, it overlooks the ocean."

"That's a good thing, wouldn't want you breaking any windows. You need to make sure you keep coming here to practice in the stations. That'll give you the feedback you need to get that swing burned into muscle memory."

"Alex, are you still happy to play right-handed?"

"Yes, I'm getting better," Catie said.

"Keep practicing."

"We will; we probably should schedule another lesson with you," Yvette said.

Victor just nodded. "I see you each got a putter."

"Yes. The clerk helped us pick them out. He said we could exchange them if you didn't like the ones he had chosen," Yvette said.

"They look fine so far. Let's see how they do when you use them." Victor led them over to the practice green. "Now putting is all about consistency. Everything is exactly the same except the length of your backstroke."

Catie and Miranda nodded; Yvette looked confused.

"You use the same grip that you use on any golf club. I recommend you relax your arms a bit, but the basics are much the same. Now line up over the ball, hip pointed toward the hole, rock your shoulder back, and drive through the stroke nice and easy."

"But what if the hole is farther away?" Yvette asked.

"You increase your backswing."

"How can that work? Just because you swing more, if everything is the same, why would the ball go farther?"

"Because when you increase your backswing, the club will be traveling faster when it hits the ball."

"Oh, so you accelerate the club throughout the swing," Catie said.

"Exactly."

"Then why didn't you say that?" Yvette asked.

"I thought I did," Victor replied. "Now, let me work with each of you to establish your stroke."

Yvette made Catie go first again. Catie had to admit that she liked it when Victor put his arms around her to guide her stroke. After a few putts, he helped Miranda out. It didn't take him long to pronounce her putting stroke as 'good to go'. Of course, Yvette had all kinds of problems getting her stroke down.

"Relax your grip on the club," Victor said.

"Oops," Yvette let the club slip out of her hands at the end of the stroke. Catie and Miranda just shook their heads.

Victor wound up spending twice as much time with Yvette as he had with Catie and Miranda combined.

"Okay, I've got to go teach my next lesson. But before I go, let me get you set up on the green. There are sensors at each corner that will register with the ball and your HUD. Once you're ready to really try some putting, they'll show you the shot you should take. Once you get comfortable, turn the feature off. The holes are done like a pool table, the ball drops below and is returned to the dispenser. You can toss a bunch of balls out in different locations and just go from one to the other making a putt," Victor explained.

"I also recommend you spend some time doing a bunch of lag shots. That will teach you to control the speed of the ball, the length of the putt," Victor added. "Have fun."

Yvette picked six balls and tossed them around the hole. Most of them landed in the five to six-foot range. She slowly went from one to the other, sinking each putt.

"You should be an actress," Miranda said. "Come on, Alex, let's try doing lag shots."

14   Excuse Me

"That's four," Yvette said as she looked back down from her HUD.

"Four?" Catie asked.

"Four messages from Gaspare today," Yvette said.

"Is that bad?"

"Five is my limit. If a man has to send you five 'I'm thinking of you' messages a day, then he's either too clingy or too insecure."

"Isn't that harsh?"

"Maybe, but there are lots of nice guys out there. Why should I put up with one that is constantly bothering me with inane messages?"

"I guess it would make you wonder why he's got so much free time to be daydreaming about you," Catie said.

"Yes, and even if he is, why doesn't he have more self-respect than to keep texting me to remind me about it all the time?" Yvette asked.

Catie met Braxton at Deogene's for dinner. He had called to set up the date right after he got back from Delphi Station, but it took until this Friday for their schedules to match up.

"Hi, Braxton."

"Hello, Alex. You should have let me pick you up. We could have walked over together, or taken a taxi."

"It's only five blocks from my dorm," Catie said. "You can walk with me on the way back. Did you check in?"

"Yes, our table should be ready." Braxton signaled the maître d' and they were quickly escorted to their table.

"Would you like to order something to drink?" the maître d' asked as he handed them the menus.

"Just a glass of water for now," Catie said.

"I'll have the same, and could we have the wine list?" Braxton asked.

"But of course," the maître d' said, signaling to the waiter to bring water and the wine menu.

"We don't need to order a bottle," Catie said. "I'll only have one glass."

"Just one glass? Come on, relax a bit; you are off duty."

"I always try to limit myself to one glass."

"I'll get a bottle anyway. You get a better selection that way."

Catie perused the menu, even though she knew what she wanted already. Once Braxton had made up his mind, she set her menu down to alert the waiter that they were ready to order. Catie ordered the Pork Chops Barbados and Braxton ordered the Jamaican Jerk Chicken. Braxton decided on a Riesling to go with dinner.

The maître d' did a nice show of serving the wine and left the bottle in an ice bucket next to the table.

"To us!" Braxton offered as a toast.

"To summer break," Catie responded.

"How is the smelter running?" Catie asked after the toast.

"It's running just fine," Braxton said. "We're working on a new problem now."

"What kind of problem?"

"We're looking into the power distribution systems here on Earth. With the fusion reactors and solar power starting to dominate power generation, distribution is the next opportunity to improve efficiency. It's amazing how much power is lost due to distribution costs. Plus, there is a lot of overcapacity because of lack of storage."

"Lack of storage?"

"Yes, you either have to have a reservoir where you can pump water up, so you can generate electricity by reversing it, or you have to have overcapacity available to generate enough power for peak demand. Right now, natural gas powerplants are the favorite to meet peak demand."

"I guess batteries are pretty expensive and bulky for mass energy storage."

"Yes, the next most-used method is compressed air storage. They pump air into a cave under pressure, then run a turbine from it. We're looking at the mercury towers they build on Artemis."

"Oh, I've heard of those," Catie said. Her father had designed the mercury towers, towers of power he'd called them. They pumped mercury up during the day and let it flow down and drive electric turbines at night.

"Sure. Well, they can store enough power in a mercury tower to handle the peak loading problem for a small town or city. We're going to take a region of the U.S. and calculate how much they can save in dollars and carbon emission by switching over."

"Come on, have another glass of wine," Braxton coaxed Catie after they both had finished their dinner. There was just over a glass left in the bottle."

"No, one is my limit," Catie said. "I told you not to order a bottle."

"If you won't help me, I'll have to finish it off by myself."

"It's your head," Catie said.

"My parents are in town tomorrow," Braxton said. "This is my last chance to relax before they start in on me."

"Start in on you?"

"Oh, I'll have to show them the whole city. They're staying the entire weekend, so we'll have to try all the various attractions around the city. We'll go up to Delphi Station on Sunday, so they can tell everyone they've been there. It'll be a bore."

"At least they care enough to come and visit you."

"I guess."

"It was a nice dinner," Catie said as she and Braxton paused outside of her dorm building.

"It was fun," Braxton said. He pulled Catie into a hug and gave her a warm kiss. He had been a bit drunk when they left the restaurant, but the walk had been enough to sober him up.

"Have fun with your parents," Catie said as she broke free of his hug. "Night!"

"How was your date?" Yvette asked when Catie entered their room.

"It was nice," Catie said.

"What did you talk about?"

"He's working on a power distribution problem at the university."

"What else?"

"A bit about some of his other classes, his parents coming to town."

"What about your space strategy class?"

"That didn't come up."

"I don't know about this Braxton guy. He should have been asking all kinds of questions about you and hanging onto your every word."

"I don't like to talk about myself," Catie said.

"That doesn't matter."

"Chief Griggs, how are the gravity drives doing?" Liz asked as she walked into the engine room.

"They're doing well. You remember Spec-three Rhodes?" Commander Griggs asked nodding to the spacer who was working with her.

"Yes; how is your first space flight going, Specialist Rhodes?" Liz asked.

"It is amazing. These gravity drives are a wonder. The amount of power each of these drives consumes could power a small city. The chief has been teaching me how to maintain the antimatter reactors," Rhodes said.

"Yes, without them, we wouldn't be able to jump this big of a ship, and it would take weeks to build up enough charge to do so," Liz said. "So do you plan on testing for your rating on the antimatter reactor?"

"As soon as the chief says I'm ready. There is a lot to learn."

"Carry on, Rhodes," Commander Griggs said. "Captain, why don't we go to my office?"

Commander Griggs poured a finger of scotch for them both, "So what brings you down here?"

"I'd like to talk about the crew staffing level," Liz said. "Things were so crazy during the reload, that we never had a chance to go over some things."

"Did you get a chance to catch up with Catie?"

"Just a day. Of course we chat on our Comms all the time."

"So what do you want to ask?"

"Catie is pushing to start up a second ship," Liz said. "I wondered if you had suggestions about crew staffing levels and rotations."

"Are the ships going to be identical?"

"Yes."

"That's good. You want to keep the crews together as a unit, but you don't want them to be switching ships and getting confused."

"Makes sense."

"If you run three crews in rotation, you can give every crew one trip off after every two trips. It'll be more complex than that with the length of the trips varying, but you should be able to let everyone get a few weeks of shore leave after twenty to thirty weeks in space."

"Oh, that's a great suggestion. I could put up with that," Liz said. "So we're going to need to hire at least one more captain, are you interested?"

"Nope, I like being the chief engineer," Commander Griggs said. "But I've got a couple of recommendations for you."

"That would be nice. Catie and I don't know that many people who have the right kinds of skills."

"No problem, I'll send their files to you right away."

"Thanks."

"Oh, one more thing," Commander Griggs said.

"Yes?"

"You do realize you're over-crewed for a civilian cargo ship?"

"We are?"

"Yes. You're crewed like a naval vessel. You can get by with a lot fewer people. Watch standers just need to know enough to call for help. So you're about thirty percent over what you really need."

"That should help," Liz said. "I'll go over it with Catie; she might want to talk with you about it."

"I'm always available."

"Let's walk over to my place," Braxton suggested. "You can take a cab from there."

"Sure," Catie replied. "You're right across from the cherry tree park, aren't you?"

"Yes, we can stroll through it if you'd like."

"That'd be nice."

Catie and Braxton held hands as they walked the four blocks to the park. They entered it on its southeast corner and starting meandering along the pathways between the trees.

"This is one of my favorite parks," Catie said.

"It is, why is that?"

"The cherry blossoms. They're really beautiful in the spring."

"I'd guess so, I never really noticed."

They walked a bit more before approaching the edge of the park where Braxton's dorm building was. "Alex, my roommates are gone this week. Do you want to come up?"

"I don't think so."

"Oh, come on," Braxton said, pulling Catie into an embrace. He kissed her slowly. He raised his hand along her side and started to caress her breast. Catie flinched and used her elbow to push his hand lower. It took all her self-control not to grab his wrist and break it.

"Sorry," Braxton muttered as he deepened the kiss.

"What!" Catie sputtered when Braxton's tongue bumped into hers. She pushed him away. "Hey!"

"What's the problem, it's just a little French kiss!"

"Well, I don't know you well enough to be doing that."

"What do you mean, this is our third date?"

"So, what does that mean?"

"Well, the third date is when you take the relationship to the next level. Don't you want to do it?"

Catie's face flushed. She was glad that it was dark and he couldn't see.

"No!" she said turning away and walking toward the other side of the park.

"What's the matter? I thought you liked me."

"That doesn't mean I want to sleep with you," Catie spat as she continued to walk away.

Braxton started to walk after her, but some other walker brushed by him, almost knocking him down.

"Hey, watch where you're going!"

"You should watch where you're going," the woman said as she kept walking away.

With the woman now between him and Catie, Braxton gave up and turned back toward his dorm.

As the woman walked by Catie, Catie whispered, "Thanks, Morgan."

"Just my job. I'm just glad I didn't have to call an ambulance for him."

Catie walked to her dorm, mad and embarrassed at the same time.

"How was your date?" Yvette asked.

"Terrible!"

"What happened?"

"He made a pass. Said something about a third date."

"Oh Chérie, you are such an ingénue, and he is such a cad."

"What do you mean?"

"Many people think of the third date as when you should have sex. It's really that you shouldn't have sex before the third date, otherwise you are, what do you say, a slut. But some men think that it is their right after three dates."

"That is ludicrous."

"Yes it is. And if he made a pass to ask you to have sex with him, then he is an imbecile. Are you okay?"

"Yes, I'm just mad!"

"See, I told you he was too into himself. If he wasn't interested in what you do and care about, then he's not worth your time. There are plenty of men out there."

15 Justice

Sophia had Chaz filming her in front of the courthouse.

"Today, Ms. Dorothea Randall gets her day in court. Under Delphi law, once a suspect is arrested, the Delphi Prosecutor has thirty days to present the evidence to the defense and a judge at a hearing. It has been twenty-five days since her arrest.

"Unfortunately, we won't be able to film the hearing or even report on it. Delphi Law only allows the defense, the prosecution, and the judge to be present. If there are any witnesses called by the prosecution, they are only allowed in the courtroom during their testimony."

Sophia moved up the steps of the courthouse before continuing.

"After the hearing, the judge will decide if Ms. Randall will be held over for trial, or have the charges against her dismissed. The judge could even enter a verdict of not guilty, which would prevent any further prosecution of Ms. Randall by the DA. This reporter is confident that the DA will present a compelling case.

"It may interest viewers to know that Ms. Randall has been released under her own recognizance while awaiting this hearing. She has had a subdermal tracking chip inserted, is being required to wear a Comm at all times, and has to report to the police once a day. Delphi law is very kind to the accused. Those and the confiscation of her passport were the only conditions placed on her release. It will be interesting to see how Delphi City handles someone once they've been found guilty and has to be sent to prison."

"Your honor, I wish to present to you the facts of the case as we have reconstructed them."

"Please proceed," the judge said.

"The defendant, Dorothea Randall, was having an affair with the victim, William Markham. We have here sworn affidavits from a hotel in Wellington where on six separate occasions they checked in under assumed names. We also have affidavits from the staff at five other hotels that state that despite checking into separate rooms, the defendant and Mr. Markham did in fact share the same room.

"We also have an affidavit from the superintendent of Ms. Randall's condo building that states that Ms. Randall was in the habit of personally admitting an unknown man into the building and taking him up to her condo. We can substantiate that on five of those occasions, Mr. Markham received a text from an unknown phone telling him to 'come over.' We can trace his movements from his condo to Ms. Randall's building."

The DA gave Ms. Randall a knowing look. She just stared ahead.

"On the night of his death, Mr. Markham received a text from an individual in Vancouver, British Columbia, Canada. Upon contacting that individual, we confirmed that he had been paid five hundred dollars to send the text on Sunday, the fifth of March at twelve forty A.M. CKT, with a promise of another five hundred dollars after the text was delivered. He agreed to do so. He was told where to find the five hundred dollars. It was hidden in a park in Vancouver, British Columbia; the second installment was hidden in another park in the same city. This occurred two days after Ms. Randall was in Vancouver on business.

"On the night of the murder, Ms. Randall was present at the party with Mr. Markham for approximately one hour. She then left the party to attend a charity event at the Four Seasons Hotel. The victim's condo is only three blocks away from the Four Seasons.

"The police have interviewed the other attendees of the event at the Four Seasons. Everyone remembers Ms. Randall's attendance. Several witnesses swore that she excused herself around twelve forty A.M. to use the facilities. No one can remember seeing her between then and two o'clock.

"We have surveillance video that shows an individual matching Ms. Randall's general height and build, leaving the Four Seasons just after twelve fifty A.M. and reentering the facility just after one thirty A.M."

"Your Honor, the prosecution weaves a fine story. But it is ridiculous to say that my client, who was dressed in a formal gown and high heels, made her way across four blocks, entered the victim's building, killed him, and returned to the party without anyone noticing, or getting blood on her gown."

"If it pleases Your Honor, I'm just getting to that," the DA said.

"Please proceed."

"A search of Ms. Randall's condos revealed several items. First, a microfiber hood, which can be folded up into a package smaller than a package of Kleenex. Second, it revealed a black microfiber hoodie which can be folded into a similar sized package. And third, a pair of microfiber pants which would allow the legs to be pulled up over themselves so that they hugged the defendant's thighs and would have been above the hem of her gown.

"We surmise, that the defendant entered the lady's room at the hotel, removed the hood and hoodie from her handbag, as well as the weapon and a pair of slippers that all our women wear when they want to carry their heels while walking on the street. She then removed her gown, folded it, and secreted it and her handbag in the bottom of the trash bin, beneath the liner. Then after lowering the pantlegs, she put the hood on her head to protect her hair, donned the hoodie and slipped out the back way, with the weapon secreted in the pocket of the hoodie.

"She then entered the victim's condo building, tailgating on a group of residents that were coming home from work. She then made her way to the service entrance and waited for the victim, who she knew would be coming to meet her due to a text message he'd just received.

"When the victim entered the building via the service entrance, which provided the shortest path to the elevator from the party he had just left, she came up behind him and stabbed him in the throat with the murder weapon."

"What murder weapon?" the defense demanded. "The kitchen knife that the prosecution has presented does not match the wounds."

"The kitchen knife, a chef's knife to be exact, has a six-inch blade that is two and a half inches wide. It shows signs of having been sharpened on the back side, then dulled afterward. It matches the wound exactly if you assume the sharpened edge, which we postulate the defendant added using the knife sharpener she had delivered to her condo one week before the murder."

The DA closed the folder containing the notes he had been using during his presentation. "Your Honor, that is our case. We await your ruling."

"Does the defense wish to make a statement at this time?" the judge asked.

The defense attorney stood up and flipped through the notes he had been taking during the prosecution's presentation. "Your Honor. The prosecution's case rests on the vivid imagination of the Chief of Police and a reporter. Their leading questions to witnesses have added to this house of cards. I submit that this case should be dismissed and that you should enter a verdict of not guilty on behalf of my client." With that the defense attorney sat down.

"If there is nothing else, I will end this hearing. You will have my ruling by the end of the week," the judge announced.

"Ms. Randall, what did you think of the prosecution's case?" a reporter asked while running beside her and jamming a microphone into her face.

Her lawyer stepped between her and the reporter, allowing Ms. Randall to get into the taxi. "My client will not make a statement. But I am looking forward to the dismissal of this ridiculous case," the defense attorney said. Then he got into the taxi with Ms. Randall and they were driven off.

16   Simulations

Catie walked into the simulation room. This was to be the first group simulation exercise. Until now, all the simulations had been individual events. She was curious how they were supposed to manage a group simulation. Everyone had just been given a room and time to show up.

"Hi, Miranda," Catie acknowledged the Cadet Colonel as she entered the simulation room right behind her.

"Hi, Alex. Anyone else here yet?"

"It's early, I think the rest of them are worried about getting trapped with the professor. But here they come."

"Hi, weird instructions; just show up on time, no prep work or anything," Cadet Major Baker said.

"Yes, they are," Miranda replied. "We don't even know who will be in the group until they show up."

The rest of the group slowly filed in. Catie groaned as Cadet Jamison walked in. *"Why did he have to be in my group?"*

The monitor in the front of the room lit up and Captain Clark started talking. "Hello, welcome to your first group simulation exercise. For this exercise you have to provide all the structure. You'll be the command staff for a fleet; figure out the roles and divide them up. You need to pick an admiral, then assign the other roles. Good luck."

"What does he mean pick an admiral?" Cadet Jamison asked.

"I think he means we vote on who we want to lead us," Miranda answered.

"Why, everyone knows you're going to be the admiral."

"I don't think so. And for my part I would nominate Cadet MacGregor to be the admiral," Miranda said.

"Why? She's just a second-class!"

"Because she's got the best aggregate score on the individual simulations," Miranda said. "In fact, her scores are so much higher than the rest of ours, she could probably win this thing if we all sat in the corner."

"You expect me to take orders from a second-class cadet? You're insane!" Jamison said.

"Hey, it's up to the group. I'll do whatever we decide. But although they say failure is the best teacher, I'm not all that fond of that method. I like to do my learning while I'm winning," Miranda said.

"I agree with her," Baker added. "What about the rest of you?"

It only took a minute before everyone except Jamison agreed. He just stood there looking mad while each of the others confirmed Catie as the admiral.

"Admiral MacGregor, what are your orders?" Miranda asked.

"Are you sure you shouldn't be the Admiral?" Catie asked. "I don't think I could have done what you did to get us organized on the schooner."

"That was then, this is now. We're all here to help. Right Jamison!" Miranda said.

"Sure, sure."

"Okay, then let's figure out the rest of the roles. We need a captain for the carrier, a wing commander, a captain for frigate A, one for frigate B, someone in charge of the Marines, and a squadron commander for each of our two squadrons. Suggestions?" Catie asked.

"I'd be happy to command the Marines," Baker said.

"Thank you," Catie said as she examined the scores for each of the seven cadets she was now supposed to lead.

"I did well in the simulation where we ran the frigates," Cadet Julie Delacroix said.

"Why don't you take frigate Alfa," Catie said.

"Wait, we just get to choose?" Jamison said.

"I think the Admiral is reviewing our simulation results," Miranda said.

Catie just nodded her head.

"I did almost as well as Julie on the frigate simulation," Hector Muñoz said.

Catie looked around the room; seeing general agreement, she turned to Hector, "Then you have frigate Bravo. So, captain for the carrier and the flight wing commander," Catie prompted.

"I'd like the flight wing," Cadet Ivan Castel said.

"You would, but your scores on those simulations aren't that good," Catie said.

"They weren't that bad," Ivan countered.

"Winning!" Miranda said.

"Okay, where would you put me?" Ivan asked.

"Captain of the carrier," Catie said. "You excelled in fleet maneuvers and managing fleet defenses."

"Wow, sure."

"Flight wing commander," Catie prompted looking at Miranda.

"Those are my best simulations," Miranda said.

"So that puts Jamison and Harris in charge of the squadrons," Catie said. "Any suggestions, or problems?"

"I'm *fine*," Jamison said without much enthusiasm.

"Okay, apparently they allocated the whole hour for this part of the exercise, so the simulator is locked. We all now have access to the files on the fleet and specifically on your command. You have two days to review them then we'll be back here where we'll begin our training exercises," Catie said.

"Since we're done early and this is our last class, I suggest the admiral buy us all drinks," Miranda said.

"You've been trying to get me to buy drinks all semester," Catie whined.

"Winning!"

◆ ◆ ◆

"Did you get everyone in the positions you wanted?" Miranda asked in a whisper.

"Yes."

"Even Jamison?"

"Well, he's your problem now," Catie whispered back.

"Maldito!"

Catie led the group to the Fox and Hound, a favorite pub for all the cadets. It was right next to the campus and served a great fish and chips as well as burgers and such. She dutifully bought a round of beers for everyone and sat back while they all chatted about the upcoming series of simulations.

◆ ◆ ◆

The next day, Catie met with Miranda and Baker to talk about tactics for the two weeks they had for training before live team-on-team battles started. They decided to separate the team into two groups. Baker would join Catie's team, and he and Catie would work on boarding strategies. Miranda would take her two squadron commanders to one simulation room to work on flight maneuvers, while Catie took the captain to another to go over fleet maneuvers. After a week, they would run two training exercises as a full unit.

◆ ◆ ◆

All the teams had been given two weeks to train. Now they would enter a double-elimination competition. There were sixty-four teams, so the winner would have to win seven simulations, eight if everyone lost once. With two simulations per week, it would take a month to get through them all. Catie and Miranda as well as the rest of their team were figuring on being the last team standing.

They had breezed through their first week of simulations, but now they were supposed to get harder, and, of course, they were facing teams that had also won the first two rounds. Each simulation exercise would consist of two parts. First, they would take in the parameters of the exercise and configure their fleet. The exercise would proceed until the first sensor contact with the enemy. Second, after a day of prep outside the simulation room, they would meet again and engage the enemy. Then events would proceed in accelerated time, based on the square of the distance between the opposing forces. Once actual contact with the enemy was made, things would drop back to 4X time.

"Are we ready?" Catie asked.

"Yes, Admiral," the three captains, Baker, and Miranda informed Catie. Catie pressed the ready button and they received the dump of information about their position, speed, and mission objective. For this mission, they were to attack a waiting force in orbit around a star.

"We get to play the Paraxeans," Catie thought, going back to the Paraxean war where they had fought to prevent the Paraxean rebel fleet from entering Sol's system. *"It'll be interesting to see what they did wrong."*

"The standard engagement model is for us to establish an orbit just inside the gravity well and for the enemy to match that. Then we would be able to send sorties against them," Catie said, as she and the team began to discuss tactics.

"How far apart?" Miranda asked.

"One to two hours of flight time for the fighters," Catie said.

"But that's not what you want to do," Baker suggested.

"Right. I want to come in high above the ecliptic, but still with a significant velocity toward the planet. Once we can get a good read on their force deployment, I want to continue toward the planet at speed. Force them to try to catch us."

"We shouldn't go outside the ecliptic plane," Jamison said.

"Why? Gravity is the same everywhere. We don't need to catch one of their gas giants to use for acceleration, and we'll get a better sensor read on their forces."

"But . . . but," Jamison stuttered, then he looked away, muttering to himself.

"It will leave us fully exposed," Julie said.

"Yes, but we're already fully exposed since we would be in an outer orbit, beyond any of their planets."

After some further discussion, Catie gave the order to enter the system, ten degrees above the ecliptic plane. There would be fighters out for pickets, and a group surrounding each frigate in a tight cluster. The hope was that the fighters would shield the frigates from sensors.

"Contact!" Miranda announced. "My picket fighter is relaying the sensor reading now."

"They have two carriers," Captain Castel reported. "They are traveling in orbit at fifty AUs on the ecliptic. One is currently ten million kilometers counter-orbit of us, the other twelve million kilometers further in the orbit."

"Thank you, Captain," Catie said.

"Commander Cordova, let's get their attention."

"Jamison, take a squadron and set an attack vector on the carriers," Miranda ordered.

"What, I'm going to be a sacrificial lamb?! Bullshit!"

"You have your orders," Miranda said.

"We should hold my squadron with the carrier to protect it!" Jamison complained. "We'll lose points if we sacrifice a squadron of fighters."

"You'll barely be able to close the distance with all the in-system velocity you'll have," Catie announced. "We just want to cause a distraction."

"Then fire missiles!"

"*Relieve him,*" Catie texted Miranda.

"Jamison, you're relieved!" Miranda ordered.

"You cannot relieve me!" Jamison shouted just as his simulation table locked up. "Damn it, you cannot do that!" Jamison started toward Catie. "I know it's you!"

"Stand down!" Catie ordered.

Jamison kept moving toward Catie until his feet shot out from under him. Baker had grabbed him by the collar and yanked him back and to the floor.

"You can either go back to your table and watch so you might learn something, or you can leave the room," Baker snarled.

Jamison started to struggle, but Baker wrenched his arm up behind his back. "Make your choice or I'll break your arm."

"I'll leave," Jamison said.

"Good."

"I'm going to report this!" Jamison shouted as he left the room.

"The one carrier has launched fighters to counter ours," Miranda reported.

"Time to contact?"

"Three hours."

"Captain Ivan Castel, match our speed to our fighters," Catie ordered. "Julie and Hector make speed for the planet. Keep your fighter shields in place."

"The second carrier is attempting to accelerate to close with the first carrier," Ivan reported.

"Good. Let's see how long we can keep their attention. Do we have a full read of the defenses?"

"Yes, ma'am. They have one small ship and a space station around the planet. The carriers seem to be their only large ships. We don't have a good read behind the gas giant on this side of the system. I'm sending a probe to make sure nothing is hiding behind it," Ivan reported.

"Thank you, Captain. Proceed."

By the time the defensive forces realized that the two frigates were making for the planet, it was too late to catch them. They tried to do a highspeed flyby to take the frigates out, but the fighters were able to handle the missiles, and at the delta speed the enemy carriers' lasers and plasma cannons were ineffective.

"I've taken out the enemy's corvette," Julie reported. "We're ranging on the space station now."

"Demand their surrender," Catie ordered.

"They fired on us!"

"Then take it out!"

"Alright, our first win!" Miranda started the celebration.

"Nice plan, Admiral," Baker said. "I wonder what that tiff with Jamison will cost us?"

"I don't know, but our score is coming in now," Catie said. "We lost twenty points for not relieving him sooner."

"My bad," Miranda said. "I shouldn't have hesitated. I was just so shocked."

"Now let's go find out if he really had a meltdown or if that was part of the simulation," Catie said.

"It was not part of the simulation, Cer Catie," ADI reported.

Jamison was waiting for everyone to leave the room. He walked up to Catie and got right in her face. "You bitch, I won't let you get away with that!"

Catie pointed to her specs to let Jamison know that he was being recorded.

"I don't care. You had no right! And remember this, I'm always going to outrank you! So just wait!" Jamison snapped, then he turned and stalked off.

"Not if he gets thrown out of the Academy," Miranda said.

"Forget him. Let's go celebrate our first win," Catie said.

17 Jump Reset

"Hi, Daddy," Catie said as they connected via their Comms. "How's Sam doing?"

"She's doing fine. We're both a bit stir crazy because we're under lockdown."

"Why are you under lockdown?"

"Oh, we've got an insect infestation we're dealing with."

"Why does that mean you have to be under lockdown?"

"Because when they sting you, they plant eggs under your skin. Those grow into larvae in a few days and then burst out of your skin and fly off to feed on our crops," Marc said.

"That's gross!"

"It is, which is why we're locked down. You have to wear an exosuit to go out."

"What are you doing about it?"

"Dr. Teltar has developed a trap for them. It simulates the perfect host. They sting it, plant their eggs, then die. The eggs are absorbed by the trap. He says we should have the infestation under control in another week."

"That's good. I guess colonizing another planet isn't all fun and games."

"Well, if this is the worst thing we have to deal with, we'll count ourselves lucky."

"Did you forget about the aliens that are heading your way?"

"No, I didn't forget," Marc sighed. "I just try to compartmentalize that into a separate category."

"Hi, Catie," Samantha said when she linked into the call.

"Hi, Sam. How's the baby doing?"

"The baby is just fine," Samantha said, patting her stomach. It was just barely pooching out. "I'm just five months. Now, how are you doing?"

"I'm fine."

"I heard you were dating," Samantha said.

"I just had a few dates with this guy," Catie said, her voice sounded a little dejected.

"Are you still dating him?"

"No, we didn't really click," Catie said, not mentioning the fact that Braxton seemed to be more interested in getting her into bed that what was going on in her life.

"So, is there a reason for your call, or did you just want to check in with Sam and the baby?" Marc asked.

"That, for sure, but I've also just spent the weekend with Dr. McDowell. We have a little bad news."

"Oh, what would that be?"

"The Paraxean asteroid is too big."

"That's terrible news," Samantha said. "Oh, you have a solution, don't you? You're just being mean. You know shock is not good for the baby."

"Sorry, I couldn't resist. But I think I have an answer. When Liz described the asteroid to me after her trip to pick up the colonists, she said that their stasis pods were mostly in the same place. I've examined the images we have of it and it seems like that's true," Catie said.

"That's my understanding," Marc said.

"So we can make it smaller. I've drawn up a plan of what parts we should lop off, but we need a better survey done."

"That's not too bad. Why don't you talk to your Uncle Blake, and he can send Jimmy Gaines out to survey it and figure out how to lop off those parts."

"Okay. Bye, Daddy, bye Sam."

"Bye, Sweetie."

Once Catie was off the call, Marc turned to Samantha. "She sounded a little depressed about the guy."

"I'm surprised you noticed, but yes, she did. She'll have to get used to the ups and downs of dating."

◆ ◆ ◆

"Hello, Katya, aren't you supposed to be making deliveries?" Dr. Teltar asked as he sat down next to her. Katya had set up on a hill overlooking the plain. A herd of gazelles was grazing off in the distance.

"Nope, Sabrina and Demi are taking care of it today."

"Demi?"

"We hired her so we could get a day off."

"And you decided to spend your day with me?"

"You decided to spend your day with me; I got here first," Katya said.

"You're right, I guess I *have* decided to spend my day with you."

"I knew you were coming. I got here first because I rode my bike."

"How did you know I was coming?"

"There's a big cat out there stalking those gazelles. I subscribed to your alarm. When the probe detected the cat, I heard about it at the same time you did."

"Clever girl."

"Hey, why are girls smarter than boys?"

"You think girls are smarter?"

"Sure, the boys are running around screaming and acting crazy all the time, while we girls are studying things."

"Oh, that's how you see it."

"Why else would the boys be acting crazy?"

"I think it's because your culture is biased to the males doing all the crazy things, like being spies, warriors, and stuff like that. The boys are just behaving like the men they see on your TV."

"Oh."

"Not convinced?"

"No."

"Well, you might be right. Girls are pretty smart. That's a female out there hunting the gazelles."

"I know. Why don't the males hunt? They're usually bigger."

"Well, because they're bigger, they're not as fast."

"That sounds dumb."

"Well, the females like it that the males are bigger, because then they can fight off anything that threatens their pride. In exchange, they do most of the hunting."

"Sounds like the females have to do all the work."

"It does. I'm sure you won't make a bargain like that."

"Nope. I'm going learn Aikido and Krav Maga like Princess Catie. That way I can fight my own battles."

"We'll Princess Catie is a good role model. She certainly fights her own battles," Dr. Teltar said.

"Do you know her?"

"I was on the mission that discovered Artemis with her. She was one of the leaders."

"Cool."

"Do you think the cat will get a gazelle?"

"I'm not sure. The gazelles all seem to be healthy, so I'm not sure the cat will be fast enough."

Katya and Dr. Teltar had been sitting for over an hour watching to see if the big cat would get a gazelle. Katya was getting a bit bored so she decided to ask some questions. "How do we know that there isn't any intelligent life on this planet?"

"There is intelligent life on this planet. That cat out there is very intelligent."

"You know what I mean!"

"You mean sentient life."

"Right."

"We assume sentience requires high intelligence. There is a possibility that there was sentient life before the asteroid catastrophe but we don't think so."

"Why not?"

"One would have expected a highly evolved intelligence to survive the catastrophe."

"How do you know one didn't?"

"No fire."

"No fire?"

"Fire is one of the most powerful tools that an intelligent life can develop. It can keep you warm during the winter. Cooking your food, reduces the risk of catching a disease, and fire is very useful in making other tools."

"So you're saying fire is a requirement for smart animals."

"No, but it is a significant indicator. Lots of animals use tools, only sentient animals use them to the extent that Humans and Paraxeans do. Learning and adapting to tools drives the evolution of the brain."

"Then why are dolphins so smart?" Katya asked.

"Echolocation," Doctor Teltar said.

"What?"

"Echolocation. Dolphins emit high frequency clicks, sound that bounces off of objects in the water. They use the difference in the time it takes for the sound to return to each of their ears to determine where the object is. It's like sonar."

"So why does that make them smart?"

"I hypothesize that their brain's growth was spurred by the enormous benefit that echolocation provided. The better they could interpret the signals, the more food they could acquire. Once their brain was big, there was plenty of extra capacity to start developing complex social interactions; that further spurred brain development and their evolution."

"Then why aren't bats smart? They use sonar."

"They are pretty smart. But sound travels over four times faster than in water, so it takes more brainpower to interpret the signals."

"I didn't realize bats were so smart."

"They are, but rats take the prize for intelligence among small mammals."

"Yuck!" Katya squealed. "Why didn't dolphins and whales get even smarter?"

"No hands. They can't make good use of tools, so there was a limit to how much advantage they were able to garner by being smarter. So brain development was capped once they maximized the benefit from echolocation and social behavior."

"So, is that why humans are so smart?"

"Yes, that and opposable thumbs mean humans can make use of complex tools. Complex tools require a lot of reasoning to maximize the benefit. So human development wasn't capped. Being smarter continued, and continues to be an advantage."

"Hmm."

"They're she goes!" Doctor Teltar yelled as the cat made a dash for one of the gazelles.

"It got away!"

"It was too healthy for the cat. Maybe next time."

18   Board Meeting – May 2nd

"Let's get this meeting started," Marc said once everyone had joined the Comm conference call. "I assume everyone has been keeping up with the situation on our murder. ADI assures me that she'll be convicted. Now, first order of business, Catie has an update on the jump ships."

"Dr. McDowell has finished calibrating the drives and the jump ships. The good news is that they can handle the Victory and the other carriers, the bad news is that the Paraxean asteroid is too big," Catie said.

"How much too big?" Liz asked.

"A lot too big. As you know, it's not the mass, but the girth that matters. Uncle Blake has Jimmy Gaines looking at how to cut down the asteroid. It should be possible to make it small enough based on the locations of the stasis pods."

"That's a good thing, we definitely don't want to have to move all those pods. It must have taken the Paraxeans a year to get them all moved to that asteroid," Liz added. "When will Jimmy know?"

"He headed out two days ago. He should be there before the end of the week," Blake said. "He thinks he'll need about a week to map things out."

"Catie, can you go back and explain about the Victory?"

"Sure. You know the problem with the jump drive is that the size of the drive goes up as a cube of the girth. The Victory would lose about a third of her internal space if we tried to put the drives in her, and even then, it'd be iffy. But with the jump ships, we can open a wormhole and expand it big enough for her to go through, they're just one big reactor and a big gravity drive. The four ships make one huge jump drive. We've also learned that we can open a wormhole between two drive sets, which opens up some interesting possibilities."

"Whoa, back up," Blake said. "You can open a wormhole between two drive sets?"

"Yes, if we open a wormhole in a system that has a jump drive in it. When that jump drive goes active, the wormhole jumps to it."

"Too many jumps in that," Liz said.

"The wormhole goes to the lowest gravity point in the area. The jump drives create gravity voids, so that's where the wormhole wants to be. And if you open two wormholes to the same system, they combine into one between the two source systems. I think we can build a set of gates that will allow us to jump directly from Sol to Artemis Prime."

"That's huge," Blake said.

"It is. That will take five days off of the transition," Liz said. "And skipping all that low gravity time will make the trip more comfortable."

"I'm thinking about the combat strategy options it opens," Blake said. "If we can choose exactly where the Victory comes out, it gives us a major advantage."

"Okay, put it in your simulation," Marc said. "Let's keep moving."

"Just one last thing," Blake said. "How many jump ships do we have?"

"We have four, but Ajda is making it a top priority to make another four."

"Good. I'd like to have more than that. Marc, do you agree?"

"Yes."

"Catie?"

"I'll tell Ajda to make it a priority to get, what, twelve more built?"

"That will work for now," Blake said. "I assume this will work with the drives in the Roebuck and the Sakira."

"Yes, you just can't send another ship through," Catie said.

"Okay. Back to you, Marc."

"Thanks. With our current situation, I think we want to skip any further mods to the Victory and get her fully crewed and out here," Marc said.

"I agree. Do you want us to pull out the cabins that we've installed in the flight bay?" Blake asked.

"No, let's just not have any delay before we get it out here, we can pull those cabins later and use them."

"Okay. What about the Paraxean carrier?"

"I don't see any reason to change their plans. But we should think about whether we want to bring the Enterprise over here as well."

"Let's see what we learn in the simulation," Blake said. "The security council will have apoplexy if we take the Enterprise out of Sol."

"We'll do what we must, but I'm okay with waiting until we learn more," Marc said. "Everyone should have the script for the reply to the aliens. Let me know if you want changes. I plan to record it and send it out tomorrow or Wednesday."

"There's a big celebration planned by the U.N. to commemorate the discovery of Artemis," Fred said. "It'll be Blake's and my first chance to be the big cheeses at the party."

"You can have it," Marc said. "How are our friends doing?"

"We've finalized the language on the treaty about cross-system sharing of intellectual property. It looks like China and Russia are on board," Blake said.

"That's good to hear; what changed their minds?" Marc asked.

"For the Russians, it's probably the new lubricant they developed. It reduces friction by another twenty percent over standard oil. So you get a big increase in engine efficiencies," Fred said. "I suspect they think they'll find customers in other systems for it."

"Developed on Delphi Station?"

"Yes, seems you can get strong hydrocarbon bonds in microgravity," Fred explained.

"And the Chinese?"

"I think they see the writing on the wall. They've also asked for space on Delphi Station."

"Good, same rules as we used for the Russians," Marc said. "Kal, do we have enough security up there?"

"We will," Kal said. "I'm going to add another full squad of Marines."

"Admiral Michaels?" Marc prompted.

"I seemed to have picked up interfacing with Maggie. It makes sense since there's crossover with the alliance. Anyway, there is serious discussion about doing something in Africa. I'll have more next month. But the U.N. wants to prove that it can do something about these failed states," Admiral Michaels said.

"It's about time," Samantha said.

"They're actually cutting off all arms shipments to the various countries around the world that are having civil wars."

"To both sides?"

"Yes. Everyone figures if they're reduced to throwing rocks, they might sit down and talk. It also paves the way for a peacekeeping force to step in."

"How are they cutting off the arms shipments?"

"It's amazing what you can accomplish when you're not worried about prosecution. They're just interdicting the shipments on the water. And with no official governments supplying the arms, that has been pretty effective."

"Governor Paratar, we should make orbit in three days. How are your preparations going?" Liz asked.

"Captain Farmer, we have all of the cargo pods ready for you. Unfortunately, one third of them are empty."

"I understand. It takes time to establish a new world. I hope you're ready for all of your new colonists."

"We are eagerly awaiting their arrival."

"I'll call again just after we make orbit. Good day."

"To you also, Captain."

Lieutenant Payne, Captain of the Roebuck, was asking permission for his Lynx to land in the Dutchman's flight bay one hour after the Dutchman slipped into orbit behind the Roebuck.

"Derek, you're sure in a hurry," Liz said.

"We've been here for almost a year. We're all getting tired of each other," Derek said.

"Is that all?"

"No, please tell me you've brought the case of Scotch I asked for?"

"I have it. I didn't know you were such a heavy drinker."

"I'm not, but there are a few things that can only get done after the exchange of a bottle of scotch. And I've been out for three months."

"In that case, you'll be glad to hear we brought two cases for you, compliments of Catie."

"Oh, I'll be sure to thank her on our next Comm call."

"You can also let your crew know that we have managed to stash quite a few luxury items from Earth. They'll be available for sale starting tomorrow. We'll send the list out today."

"You are a pirate!"

"Hey, a girl's got to make a living."

"I'm sure you'll have a lot of eager customers. Just don't gouge them too much?"

"Catie and I agreed on two hundred fifty percent of cost," Liz said.

"I was wrong, you're both pirates," Derek laughed.

"Just to show you how wrong you are, let's go to my cabin and I'll pour you a scotch."

"Not rum?"

"We're Scottish pirates."

"Why have you built the city so dense?" Liz asked.

"Paraxeans are a gregarious race. And especially after coming out of stasis, they want to be close to their fellow Paraxeans," Governor Paratar said.

"Why is that?"

"We don't understand it that well ourselves, but the experience of stasis seems to make you lonely."

"Aren't you just frozen?"

"Oh, we do not freeze ourselves. Long-term freezing leads to too much cell damage. It takes months to recover from that, and even then you never fully recover."

"So if you don't freeze yourselves, what do you do?"

"I'll try to explain, of course one of our doctors could do a better job."

"I'm sure your explanation will be just fine. A doctor's would probably be too technical."

"Okay, I'll try. When you enter a stasis chamber, you're connected to an IV that provides all the nutrients your body needs. It also circulates the blood through the system which removes all the waste and re-oxygenates it. In addition, it removes enzymes that would eat away your muscles, so you generally wake up as fit as you were when you went in. Once all the connections are complete, the chamber is filled with fluid, similar to the liquid breathing you people use for deep diving."

"If your blood is being re-oxygenated, why do you have to do the liquid breathing?"

"We need to make sure that your lungs are happy. They will quit working after a short time, but the liquid breathing is critical for when you start the stasis as well as when you are brought out of stasis. Once everything is established, they start to lower the temperature of the liquid. It is taken down to ten degrees Celsius. At that temperature, with all your body's needs taken care of, your body goes into a kind of hibernation. All activity slows down and aging almost stops."

"Almost stops?"

"Dr. Metra says it's much like your Galapagos tortoise. Things are so slow that there is little cell damage; your body doesn't need to regenerate your cells, so it requires fewer nutrients and less oxygen. Eventually it reaches the state we call stasis proximal. At that point, the probes attached to your brain start to manipulate your brain waves, putting you into a deep sleep. You don't dream, so there shouldn't be any sensation of time passing, but there is. When you wake from stasis, you feel that passage of time, and it feels like it was a very lonely time."

"That sounds lonely," Liz said.

"Yes it does. Therefore, after waking from stasis, Paraxeans crave the company of other Paraxeans. It takes over a year before your psyche recovers. So in a few years, we'll spread the city out, and many of these buildings will be converted to office buildings, though some will remain condos. Of course, we cannot do that until we've brought all the colonists out of stasis."

"I see. Will you build other cities?"

"Yes, but they will be built and populated by Paraxeans who are ready to leave here and move to a new place. This will always be where we bring the new colonists after they come out of stasis."

"I hope that on your next trip, we'll be ready for my wife and children to accompany you," Governor Paratar said.

"I'm sure they're just as anxious as you are. Do you call them often?" Liz asked.

"Not too often, we cannot abuse the bandwidth you allow us to use. But at least once a week."

"The Paraxean children seem to be doing well; they've all joined in the exercise and training classes that Samantha has our colonists taking."

"That is good. How is their English?"

"They seem to be doing well. All the Paraxeans seem to enjoy the movies and TV shows we provide. Most of them are in English."

"That is good. We are encouraging all of our colonists to learn English. It is obvious that it will become the language of trade. How are your people interacting with the Paraxeans?"

"The children are doing great. I saw them playing in the parks and generally having a good time. The trainers say the Paraxean children are excellent students."

"And the adults?"

"There's not as much interaction, but I saw several mixed groups when I went to dinner."

"That sounds promising. I hope our peoples can become good friends."

"I'm sure we will. We have so much in common. Your colonists were excellent guests on the Dutchman."

"I'm glad to hear that."

There were numerous large celebrations set up to recognize the discovery of Artemis. With Marc and Liz off-planet and Catie in disguise, Blake was left as the one to represent MacKenzie Discoveries.

"I cannot believe you agreed to this," Jackie said.

"Hey, you're the one who said she wanted to go to a few royal balls," Blake said.

"But six in one day, that's insane."

"It won't be too bad. Fred and Latoya will be with us. And we can rest on the Lynx."

"But twenty-two hours of parties?"

Blake laughed, "Yes, six cities, six time zones and four continents. We'll set a record."

"If we survive it."

"And you get to wear six different dresses with six different sets of jewelry."

"Yes, while you get away with one tuxedo."

"Well, six actually; they're mostly the same, but even I wouldn't wear one tuxedo for twenty-two hours."

"So, the first one is in Tokyo at the royal palace," Jackie said.

"Yes, we get to meet the Emperor and his wife."

"I'm sure that will be exciting," Jackie said, expressing her boredom at the thought.

"Then next we'll be in Beijing; it's a good thing the Chinese like to party late. We won't get there until ten."

"So we won't get to see the Forbidden City?"

"No, it's forbidden," Blake joked. "We'll be in Zhongnanhai, it's right next door. After that we've got a four-hour break while we fly to Paris."

"Where we'll again not get to see the city," Jackie complained.

"We can go back anytime you want. But you're going to get to meet most of the European leaders and a lot of royalty."

"Oh joy, then after a couple of hours of partying in Paris, most of which will be taken up with the introductions, we fly to New York."

"Right, there you get to meet President Novak and the Canadian Prime Minister. Then we jet to L.A."

"How do we make that in time?" Jackie asked.

"The president is allowing us to go supersonic for the flight to L.A. and we arrive there at eleven."

"How do we make it back to Delphi City in time?"

"Mach five, baby. Except for our flight from Beijing, all of them are about 1½ hours. And with a Hover Lynx, we get to leave from the nearest helipad."

"Hello, again," Marc said. He was wearing the governor's uniform that Blake had created and was sitting in his office in the city. This communication would be all business, no niceties.

"I would like to reinforce my request that you enter an outer orbit of our solar system when you arrive. We feel that you should be able to establish one at sixty AUs. An AU is the distance that Artemis is from our sun, Artemis Prime. We'll be out there to meet you and provide any assistance that you may need."

Marc paused the video to handle some business from a very military-looking pair of officers, then continued. "I've been informed that the Victory, a starship from our naval fleet, is due to arrive in a few weeks. It is much more capable than the one we have here, so it should be able to help with any repairs or replenishments that you may require. We are concerned that your recent course change will make it difficult for you to decelerate enough to stop in our system."

Marc squared himself to the camera and leaned forward. "I cannot impress upon you enough how much we look forward to establishing a friendly and mutually beneficial trade between our two civilizations. Please let me know if there is anything we can do for you."

"How can he know about our course change?!" Captain Shakaban demanded after he had finished reviewing the message from Marc. "There hasn't been enough time for the light to reach him, much less for them to discern the change."

"Maybe he's guessing," Lieutenant Lantaq suggested.

"And he says he wants to help us. If he wants to help us, he can leave that system!" Captain Shakaban yelled.

"It doesn't look as if he's willing to do that," Lieutenant Lantaq said.

"Well, we'll be changing his mind soon!"

"What do you think about his claim that the warship Victory will be arriving soon?"

"Lies! He is trying to intimidate us. Well, it won't work."

"Hello, Governor McCormack," Captain Shakaban said. "It always amazes me the stories that the governors of worlds we've encountered make up to try to dissuade us from visiting their systems. One would think that starships grow on trees and travel at ten times the speed of light."

The captain paused, giving the camera a feral grin.

"We will be happy to have you meet us on your fringe, sixty AUs you said. And I continue to hope we can come to terms on the rules for trade. The Empire does not trade with many of our neighbors, except of course those that have joined the Empire.

"We are now getting very detailed sensor readings from Zagawani, and we don't see signs of the vibrant colony that you describe. Possibly those words have different meanings in our languages. I look forward to meeting you face-to-face. Until then."

"You are inviting him to meet you with his entire fleet!" Lieutenant Lantaq said.

"That is exactly what I am doing. Wake all of our crew from stasis. We have six weeks to prepare."

"Ms. Randall, can I get you anything?" the attorney asked as he escorted her to his office.

"No."

"I have to tell you, after reviewing the prosecution's case, I find it is very compelling."

"I know," Ms. Randall whispered.

"Is there anything you wish me to do?"

"Get me a deal."

"Is there anything you can tell me that would be of benefit in making a deal?"

"I told that son of a bitch that nobody dumps me!"

"I think we'll keep that to ourselves. Anything else?"

"No."

Sophia was again at the courthouse recording a story.

"Today, Ms. Dorothea Randall entered a plea of guilty. As part of the plea deal, she was sentenced to ten years. This reporter has learned the terms of her sentence. She has had to refund Delphi for the cost of the police investigation into her crime as well as the cost of the prosecution. She will be housed in the city jail. She will be given a job working in the recycling plant at the airport. She will travel to and from her jail cell each day on her own. She will have a tracking device inserted under her skin as well as being required to wear a Comm at all times. She has to proceed directly to and from her job via taxi or walking, and is not allowed any side trips.

"This reporter wonders if that is sufficient punishment for murder? It will obviously be a minimal burden on the state, but how will the victim's family feel?"

19   Asteroid Surgery

Jimmy Gaines took a small crew and an Oryx and headed out to the fringe to examine the Paraxean asteroid. He wasn't looking forward to this assignment. The trip out under a high-G profile would be uncomfortable; then they wouldn't have any gravity for the week or so it would take to survey the asteroid. *"I'm getting too old for this,"* he thought. He spent the trip out studying the notes that Catie had made and the specs the Paraxeans had given him.

"Your asteroid is in sight," Hassam, the pilot, informed Gaines.

"Alright, boys, time to suit up," Jimmy said to roust the crew from their naps or video watching. Everyone was wearing a shipsuit, but now it was time to put on their exosuits and prepare for the EVA to the asteroid.

"We're all going?" Jacko asked.

"No, but we're going to decompress the cargo bay, so you'll want to be suited up for safety. Billy and I will make the first survey."

Jacko reached over and grabbed his exosuit body piece and his helmet. "I'll put them on when you start decompressing," he said, then he went back to watching his video.

Jimmy and Billy suited up and exited the crew area of the Oryx and then entered the cargo bay. The bay was filled with the survey equipment they would use to analyze the asteroid. There were kits with small explosives so they could take seismic readings to find any fissures, as well as x-ray equipment to examine those fissures in more detail.

"What are we taking with us?" Billy asked.

"Nothing, we're going to just make a visual inspection, get the lay of the land."

"You mean the lay of the asteroid."

"Billy, don't be a smart ass or you won't be coming back from this survey mission."

"Sorry," Billy gulped.

"Don't be, I'm just a bit frustrated. This is a long way to come to look at a damn asteroid."

"The bay is decompressed," Billy announced.

"Alright, open the big doors and let's see what this thing looks like."

When the doors opened, they saw the asteroid floating next to the Oryx, or one should say the Oryx floating next to the asteroid since the asteroid was hundreds of times bigger than the Oryx.

Jimmy knew the asteroid was over one thousand meters in length and about five hundred meters across and one hundred fifty meters deep, but floating next to it, it seemed even bigger.

"That is a big asteroid," Billy said.

"Damn, it sure is. And apparently it's too big," Jimmy said as he continued to gaze out at the rocky surface. "Hey Hassam, I thought there were supposed to be a bunch of stasis pods on this thing. Did you bring us to the right position?"

"Jimmy, are you trying to tell me how to fly this thing?"

"No, but I don't see no stasis pods."

"They're in a big trench in the middle of the asteroid. We're not allowed to get too close to them. I guess they're afraid some idiot might fly into them. Anyway, look out about one hundred meters, you should just be able to see the edge of the trench."

"Oh, I guess I see it. Well, Billy, looks like we have to take a walk. Let's go."

Jimmy walked to the edge of the cargo door, turned off the magnetic couplings in his boots, leaned forward and rotating his feet around the lip of the door, pushed off. He allowed himself to fly just above the surface of the asteroid for about fifty meters before he engaged his thrusters and brought himself down to the asteroid's surface.

When he touched down, he engaged the magnetic couplings in his boots, thinking, "*Hey, might as well try.*" But he got no joy, as there wasn't enough metal in the asteroid for the magnetic coupling to grab. Turning the coupling back off, he hopped and skipped over to the edge of the trench. All this time he had been keeping an eye on Billy, who had been copying Jimmy's moves as best as he could. Billy had only been mining asteroids for a few months, so he wasn't as graceful as Jimmy, but he did manage to catch up to Jimmy about the time Jimmy got to the edge of the trench.

"What the hell," Billy said. "I never seen anything like that before."

"Well, Pohawk isn't known for having anything but a coal mine," Jimmy said. "But this does take the blue ribbon over anything I've ever seen."

They were looking down on a maze of metal. The gaps between the towering walls was three meters which seemed like it should feel spacious, but when Jimmy's sonar meter came back with twenty-five meters for the wall height, it clarified why the space looked so tight.

"My gawd, what is that?" Billy gasped.

"Those are stasis pods stacked to hell and back," Jimmy said.

"How many are there?"

"There's supposed to be 1.2 million pods down there, less the twenty thousand or so that they've pulled out."

"And what are we supposed to do again?"

"The damn asteroid is too big. It's over five hundred meters wide and they want it to be three hundred meters wide."

"How wide is this channel?"

"That's going to be a problem. It's four hundred meters wide," Jimmy said. "Comm, call Catie."

"Hi, Jimmy."

"Can you talk?"

"Sure, I've got a few minutes," Catie said. She was using her avatar to talk for her while she messaged her answers.

"You do realize that the channel with those stasis pods in it is over four hundred meters wide?"

"Yes, that's what I remember."

"And you also know that four hundred is bigger than three hundred?"

"Yes."

"So you're expecting us to remove a bunch of these pods?"

"Yeah, I guess that's right. Will that be a problem?"

"I'm sure it will be. It'll definitely be a pain in the ass," Jimmy said.

"Sorry."

"How are these pods connected?"

"Their wiring is below the floor level. It's only power, each pod has its own control module."

"If we disconnect power, what happens to the stasis pod?"

"You have to provide another source of power, or wake the person up first. You do know that ADI can answer all these questions?"

"Yeah, I know, but she gives me weird answers, so . . ."

"I beg your pardon," ADI interjected.

"Sorry, ADI," Jimmy said. "But you know I never understand your answers."

"It's not my problem that you do not phrase your questions correctly so are unhappy that I didn't answer the question you wanted to ask instead of the one you did," ADI said.

"Yeah, I know, but Catie knows what I want to ask, so it's easier this way."

"It's okay, Jimmy," Catie said. "ADI, don't pick on him."

"Humph," ADI said as she closed her channel. Of course, she continued to listen in.

"So how have they been getting the colonists out of these things?" Jimmy asked.

"They've been pulling the stasis pod. They take a battery system, connect it up, then pull the pod. They take it to the Oryx where they collect them until they have a full load. Then they wake the colonists up while they're ferrying the pods to one of the carriers."

"That sounds like a lot of work. Why don't they just wake them up here and leave the pods in place?"

"Because it would be a lot of work to put a pressure bubble over each pod so you could bring the colonist out of stasis, and they've been picking people out that are all over the place, not in nice groupings that would make it easy."

"Well, we're going to have to yank out like twenty rows of these pods to slim this thing down. I'm thinking we'll just put a big tarp over this thing, and seal it, pressurize the whole area, then start pulling colonists out of the pods in the area that we need to cut off."

"Governor Paratar was asking us to move the pods around so he could still select the colonists he wants," Catie said.

"You can tell that governor where he can put that idea," Jimmy said. "We won't be having time to do that kind of work. He'll just have to take them as they come. We're going to have to remove something like 120 thousand pods."

"That many?"

"Yes. I'm, having a hard time imagining how we're going to do that."

"Yes, and where are we going to put all those colonists?"

"You're asking me?"

"No, just wondering," Catie said. "Is there any way you can slice off the sections without having to wake the colonists?"

"I'll look into it," Jimmy said. "Thanks for your help, I think."

"Bye, Jimmy."

"Well, Billy, I don't think there's anything to do but jump down there and look around," Jimmy said.

"I'll be right behind you."

"You would, wouldn't you?" Jimmy jumped and then used his thrusters to push himself down the two meters until he landed on the first stack of stasis pods. "Your boots will grab onto these things," he shouted up at Billy.

Billy nodded his head and jumped, maneuvering himself to land next to Jimmy. "After you," he said motioning for Jimmy to go ahead and jump the twenty-five meters to the floor of the maze.

Jimmy moved to the edge and used his thrusters to move downward. He slowly floated until he hit the floor, where his boots grabbed on. He turned and waved Billy down.

Billy followed, landing next to him. He looked around at the enormous wall of stasis pods. "How did they move all these things?" he asked.

"I have no idea," Jimmy said. Then giving himself a mental push, he Commed ADI. "ADI, do we have any data on how the Paraxeans moved the pods onto this asteroid?"

"Jimmy, there is no data on that. Neither DI from the Paraxean carriers has any record showing how they moved the pods. Did I answer the correct question?"

"Yes you did, sorry for complaining about you. Are there any records from the colony ship?"

"No, they did not preserve anything from the colony ship DI. I have to assume it was damaged or destroyed during the attack."

"Thanks, ADI."

"You're welcome."

"You know, Jimmy, I'm looking at these walls, and I'd swear that they were built like this, not assembled later after they moved them."

"You think so?"

"Yeah. Look at how tight these seams between the pods are. The frame looks like it's monolithic."

"I think you're right."

Billy lay down on the floor, "And look here, the seam to the floor is perfect. I don't see how they would have done such a nice job if they were working in microgravity after an attack on their ship."

"Are you suggesting that this is part of the colony ship, and they just stuck it into this asteroid?"

"Yeah. They could have cut out this big room, it's kind of like a cargo bay. Anyway, they could have cut it out of the colony ship, then found this asteroid and dug out the channel and then slipped it into it."

"How do you think they cut this channel out?"

"They could have used the plasma cannons on one of those carriers. Used that to do the big work, then come down with hand-held cannons and trimmed it up. It looks like there's some kind of foam between the walls and the asteroid."

"You know, Billy, you're not as dumb as you look," Jimmy said.

"Hey, I look pretty much like you do, we're cousins after all."

"Like I said. You're not as dumb as you look. So if we slice off the sides, we could trim this down to the three hundred meters they want, and the two sides would only be one hundred meters each."

"If we're going to do all that work, why don't we just cut the thing in half. Then we'd have two pieces, two hundred fifty meters each. They could even glue it back together after they jump it. That'd keep the pods protected."

"Billy, now you're just showing off. Let's go find the reactor so we can figure out where to cut this thing up."

They found the reactor, actually a pair of them at the head of the asteroid. There was a small room built behind the main wall.

"Hey, it's looks like they anticipated our needs," Jimmy joked. "There's a backup reactor here. We can rewire it so that each reactor supplies half the pods, then split it all in half."

"How do we split this room in half?"

"We don't, we move over ten meters and cut out a second room, move the backup reactor, then split the feeds."

"That seems safer," Billy said. "The power runs under the floor?"

"That's right. Start pulling up some of these floor panels and map out the wiring. It looks like it just goes to each row, from the power room then down the row. So we shouldn't have too much of a problem doing the rewiring, but we don't want to be cutting into any power lines when we cut through this floor."

"Alright."

Billy spent the next hour mapping out the wiring, and recording it in his HUD, while Jimmy drew up the plans for the new reactor room they needed. He also drew a line down the center of the aisle where he was planning to cut the floor.

"You ready to head back and get some chow and rest up?" Jimmy asked.

"Yep, I'll be right behind you," Billy said.

"You know, one of these days I'm going to make you lead."

"Yep, but until then, I'll be right behind you. Don't want to get in your way."

◆ ◆ ◆

"Call Catie," Jimmy instructed his Comm.

"Hey, Jimmy, what did you figure out?"

"Actually it was Billy that figured it out. But it looks like we can cut the asteroid right down the middle. Make two halves that will fit through your wormhole. Then after they're through, we can kind of glue them back together."

"Really, that would save a lot."

"Do you want us to go ahead and do it now?"

"Are you sure you can?"

"Pretty damn sure."

"ADI, get me Uncle Blake."

"He'll be with you in a minute," ADI reported.

"What's up?" Blake asked when he finally came on the line.

"Jimmy says he can cut the asteroid in half, and he thinks he can start the job now."

"Jimmy, I'll buy you a case of scotch if you can pull that off," Blake said. "How long would it take you?"

"I figure two weeks," Jimmy said. "We have to go kind of slow so we don't fracture the asteroid. I also need to come up with a big plasma cannon."

"Why don't you just use one of the Foxes? They've got a big cannon, and we've got a whole squadron of them out there on the Enterprise," Blake suggested.

"You think they're powerful enough to cut this asteroid in half?"

"You'll have to cut a shallow channel and keep making it deeper, but they'll cut it."

"Okay, why don't you arrange for the Foxes and pilots, and I'll get these boys started with rewiring the reactors and getting ready to cut that big room in half."

"I'll get right on it," Blake said.

"Uncle Blake," Catie interrupted.

"Catie, I can guess, you're going to suggest that we tell Governor Paratar that we'll bring the asteroid soon, so we can stop the mods on the Galileo."

"It would make Daddy happy."

"I plan on telling the governor that's what we're going to do. Giving him a choice is just inviting the wrong answer."

After lunch and a bit of a rest, Jimmy took Jocko out and did the survey of the backside of the asteroid. They placed a few marker beacons on the asteroid and digitally marked the line where he wanted the Foxes to cut away the rock so they could split the asteroid. He also found the three gravity drives and the fusion reactor which had been used to drive the asteroid.

"Hey, Billy, I've marked the gravity drives and the reactor they were using to fly this asteroid. Grab a couple of guys and come out here and remove them."

"Sure," Billy replied. "It's going to be a late dinner, huh."

"Maybe, but it should be faster removing them than it is to put them in, so you've still got a shot at making dinner on time."

"You might be right. We'll be out in just a minute."

By the time Billy finished removing the reactor and drives, Jimmy had finished his survey. He'd set off a couple of small explosions to map all the fissures in the asteroid. They were eating dinner when the Fox pilot called.

"Hey, I hear you guys want a portable plasma cannon," the pilot said.

"I do," Jimmy said. "But can you come tomorrow? We're calling it a day now."

"I can, but it's day time to me. You want me to go ahead and start?"

"Nope, I don't want anybody blasting away at that asteroid lessen I'm there to keep an eye on it. Don't want any accidents."

"Got it. It'll be someone else tomorrow, what time you want them to fly over?"

"Six o'clock."

"Is that Delphi Standard time?"

"Yep."

The next day, Jimmy met the Fox pilot out on the asteroid; well he was on the asteroid, the pilot was in his Fox hovering two meters over Jimmy's head.

"You ready to do some work?" Jimmy asked.

"Sure, what do you want me to do?"

"Well, just for grins, let's see what that laser of yours will do. We want to cut a narrow slot all the way across this asteroid."

"We can try, but I'm pretty sure it won't do anything," the pilot said.

"Can't hurt to try. Give it a go."

The pilot moved the Fox over to the edge of the asteroid and fired the laser along the line that Jimmy had mapped.

"I'm not seeing anything from my end," the pilot said.

"You're right, the rock is dissipating the heat; okay, switch over to the plasma cannon, use the narrowest beam you can."

"Okay, here goes."

A plume of debris started shooting into space as the plasma cannon started to eat away at the asteroid.

"Hold up now," Jimmy ordered.

"Cannon is off."

Jimmy used his thrusters to take him over to the slot the Fox was cutting. He measured the size and depth and checked out the sides. "Hey, dial back on the power about twenty percent and try again."

"Do you want me to dig deeper, or keep moving down the line?"

"Keep going down the line."

It took the Fox all day to get the first level of the slot blown away. It was six more days before they had the slot down the hundred twenty meters or so to the floor of the room holding the stasis pods.

Four days later they had cut the metal walls to separate the asteroid into two halves.

"We've finished it. What do you want us to do now?" Jimmy asked Blake.

"Can you stabilize it so it stays together? We won't move it over to Mangkatar for a couple of months."

"We can glue it together. Someone will have to use a laser to slice it back in half, but that shouldn't be a problem."

"Do that, then head home," Blake said.

20 Final Simulations

This was round six of the simulation tournament. Team Charlie was still undefeated. After the incident with Jamison, they had been allowed to replace him with Cadet Morrison. If they won the next two exercises they would win the tournament. They had just received the parameters for the exercise.

"This is a suicide mission," Julie declared.

"Don't give up yet," Miranda said. "Even if we lose this one, we still have one loss to go."

"Hey, stop that negative thinking," Catie ordered. She put the parameters up on the display.

"We have only one ship," Catie read off. "That's going to play hell with our command structure." All the previous simulations had given them three ships. Now Catie had two extra captains to deal with. "Julie, you take weapons systems, Ivan take the sensors, Hector take navigation."

"Aye, Admiral."

"We also only have ten fighters," Miranda said.

"Then you take them. We'll put Harris on engines and Morrison on defensive weapons," Catie ordered.

"What's the objective?" Baker asked. "Capture solar system seems vague."

"Here it is. We are to take the system so we can harvest the resources from it. The total period of the exercise is two years!" Hector Muñoz said.

"Two years! That doesn't make sense," Julie said. "Why would it take two years to win or lose; most likely lose. It says the defenders have five starships."

"This looks suspiciously like the Artemis situation," Catie messaged ADI.

"I concur. I look forward to seeing how you solve the problem," ADI replied.

"Weapons?" Catie asked.

"We have forty missiles launchable from the starship. They have a yield of one hundred megatons. The fighters have ten missiles each with yield of ten megatons."

"What about our defenses?" Catie had read the data already, but asking the question helped everyone focus.

"Point laser defenses on both the starship and the fighters."

"Our engine status and speed?"

"We are at 0.4 times the speed of light. Our grav drives are gutless out where we are. We won't be able to start decelerating until we get inside the 60 AU limit."

"Reaction mass?"

"Ten percent of our ship's mass is available."

"How are we approaching the system?" Catie asked.

"We're heading directly into the sun, on the ecliptic, . . ."

"So, all we're supposed to care about is the ability to harvest resources from the system. What does that mean?" Catie asked.

"It depends on what the enemy is there for," Baker said. "If they have the same objective, then what resources will they have put in place to defend it?"

"Let's assume they've just colonized the system."

"Then their goal will be to defend the planet."

"Do we need the planet?"

"Not really, we just need to be able to mine resources from the sun or one of the gas giants. That and have enough to feed our crews while we extract what we're after from the asteroid belt or the planet."

"How would we do that without a planet?" Catie asked.

"It's not pretty, but you can literally regenerate all the hydrocarbons. You just have to add some minerals and have access to water and you can go on forever. Won't be appetizing, but if you have the energy..."

"Yuck!" Julie said.

"So, they need the planet and we don't," Catie said. "Oh, my god!"

"What?!"

"ADI, end this simulation and get me Daddy and Uncle Blake!" Catie messaged.

"Simulation is terminated," the simulators notified everyone in the room. "Please exit the room."

"What's going on?" Miranda asked.

"This is a drill!" Alarms were sounding in the background.

"Fire drill," Catie suggested.

◆ ◆ ◆

"What's going on?!" Marc asked. "It's 0300 here!"

"Daddy, I know why the aliens changed course," Catie declared. "I know what they're going to do."

"What?!" Blake asked.

"They're going to bomb Artemis!"

"But changing course probably makes it impossible for them to even decelerate enough to stay in the system, unless they can sustain more gravitation force than we can," Blake said.

"They don't care about staying in the system!" Catie said. She had Artemis Prime and its system up on the simulation table.

"Why not?!"

"Yes, their new vector will take them right by Artemis, almost head on."

"Why would they do that?"

"Imagine a one-hundred-megaton missile hitting the atmosphere," Catie said.

"It would burn up," Blake said.

"But set it to explode before it burns up."

"Hmm . . . Oh shit!" Blake said.

"Someone explain it to me," Marc demanded.

"If a missile traveling at 0.6 the speed of light explodes in the atmosphere, it will rip off a chunk of air and push it into space."

"So?"

"Now, imagine twenty of them, one after the other!" Catie said.

"Oh, the planet would be uninhabitable."

"Yes, not only would you lose a large percent of the atmosphere, but the warheads will likely pollute what's left of the atmosphere."

"And the loss of atmosphere would make the solar radiation problematic."

"Right!"

"So how do we defend against that?" Marc asked.

"Easy," Catie said.

"How?"

"Drop an asteroid in front of it."

"it's traveling at 0.25 times the speed of light, how's that going to work?" Blake asked.

"Use a probe. Ramp it up to speed in Proxima Artemis; jump it in and use its grav drives to maneuver it in front of the alien ship. Then open a wormhole between our jump ships in Proxima Artemis and the probe; push an asteroid through, and bam."

"That would definitely eliminate the threat," Blake said.

"Okay, get us set up to do that, but I want a scenario where we can capture them or force them to surrender," Marc ordered.

"That's not going to be as easy," Blake said.

"Make all the teams try to come up with a plan against Catie's invasion scenario. Someone will come up with a way."

"My team's going to come up with it!" Cate declared. "But to be fair, we should give all the teams access to ADI; that would improve our odds."

"Fine," Marc said. "Pull out all the stops, full access to the simulators, and plenty of time."

"Wait, we're still in the offensive scenario," Catie said.

"I don't care about the tournament," Marc said.

"But we do!"

"I'll handle it," Blake said. "Go join your friends. Be prepared to run your simulation tomorrow at 0800."

"Where were you?" Miranda asked when Catie walked into her cabin. Miranda was there talking to Yvette.

"I went out the back way," Catie said. "I found a spot to sit and ran the scenarios using my HUD."

"And?!"

"Easy, peasy."

"What does that mean?" Yvette asked.

"Simple comme bonjour," Catie replied.

"How?"

"Destroy the planet's atmosphere."

"Again, how?"

"Speed up, aim at the planet, launch missiles at it one after the other."

"I still don't get it," Yvette said.

"Oh, over half the speed of light; yeah, that would do it," Miranda said. "You are an evil genius."

"Thanks, I think," Catie said. "We get to run it tomorrow at 0800."

"When did you hear that? Oh, I just got it, how did you the notification before me?" Miranda asked.

Team Charlie was the only one to win the engagement the next day. The other teams ended in ties when the time was called. Blake had only given everyone four hours of simulator time to prove out their method. Since Team Charlie never actually engaged the enemy directly, their simulation was carried out in accelerated time and finished within an hour. Now every team had been given the mission of defending the system against the attack Catie had mapped out.

"Okay, so we know the scenario that the enemy is going to use. How do you propose we defend against it?" Miranda asked.

"We're back to three ships and full flight wings, so everyone assumes their previous roles," Catie instructed.

"Okay, but when we finished the attack scenario, you called the defenders idiots," Miranda said. "So you must know how to defend against it."

Catie shook her head, "Yeah, easy. Drop an asteroid in front of the ship."

"What?"

"Drop an asteroid in front of the ship."

"And how do we do that?"

"We have the jump ships," Catie said.

"But they're not that accurate. They only open a wormhole up within a few thousand kilometers. How will that work?"

"Oh, you send a probe through, position it, have it anchor the wormhole, then push the asteroid through from the other end."

"You can anchor the wormhole with a probe?" Baker asked. "Where did you come up with that?"

"It's in the document on the jump ships," Catie said. She knew it was there because she'd written the document.

"Wait a second," Julie said as she frantically read the document. ". . . okay, I see it here, but it also says you have to stay a few hundred thousand kilometers away from a mass that's moving that fast."

"Yeah, but once you open the wormhole, you can maneuver the probe and the end of the wormhole. So, you open it up, then fly the probe until it's in front of the ship. Then you push the asteroid through."

"Okay, so we should have a lock on this mission. Do we want to run it?" Miranda asked.

"What about the bonus points for capturing the ship?" Ivan asked.

"Do we really think anyone is going to get that far?" Miranda asked. "We're the only undefeated team. We can afford a loss, but I don't think anyone's going to pull out all that detail. Which begs the question, Alex MacGregor, how have you come up with all this?"

"I like jump ships," Catie said. "I've been reading up on them since they first read us in on them."

"So why are you so distracted now?" Miranda asked.

"I'm trying to figure out how to get the bonus points," Catie said.

"So you don't want to run the easy scenario?"

"Oh, sure we should. But they're going to make us keep running scenarios until someone scores the bonus points."

"How do you know that?"

"Isn't it in the communication about continuing the tournament?"

"It is now," ADI said. "You'll have to say you checked it again when you arrived."

"I see it. There was an update put out this morning. It says everyone is running the defense scenario against the computer and that the exercises will continue until someone comes up with a solution that captures the alien starship," Julie announced.

"Oh, then why don't we run the first scenario, then we can start working on the bonus points," Miranda suggested. "We might as well nail down the win."

"Sure," Catie said. "Baker, you need to get us an asteroid; pick an iron one, about 100 meters in diameter. You'll have to mount three gravity drives, a fusion plant, and a control module on it. Then get it out to the fringe of the system."

"On it!"

"Miranda, you can fly the jump ships; we'll need them by the asteroid. We don't want them moving in relation to each other, so they should be able to be close. The tables should be in the mission brief."

"Yes, ma'am."

"Harris, you can get the probe built or pull it from stores if we already have one. You'll fly it. Julie, you fly the frigate that will be managing the probe. Hector fly the one Miranda and Baker will use to handle the asteroid."

"Aye-aye."

"Let me know when we're ready," Catie said as she turned back to studying the scenarios that would let them capture the starship, or have it surrender, which she guessed would be the same thing. *"ADI, can you clarify if surrender is the same as capture?"*

"Cer Blake says that surrender is worth more," ADI told Catie.

It was an hour before the team announced that they were ready to run the simulation.

"All ships in place?" Catie asked.

"Yes."

"Is your asteroid ready?"

"Yes, ma'am."

"Then let's do it. Jump Frigate Alfa next to and in front of the enemy vessel."

"Jump complete. Now maneuvering so we can release the probe," Julie announced.

"Maneuvering probe, . . . ready to open wormhole!" the computer announced.

"Open it."

"Wormhole open!"

"Good, now maneuver the probe to within fifty million kilometers of the alien ship and match velocities."

"Probe in place."

"Isn't that too far? Won't they be able to maneuver away?"

"The asteroid is going to show up with almost zero relative velocity," Catie said.

"Ah, and at half the speed of light, that's only a few tenths of a second."

"Okay, send the asteroid through."

"Sending asteroid through," Baker announced.

"Blam!" Hector yelled. "Nice special effects!"

"Great. Miranda, would you take care of completing the simulation," Catie said as she turned back to her table and started mapping out data associated with the capture scenario.

"Okay, my evil master," Miranda joked. "Tell us how we capture them?"

"I think we need to let them avoid the asteroid," Catie said.

"How does that help; they'll just keep going toward the planet."

"I don't think they'll be able to," Catie said. "If we force them to turn outside the gravity well, then they'll have to use reaction mass to steer back. How much mass would it take to make that ship turn three degrees?"

"At half the speed of light, a lot," Julie said.

"Once they turn that much, they'll be heading out of the well, and probably won't have enough reaction mass to turn back into it. And they'll be heading too far away from the planet to launch missiles at it."

"Why won't they be able to launch missiles at it?"

"Too much velocity and not enough reaction mass in the missiles. If they launch far enough away that they can hope to reach the planet, our fighters can take the missiles out."

"So?"

"We don't leave them a choice but to surrender. They either surrender or take all that velocity into deep space away from the gravity well. They won't have enough reaction mass to maneuver toward another star system, and no hope of slowing down."

"Okay, let's start working up scenarios. We need to figure out what they'll do when we mess up their plans," Miranda said.

"Good idea. I'll play the alien captain, you take over the defenses," Catie said.

21 The Victory Arrives

"The aliens reach Artemis Prime's fringe in four weeks. We have until then to be prepared" Blake said, as he opened the meeting.

"You have to allocate time to get everything up to their velocity," Catie said.

"I understand. I want to bring the Roebuck to Artemis also."

"That means we need to send the Galileo to Mangkatar," Samantha said.

"It's ready," Blake said.

"Do we have a crew identified?" Marc asked.

"Yes, Captain Westport will take command, he's new, but comes with enough experience. Half the crew will be Paraxeans. All the fighter pilots will be Terrans," Blake said.

"Terrans?"

"Human sounds weird, I keep hearing Quark saying 'Hu Man'. I like the sound of Terrans," Blake explained.

"Who's going to be captain of the Victory?"

"I'm leaving its command staff in place. That gives us Captain Clements, with Frankham as XO and Fitzgerald as wing commander."

"For the Roebuck?"

"No reason to change. Lieutenant Payne can handle the mission I have in mind."

"Can you set the timing on the Galileo so that it would be ready to come to Artemis if you need it?"

"I'll work with Governor Paratar to make sure they expedite the unloading of the colonists," Samantha said.

"Thanks. It'll be okay if they don't get all of the cabins out of the one flight bay, three fighter wings will be enough."

"Are you coming?" Marc asked.

"I'm already on my way," Blake said. "I'll reach the Victory in three days."

"Then a week to get here."

"Right. I'd like to practice that high-speed jump at least once," Blake said.

"You won't have time. The only way you can reach the right speed in a ship with people on it is to cut across the system fringe-to-fringe at full acceleration. That takes three weeks," Catie said.

"I know!"

"Sorry."

"Forget about it. Yes, we won't be able to do an actual full speed trial, but I'm going to have the Victory build up as much speed as we can so we can at least try it at high speed. I want you to set up a probe and the jump ships to do a full speed test."

"Yes, sir!" Catie said.

"Have you picked the system you want us to come out of?" Blake asked.

"Yes," Catie said. "We're going to use Artemis Proxima. We'll have to route you through another star system, so you enter on the right side, then we'll be able to jump you when you're ready."

"How about our asteroid?" Blake asked.

"We'll jump it from the same system. I've already put it there; it's building up speed now. We don't have to get it all the way up to quarter light speed, so we'll be okay."

"Just make sure you go over the numbers."

"ADI and I are running them and looking for any chance of an error."

"Good. Will you have the Roebuck coming from Artemis Proxima also?"

"Yes, he'll get there about the same time as you get there."

"Payne, do you know your part?"

"Yes, sir. I have my staff running simulations twice a day," Lieutenant Payne said.

"Good man," Blake said. "Okay, everyone knows their role. Call with questions, and I want a status report every day."

"Yes, sir!"

22   Board Meeting – June 6th

"Now that everyone is here, let's begin," Marc said.

"Sorry, I had a class," Catie said, explaining why everyone had had to wait on her.

"It's okay, we're all a bit tense," Marc apologized. "I've recorded our final message to the aliens. We'll send it tomorrow. Blake, is everything ready?"

"We just jumped into Artemis Proxima; we're starting our acceleration," Blake said. "The Roebuck is jumping in tomorrow."

"The Paraxean asteroid is ready to jump," Catie informed everyone.

"Thanks, I've heard. But I want to wait until after this alien ship is taken care of," Marc said. "I'll tell Governor Paratar that we'll take care of it next month."

"Your funeral," Blake said.

"Probably. Now, let's review where we are with the U.N. Admiral Michaels?"

"The U.N. has committed to intervention in Somalia. They plan to cut the country in half, and focus on the area around Mogadishu. They'll isolate the rest and let the arms embargo take effect," Admiral Michaels said.

"How is that going to be enough?" Samantha asked.

"That's where we come in. They're asking us to provide two fusion power plants to Somalia and six for Egypt."

"Egypt?"

"It's a large, impoverished population; members of the security council are committed to putting in factories to raise employment. With the fusion plants, Egypt will be able to expand how much of the Nile basin they irrigate. They'll be able to increase food production as well as cotton," Admiral Michaels said.

"How does this help Somalia?"

"They will put parts plants in Somalia that will supply the factories in Egypt. They want to create a dependency between the two countries.

With that established, they hope to bring Ethiopia and Sudan into the sphere."

"Ambitious."

"You have to start somewhere. Are you okay with delivering the power plants?"

"Yes," Marc said. "Fred, can we find something to locate in that region?"

"I'll look into it. We should have something that will work. We can at least put in a few assembly plants for solar panels."

"Blake, where is the U.N. on dealing with colony planets?" Marc asked.

"They all must be watching *Star Trek*. They've finally figured out that they cannot control the other planets, especially once they realized that there are at least six other planets that we will eventually trade with. So now they want to form a Federation of Planets," Blake said.

"And how do they envision that working?"

"The security council will appoint the ambassador to the Federation, the other planets will do the same. They intimated that they expect the Earth colonies to line up with Earth."

"They would," Marc said.

"They'll expect economic ties and our common heritage to work in their favor," Samantha said.

"They probably will. Blake, go on."

"They would like you to propose it to the Paraxeans."

"Of course they would. I'll think about it. I suspect this is the right way to go."

"It is, Daddy. We need a governing body to manage the rules of trade."

"Says the girl with a monopoly on interstellar trade," Marc said.

"We have to find a way to share that access. I have some ideas," Catie said.

"No surprise there. Now, is the Galileo ready to head to Mangkatar?" Marc asked.

"Next week," Fred said. "We're just getting the colonists loaded up. Twenty thousand is a big crowd."

"They're getting twenty thousand into that thing!" Samantha said. "Hey, I thought we weren't going to pull any more colonists from the asteroid."

"These are all the ones we already pulled out," Fred said. "They originally wanted to bring thirty thousand, but Blake stopped them. There are lots of families, so it's crowded. And Marc, there shouldn't be a problem getting them unloaded in time to jump to Artemis if you need the Galileo. One of the flight bays might still have cabins in it, but the other three will be ready."

"I think we'll only need one flight bay anyway," Blake said.

"Okay, I'm good with that," Marc said. "Catie, we're going to want another Skylifter."

"Oh, you will?"

"Yes, and get those dollar signs out of your eyes. We'll pay the same as we did last time."

"But last time we had to use it. We've got our own now."

"I'm sure you owe us for something," Marc said.

"*Okay*, we'll give you a break. I'll have Ajda start building it now."

Four hundred colonists had decided to join Marc at Lake Diana. The level of the lake was rising noticeably now that the they had increased the delivery rate of the ice asteroids. Marc had declared a holiday and commissioned a large picnic at the lake. The rest of the colonists were taking the holiday, but had decided to watch the festivities from the comfort of a bar.

"Here comes one!" a young boy shouted, pointing to the Skylifter headed down toward the lake with an ice asteroid sitting on its tail.

"Yay!" shouted the other children as they gathered around to watch the asteroid drop into the lake.

The pilot had realized how much the children were enjoying the show, so he decided that this time he would give them something to really get excited about. At two hundred meters he rotated the Skylifter one hundred eighty degrees, letting the asteroid slip free and plummet into the lake. Dropping two hundred meters, the asteroid set up a huge splash, sending a virtual tidal wave toward the lake shores.

"Idiot," Marc shouted as he rushed to the children. "Get back! Up the hill!"

When he reached the children, he realized he needn't have worried, the lake was still too shallow to generate much of a wave. The water drew back from the shore about five hundred meters then the wave crashed onto the shore, but it was only able to swamp the lower part of the hillside that they were standing on. The lake was only fifty meters deep, and the top of the shoreline was another one hundred meters above that.

"Sorry about that," the pilot said. "I guess I shouldn't drop it from so far."

"Yes! A twenty-meter drop should generate more than enough excitement," Marc said.

"Not anymore," Samantha laughed as she pulled Marc back to their picnic blanket. "Hey, if we're getting over ten asteroids a day, why are they taking over two hours to drop one in the lake?"

"The Skylifter can't bring that many of them down this far," Marc said. "It's dropping the smaller ones in the ocean, where it can do a ten-thousand-meter drop."

"Oh, is that why you're getting another Skylifter?"

"Yes, we have this lake to fill and another one like it on the southern continent to fill, plus we want to raise the ocean level by another foot or so."

"That much?"

"We have a lot of water vapor to make up for."

"How long will it take to fill this lake?"

"We'll fill this one in about six months," Marc said. "When we get the other Skylifter, we'll start filling the other lake. Dr. Qamar says it will take two years to get the ocean level back to where we want it."

"Will that make the planet less arid?"

"Some. The increased surface area of the ocean will reflect more heat, and the two lakes will do the same. But mainly they'll affect the local climate. That will lead to more forest which will reflect more heat. We'll eventually have more clouds, which will reflect more heat. And the forest along the equatorial regions will expand, absorb more CO_2 and reflect more heat."

"So how long?"

"Fifty years," Marc said.

"Fifty years!"

"Hey, this area is already nice, it'll get even nicer when the lake is full. We won't need to expand much beyond this region for at least twenty or thirty years."

"Okay, I'll give you that," Samantha said.

Marc was taking a nap when a child's squeal woke him up. "What is that about?"

"Oh, just chasing each other around while they wait for the next drop," Samantha said.

Marc shook his head as he sat up. "Doctor Z," he called to the Paraxean doctor with the unpronounceable name. Dr. Metra had persuaded her to go Artemis Colony until their doctor was fully trained on Paraxean medical technology.

"Yes, Cer Marc?"

"Haven't you Paraxeans figured out how to have a child's voice change early, like around three?"

"You might not like hearing that high-pitched squeal, but I can assure you that any mother is happy that her child's voice is so piercing. It is a comfort to know that when they get into trouble, they are able to get your attention from afar," Dr. Z said.

"How about doing something so that it's only piercing when they're truly afraid?"

"That might be worth considering. I'll look into it," Dr. Z said, but her eyes said she was just humoring Marc.

"This is your final message," Marc said. "We warn you that if you don't deviate your course toward the sun and away from the planet, we will be forced to assume your intentions are hostile and will destroy your ship. You must start decelerating as soon as you enter the sixty AU limit."

The aliens were just days from entering Artemis Prime's gravity well. Now it was clear that the course adjustment they'd made months ago had put their course vector pointing directly at Artemis. Marc really wanted to capture them so he could learn about them, but he was perfectly willing to obliterate the starship with an asteroid if that's what it took to protect Artemis.

"They dare to threaten us!" Captain Shakaban shouted. His face was livid with anger, and his grip on the arms of his command chair was crumpling the metal. "Prepare our missiles, we will be in their system in three days! Then we'll teach them not to stand in our way!"

23 Roadblock

"Captain, we are getting a sensor ghost ahead of us," the alien sensor operator said.

"What do you mean, 'ghost'?"

"There have been several small energy spikes off of our port bow. They are at extreme sensor range."

"Several, how many?" the captain demanded.

"Five large spikes and hundreds of smaller ones since. The smaller ones look like signatures from gravity drives."

"Our friends are probably trying to move into position so they can intercept us," the captain said. "They will be very surprised when we fly right by them instead of slowing down. How long until our gravity drives will have enough power to maneuver?"

"Approximately two hours, sir."

"Is everyone ready?" Blake asked. He was on the Victory which was approaching the fringe of Artemis Proxima.

"We're ready, the wormhole is open and stable on my end," Catie reported. She was at the Academy, in one of the simulation rooms where she would be able to control the jump ships.

"We're ready, Admiral," Captain Clements, the captain of the Victory said.

"The wormhole is open and stable here in Artemis Prime," Lieutenant Payne of the Roebuck announced.

"Then, take us through!" Blake ordered.

Catie slowed the jump ships in Artemis Proxima so that the Victory plunged through the wormhole.

"Captain, a huge vessel has just appeared off our port bow!" the sensor operator yelled.

"What, that's impossible!" Captain Shakaban yelled back. "Check your sensors again!"

"It is there. It must be five hundred meters long and two hundred meters across!"

"How would they be able to move something that massive without us noticing?!" the captain demanded.

"I don't know, but it is matching our course and speed, sir."

"There is a message coming in," the communication officer announced.

"Put it on the display."

"Greetings, I'm Admiral Blake McCormack of the Delphi Starship Victory. You have been warned to adjust your course away from the planet or face being destroyed. Are you ready to comply?"

"We claim the right to Zagawani, and do not recognize your right to exclude us," Captain Shakaban snarled.

"You might not recognize our right, but do you recognize this ship that is flying just off your port bow? We have five hundred space fighters on board her, and we intend to stop you from getting close to our planet."

"You will find that we are not without teeth," the captain said, giving a wide smile that showed lots of very sharp teeth.

Blake froze the Comm. "Catie, are you ready?" Blake asked.

"We're ready."

"Then go!" Blake ordered.

Catie and Lieutenant Payne had been decelerating the jump ships since the Victory went through. She had them aligned with the asteroid. She now slowed them enough that the asteroid went through. It would have a significantly lower velocity than the alien ship when it emerged on the other side.

"It's through," Lieutenant Payne announced.

Blake turned back to the display and had the communication officer reopen the channel to the alien space ship. "You will find that we are not without teeth either. But first, I think I should point out that you're about to run into an asteroid."

"Captain, an asteroid has appeared dead ahead!" the sensor operator shouted. "We will hit it in one minute!"

"Destroy it!"

"It is too big!"

"Then avoid it, you fool! Hard to starboard!"

The alien ship started spewing reaction mass from its port side while its gravity drives gave as much as they had. They managed to turn the ship two arcseconds, barely missing the asteroid.

"Put us back on course!" Captain Shakaban ordered.

"We do not have enough reaction mass to turn back."

"Use the gravity drives then!"

"We are still too far outside the gravity well; they do not have enough power."

Captain Shakaban pounded the arm of his command chair. "Have the shuttle loaded with as many missiles as it can carry," he ordered. Then he motioned the communication officer to reopen the channel to the Victory.

"I don't know how you managed that, but rest assured we are not finished. We demand that you allow us access to Zagawani while we discuss our options."

"Demand all you want. I don't see how you're going to be able to slow down enough to stay in our system," Blake replied. "If you don't surrender now and do a maximum deceleration, we will be forced to destroy you, or maybe we'll just let you head out into open space. I wonder how many months of supplies you have."

"You would risk the lives of your crew just to keep us out of this system?"

"You would risk the lives of your crew just to avoid surrendering? If your intentions are honorable, we will release you. We don't trust you and until you comply, we have to assume you have hostile intentions."

"What could we do to you? You have an entire planet, that huge space carrier you call Victory, while all we have is our one ship."

"We don't know, and we don't intend to find out after you attempt it. Now decelerate!"

"Captain, the shuttle is ready to launch."

"Then launch it!"

"Admiral, the aliens have launched a shuttle!" the Victory's sensor operator announced.

"Commander Fitzgerald, launch your squadron!" Blake ordered.

"Launching now," Commander Fitzgerald reported. "What do you want them to do?"

"Overtake that shuttle, order the aliens to evacuate it, give them five minutes, then destroy it," Blake ordered.

"Yes, sir."

Eight Foxes flew out of the back of the Victory and banked around her and headed toward the shuttle.

"Shuttle, this is Commander Fitzgerald. You are ordered to evacuate. We will give you five minutes, then we will destroy the shuttle!" Commander Fitzgerald announced over an open channel.

"Commander Fitzgerald, we cannot evacuate the shuttle, we do not have space suits."

"That is unfortunate since you have five minutes before that shuttle blows up around you."

"Commander, even if we evacuate, your destruction of the shuttle will kill us."

"Evacuate and we'll shield you from it," Fitzgerald said. "You now have four minutes!"

Three figures jumped from the shuttle as the shuttle continued to accelerate. The distance between them and the shuttle started to grow as the shuttle continued to accelerate away from them.

"Jackson, put your Fox between them and the shuttle," Fitzgerald ordered.

"Yes, ma'am."

Fitzgerald waited the full four minutes before giving the order to launch a missile at the shuttle. It exploded in a fiery ball, giving away the fact that it was carrying a huge load of atomic weapons.

"Captain, they have destroyed the shuttle!" the alien sensor operator announced.

The captain gave a loud roar. "Helm, make course for that space carrier. We are going to ram it!"

"We don't have enough reaction mass to change course that much! Sir."

"Rotate the ship, I'll use the fighters in the flight bay. Commander Dumak, prepare your fighters for maximum burn."

"Yes, sir!"

"Belay that order!" Lieutenant Lantaq yelled. He was standing behind the captain. The captain's face was slack and he had Lieutenant Lantaq's dagger protruding from the back of his skull. "I have assumed command. Open a channel to the Victory."

"Yes, sir!" the communication officer replied with obvious relief.

"This is Captain Lantaq, I have assumed command of the Mortarka. We are now attempting to comply with your orders. We do not have enough power in our gravity drives to decelerate sufficiently to achieve orbit, and we do not have enough reaction mass to do so either."

"I believe we can help you with that," Blake announced. "Hold your course steady."

"We will comply."

"Stand down your weapons. We are going to place a probe on your ship."

"What kind of probe?" Captain Lantaq asked.

"Stand down your weapons!" Blake ordered again.

"Our weapons are down."

"Fitzgerald, have one of your Foxes place a missile warhead on their hull, attach the probe to it," Blake ordered.

"Yes, sir."

"Catie can you jump them into Artemis Proxima?" Blake asked.

"Yes, if they stay on course."

"Then let's try it."

"Payne just needs to position his jump ships and we'll be good to go," Catie said.

"Oh, right. Lieutenant Payne, please position your jump ships ahead of the alien ship; we want to send it to Artemis Proxima," Blake ordered.

"Yes sir." Payne maneuvered the ships so they were in front of the alien ship. He slowed them so the alien ship had a relative velocity of 300 meters per second. "Ready."

Catie opened the wormhole.

"Wormhole confirmed," Lieutenant Payne reported.

"We're ready," Catie informed Blake.

"Captain Lantaq, you'll see four ships in front of you; they're about two million meters away. You need to steer for the center of them," Blake communicated. "We have placed a probe with a warhead on it. If you fail to comply with any of our instructions, your vessel will be destroyed."

"We will comply. What will happen when we fly between the ships?"

"You will see," Blake said.

Two hours later the Mortarka went through the wormhole to Artemis Proxima.

"What happened?!" Captain Lantaq demanded. His entire bridge crew was scrambling at their stations to try to make sense of their sudden shift in location.

"You're in Artemis Proxima's system," Blake explained. "You should be heading toward its star. Use its gravity well to slow your ship down, then put it in orbit at the fringe. We need you to be at sixty AUs for the next step. When you reach that point, we'll get back to you and bring you over to Artemis Prime's system and complete our discussions."

"Yes, Admiral. It will take us three weeks to slow down that much, and we will be on the other side of the system when we do."

"That will be fine, just make orbit then. I will talk to you when you do," Blake said. "Please don't make me blow your ship up."

"We won't."

"Thank you," Blake said before he cut the communication channel with the alien ship. "Good work everyone. Now, stand down, and get back to work. Captain Clements, you have command. I'm going to rendezvous with the Roebuck and see if I can make it back in time for my niece's graduation."

24   Graduation

Sixty-eight graduating cadets walked out onto the parade ground to take their seats. If anyone was counting, they would have noticed that sixty-eight was one more than the number of first-class cadets. Catie had made it. She had finished all the necessary course work and had gotten a nod from Uncle Blake that she would be allowed to graduate. She'd dyed her hair back to its natural color, and had worn colored contacts for the last two weeks while her eyes returned to their natural color. She'd let her skin adjust with time, darkening to the shade she now preferred. She took her seat in the last seat on the last row.

"Who is that girl?" a cadet asked.

"I don't know. I don't remember her from class. She seems quiet, maybe we never noticed her."

"That's hard to believe, especially since she's wearing a sash that says she's graduating with honors."

"Maybe she's just a bookworm."

"Shhh!"

"I would like to welcome the families of our graduates to the Academy," Commandant Lewis said. "It is an extra-special occasion since they are our first graduating class, a distinction that they will carry with them throughout their careers. And to make the occasion even more special, Admiral Prince Blake McCormack is on stage to greet each graduate as they receive their degrees. He will be making the keynote address."

Commandant Lewis continued with her commencement speech, citing all the firsts that this class had accomplished. Finally, they started to hand out the degrees.

"Graduating with honors, our Valedictorian, Cadet Colonel Miranda Cordova."

◆ ◆ ◆

"And our last graduate, graduating with honors, Cadet Alexandra MacGregor. And it is especially my honor to announce that Cadet

MacGregor is actually Lieutenant Princess Catherine Alexandra McCormack!"

The crowd went wild as Catie walked across the stage. Blake broke protocol and gave her a hug before shaking her hand for the formal picture.

"You have some explaining to do," Commandant Lewis said as she shook Catie's hand.

Catie continued across the stage and picked up her parchment from the staff secretary and returned to her seat.

"Can you believe it, Princess Catie was in our class the whole time?!"

"Not our class, the one behind us. And that would be Lieutenant Princess Catie, and a full lieutenant, too."

"Jamison, you sure know how to pick the right people to piss off," Ensign Barkley said.

"Oh, shit. I might as well quit now; she's going to make my life hell."

"Bawk, bawk!"

"I wouldn't worry about it. I've heard she only gets even once for each transgression."

Jamison just moaned.

Blake went to the podium to give his speech.

"Good afternoon," Blake started. "First, let me explain that last announcement. Cadet McCormack's father wanted his daughter to have enough of an Academy experience that she would be able to fully internalize what it means to be a member of the Delphi Defense forces. Some of you in the audience may not understand that, but I'm sure all of our graduates do. The experience at the Academy forms a bond between cadets and between each cadet and the service. Obviously, sending Princess Catherine to the Academy was out of the question, so with some minor cosmetic surgery and a few modifications to the records, we invented Cadet MacGregor. But all of that just underscores how important the Academy is and how much these cadets in front of you have accomplished."

Once Blake finished his speech, Miranda got up to do hers.

"Oh, my. This is definitely an honor. I'd like to thank my parents, my instructors at the Academy, and my friends. This accomplishment would have been impossible without the help I received from all of you. I would like to add a comment about Cadet MacGregor. Never in my wildest dreams would I have guessed that she was the Princess. We've had a class together, and have become friends. I wouldn't be standing here if it wasn't for her help with one of my classes. And as Admiral McCormack said, it is a testament to what it means to attend the Academy that none of us knew who she really was. . . ."

The cadets were finally able to parade out into the crowd where they met their families or friends. Each was eager to have their new rank insignia attached. Catie found her mother Linda, Liz, and her Uncle Blake waiting next to Commandant Lewis.

Catie snapped off a salute to them as she approached. "Hi, I hope Uncle Blake explained everything."

"He has, but I still expect you to join me for dinner later this week and provide your own explanation," Commandant Lewis said.

"Yes, ma'am."

"Now, I'll leave you to it," she said before turning and moving toward another group of cadets.

"Mommy, will you pin my boards on?"

"Of course," Linda said. Blake handed her the box with a new set of lieutenant boards in it. She replaced Catie's cadet boards with them, then gave her a kiss.

Blake and Liz stepped back and saluted, "Lieutenant McCormack."

"Thank you, sir, ma'am," Catie replied as she returned the salutes.

"Now, go talk to your friends, I'm sure they're bursting with questions," Linda said.

"Mother, this is my friend, Lieutenant McCormack," Miranda said after she gave Catie a salute.

"Oh, my. I can't believe this," Ms. Cordova said. "Where did your father run off to?"

"Hellos Ms. Cordova, it's an honor to meet you," Catie said.

"The honor is mine."

"Oh, don't let that princess stuff get in the way. Miranda and I are friends."

"I'm glad to hear that. Here's her father, Joaquín. Joaquín, can you believe our daughter is friends with the princess?"

"It doesn't surprise me," Mr. Cordova said. "It's a pleasure to meet you, Princess."

"Just call me Catie."

"Here come Joanie and Yvette," Miranda said.

"We'll leave you girls to chat," Mr. Cordova said as he guided his wife away.

"Alex, I cannot believe you!" Joanie said. "Princess Catie, and you crawled through all that mud."

"That was fun."

"*Oh la la*, they do say that royals are sometimes a bit crazy," Yvette said. She and Joanie stepped back and gave Catie and Miranda a salute.

"As you were," Catie ordered.

"I bet Jamison messed his pants when they announced who you were," Yvette said.

"I'm sure he did," Miranda said. "I wish I could have seen the look on his face."

"I'm sure there is a video of him," Catie said.

"Of course there is," ADI said. "Would you like a copy?"

"Send one to all of us," Catie said.

"What?" her friends asked together.

"I was just informed that they caught Jamison on camera; I've asked them to send videos to all of you."

"You have spies; that makes sense, you're a princess after all," Yvette said.

243

"Oh, it's just ADI. You know, the DI for Delphi Station. She and I are friends and she has access to all the cameras," Catie said.

"Oh, friends with the all-powerful DI," Miranda said.

"We could be friends, too," ADI whispered into Miranda's Comm.

"Oops. Yes, let's be friends," Miranda said.

"So you have to tell us all your secrets," Yvette said. "Was that Liz I saw over there with Admiral Blake?"

"Yes," Catie said.

"Good, let's go and change, then the Princess can take us all out to dinner and we can talk. Possibly Liz can join us and give us some of the real dirt," Yvette suggested.

"Sure," Catie said as she sent Liz an invite.

"Catie, don't you dare leave without talking to me," Sophia yelled as she struggled to make her way through the crowd.

"Who's that?"

"Oh, I guess you'd say she's a friend," Catie said.

"You guess?"

"She's a reporter. She wrote that book, Princess Catie, The Inside Story."

"Oh, that was a good book," Miranda said. "It seemed like she liked you."

"I guess, but it messed my life up for a while."

"Hi, I'm Sophia," Sophia said as she finally reached Catie and her friends.

"Sophia, this is Miranda, but of course, you know that. This is Yvette LeClair, my roommate at the Academy, and this is Joanie McCoy, my roommate during Basic. Guys, this is Sophia Michaels, my friend from before the Academy, and the owner and reporter for the Delphi Gazette."

"Sophia Michaels, as in Admiral Michaels' daughter?" Miranda asked.

"Yes, he's my father," Sophia said. "Now Catie, will you give me a statement?"

"I am delighted to have been able to attend the Academy incognito. I will treasure the experience for the rest of my life. I am especially grateful to have developed the friendships I did with many of the Cadets. The camaraderie among the cadet core was a great asset to my ability to complete my year. I would especially like to thank Commodore Lewis for her guidance and leadership. There, is that good enough?"

"For now," Sophia said.

"Why doesn't Sophia join us for dinner?" Yvette suggested.

Catie shot daggers at Yvette, who seemed oblivious to her. "Why not, it's going to be a roast anyway, might as well bring a fire starter," Catie said.

"So Sophia, how did you meet Catie?" Yvette asked. They were at Deogene's drinking wine and waiting for their orders.

"She's the first person from Delphi that I met," Sophia said. "We met in Tijuana, Mexico, when my family was flying here because my father had pissed the president off."

"Oh, that must have been tough."

"It was. But Catie helped us out . . . got my mom and me to the clinic to get the birth control nanites, got me a Comm before everyone else."

"I can see why you became friends. How did you come to start the Delphi Gazette?" Miranda asked.

"That was Catie's idea. I suggested ADI should do a newsletter since she always knew what was going on. Catie said ADI would help me do one. That's before I knew ADI was a DI."

"Then you wrote that book," Yvette said.

Sophia winced. "Yeah, I wrote it, then hid from Catie for a few months."

"Why did you hide?"

"She has a habit of getting even when you make her mad."

"Did she get even?"

"Yes."

"I did not!"

"Oh, can it, everyone knows it was you."

Catie just smiled and shook her head.

"What did she do?" Miranda asked.

"Once things calmed down, I came back home. One morning I was taking a shower and the water turned my hair and skin green."

"How did that happen?"

"They couldn't figure out how she did it, but I know she did. I dyed my hair but my skin had a green tint for weeks after."

Catie giggled a bit.

"See, she admits it!"

"I did not, I just thought that green being the color of greed was appropriate."

Liz snorted. "That's as much of an admission as you'll ever get from her. We do know that nobody else had a motive."

"But I didn't have the means or opportunity," Catie said.

"Pfft, if anyone could pull it off, you could," Liz scoffed.

"When did this happen?" Miranda asked.

"The end of July."

"We were in Guatemala then."

"That wouldn't have stopped her."

"Let's talk about something else," Liz suggested. "Are you three telling me that you had no idea that Catie might not be who she said she was?"

"No clue," Joanie said. "She always was being nice and helping everyone."

"I was a bit curious after the simulations," Miranda said. "She seemed to know more about it than anyone else."

"I just knew the rules for the last one. And about the jump ships," Catie said.

"But that fire drill?" Miranda asked.

"Oh, that was because I figured out what the aliens were going to do at Artemis."

"The aliens?"

"Oh, you don't remember that we had an alien starship approaching Artemis?"

"Cer Catie. That information was not released. Only the U.N. security council knew."

"Oops. I'll explain later. Let's just say the simulations tournament was staged to come up with the strategy for dealing with an alien incursion into a system."

"Interesting."

"I did wonder how she was able to type all those papers so fast," Yvette said. "Did you have ADI type them?"

"No! I would never do that. I type about six hundred words a minute," Catie said, offended that they thought she would cheat.

"How can you type that fast?!"

"You didn't tell them?" Liz asked.

"I couldn't."

"Tell us what?!"

"Catie and Dr. Metra developed this process where a doctor puts nanites at the nerve endings in your coccyx that used to control your tail. Catie uses those to type," Liz explained.

"And it lets you message in your HUD and control things with it without using your hands," Catie added.

"Can we get these nanites?" Miranda asked.

"Sure, want me to set it up with Dr. Metra for you?" Catie asked.

"Please!" all three girls said at once.

"Okay, but it takes a month before you can really use them, and you have to be able to go to the clinic every week for three weeks," Catie said. "Sophia, I assume you have yours."

"I got them last month," Sophia said. "I live in Nice most of the time, so that was the first chance I got."

"Oh, you live in Nice, that's where I'm from. Alex . . . I mean Catie, why didn't we visit her while we were there?" Yvette asked.

"Because the last thing you want to do when you're trying to be in disguise, is talk to the press.'"

"Oh, I guess so."

"Catie," Joanie cooed. "Is there any chance you could help us get better summer cruises?"

"I'm not sure," Catie said. "Why, you don't like the ones you've been assigned to?"

"We don't know what they are," Yvette said.

"Yvette is being assigned to one of the surface carriers," ADI informed Catie. "Joanie is being assigned to work on Gemini Station."

"Tell them," Catie suggested.

Once ADI had told Yvette and Joanie their assignments, Catie gave them a 'well what now' look.

"I kind of like mine," Joanie said.

"Mine doesn't sound so wonderful," Yvette said.

"Why not? You could get the Mediterranean carrier and be close to home."

"I think I'm allergic to salt spray," Yvette giggled. "Two weeks on that clipper was more than enough for me."

"You can ask if they'll give you another posting."

"I will, but what if they don't have anything else?"

"Ask, then let me know," Catie said. "Miranda, do you have your first assignment yet?"

"I'm scheduled for flight training when the next class starts. That's in three weeks. Until then, I'm on leave."

"That sounds good, have you been using the simulator yet?"

"There's a long line of people wanting to use the simulators," Miranda said.

"Not those, the one in your HUD," Catie said. "That's how I learned."

"Is there a reason nobody has told us about it?" Miranda asked.

"I don't know. ADI, who is in charge of pilot training?" Catie asked.

"Lieutenant Beaulieu," ADI replied.

"Is she available?"

"Hi, Catie," Mariam Beaulieu answered her Comm. "Congratulations on finishing at the Academy. I didn't know you were going."

"Hi, Mariam. Thank you, and it was a secret. But I'm calling about the pilot training. I have a friend going to attend the next class and we wanted to know if there was a reason that you didn't point them to the HUD simulator?"

"I can't imagine why, unless Commandant Lewis doesn't want them distracted. But there are lots of other distractions to worry about."

"So, you don't mind if I show her how to use it?"

"Not at all. Take her up and let her fly one for all I care."

"Thanks."

"She says it's okay," Catie said.

"Cool. Hey, what are you doing next?"

"She's taking the Dutchman out on a cargo run to Paraxea and Artemis," Liz said, "the luxuries of being on a planet."

"Hey, Daddy said he gave you a tour of Artemis."

"Three days!" Liz said. "I've only been on the ground for ten days in the last six months."

"Blame Daddy and Uncle Blake, they're the ones who made me go to the Academy. Besides you get to go down in history as the captain of the first cargo ship to make an interstellar round trip."

"When do you leave?" Miranda asked.

"I'm supposed to make a run to the asteroid belt and back next week," Catie said. "That's two weeks. After that, I have to make the long run, which is eighteen weeks or so."

"That is a long run," Yvette said.

"Yeah, but Dr. McDowell and I think we have a way to take out ten days or so," Catie said.

"Why is it that it's only now that you have to sail the next trip that you're ready to deploy that?" Liz asked.

"We just figured it out back in March. We still have to prove it will work, then we need to make the infrastructure for it."

"Well, we should try to hire another captain to balance out the work schedule," Liz said.

"I think we need to hire more than one. Our second ship will be ready in a few months, and I want to go out on the Roebuck and check out some new systems to trade with."

"You're worse than your father, never satisfied with what you have. It's always more, more, more."

"Now you're sounding like Uncle Blake."

25 Well, Now What?

"Catie, can we talk about money?"

"Sure, you want to give me some?"

Liz snorted. "Like you need help from me."

"Hey, at least you've been getting a paycheck. I'm only getting about half of my usual check from Fred, and nothing from StarMerchants."

"Oh, cry me a river; you're worth billions and you're whining about not getting a paycheck."

"Hey, ADI won't let me use money from my savings and investments."

"It's your money!"

"A penny saved is a penny earned," ADI said.

Liz laughed. "Funny, ADI."

"The saving man becomes the free man."

"She has a whole list of them," Catie whined. "She goes through them all before I can touch any money besides my paycheck."

"Wasting is a bad habit, saving is a sure income."

"Okay, we get it!" Liz said. "Anyway, I wanted to ask how we were managing our pay from StarMerchants."

"Standard captain's pay," Catie said. "Didn't you get paid?"

"No, that's why I'm asking about it."

"Just a second." Catie dove into her HUD and looked at the records.

"Did someone forget to approve her pay package?" Catie asked when she found what she was looking for.

"What?!"

"It says here your pay is awaiting approval from the co-owner. I approved it, but you haven't."

"You've got to be kidding, why do I have to approve my pay?"

"All salaries have to be approved by both owners."

Liz groaned as she used her HUD to find the document in her in-tray. She signed it and closed the view. "I can't believe I missed that."

"Hey, open it back up and approve my pay package."

"Sure, I guess now you'll finally be able to have some money that ADI will approve of you spending."

"Don't save what is left after spending; instead spend what is left after saving," ADI quoted Warren Buffet.

"Argh!" Catie screeched.

"Catie, you do know that the cargo run to Gemini Station is about ready to go out?" Liz asked as she sat with Catie at breakfast.

"I know, I'm just waiting for them to load the last container of appliances. We should be ready to head out on Wednesday. I wanted to let everyone have an extra day planet side."

"How long is the run going to be?"

"Since we're not carrying that much cargo, we can use a higher acceleration profile, so it's five days each way. We'll spend one day there since we have passengers to disembark and a new set to bring home."

"Passengers?"

"Miners."

"Oh, right. What are we charging for them?"

"Nothing."

"What! No way you're giving them a free ride."

"I am."

"Why?"

"I'm negotiating with Daddy about making the solar probes so we can establish a single wormhole between our jumps."

"That benefits him, so why do you have to butter him up by giving free rides to the miners?" Liz asked.

"It really benefits us. He doesn't care about saving a week in the transit time."

"Two weeks when you count both ways, but I see your point. Do you think it'll work?"

"We'll see." Catie said.

"What do those probes cost?"

"Thirty million each, but they each need a quantum relay as well."

"Oh! Let me know if I can help."

"You can interview for a second crew."

"Oh no you don't, we'll interview when you get back."

"But what about all the crew from the Roebuck? Most of them are on leave and they might be reassigned before I get back."

"Tell you what, I'll work with Derek and see who we can pick up from his old crew. I assume you're okay with having him take the first mate slot."

"If he wants it," Catie said. "He's been captain of the Roebuck for over a year."

"I'll talk to him; can I tell him we'll make him a captain when we get the next StarMerchant built?"

"Definitely."

◆ ◆ ◆

"She's a vindictive bitch," the spec three at the antimatter reactor console whispered as Catie walked by.

"Captain, I'm surprised to see you back here," Commander Griggs said as she gave the spec three a disapproving stare.

"Hi, Commander Griggs," Catie said. "A gravity and a half isn't that tough. The walk will serve as my exercise for today."

"Call me Chief," Commander Griggs said. "Now come into my office and we'll chat."

Catie followed Commander Griggs into her office, glancing over her shoulder at the spec three. "Was he talking about me?"

"What? Oh, that vindictive bitch comment. Are you a vindictive bitch?"

"Some people might think so."

Commander Griggs laughed. "Liz told me about the green food coloring incident. She showed me some interesting videos of Sophia rushing out of her shower. But, no, the comment wasn't about you. It was about his ex-girlfriend. He came home after a night out with his mates to find all his stuff in plastic bags. She'd washed his clothes in red dye and put them in bags with moldy bread. He spent the next two days buying new clothes."

"That does sound vindictive."

"Yes, and that is a reputation you don't want to get," Commander Griggs said, giving Catie a knowing look. "Getting even can be funny if you do it right, but if it becomes a habit, you can fall into that trap."

"Oh, so you think I should stop getting even?"

"At least for the little stuff; it's not worth it. You should have better things to do with your time."

"I guess you're right."

"So, what did you want? I'm sure you didn't come down here for mothering."

"No, not that I don't appreciate it. But I wanted to review the crew staffing. We're going to take your advice and create a three-crew rotation between the two ships. That gives everyone at least six weeks off every thirty-six weeks."

"So, when is the second ship going to be ready?"

"Six months, but we want to get key members of the crew hired now. Liz is trying to grab as many as she can from the Roebuck now that it's back."

"That will endear you to your Uncle, the admiral."

Catie laughed. "Well, he's getting used to it. Do you know Lieutenant Payne?"

"Only by reputation."

"We're going to make him an offer to be first mate for the second crew, and captain when we start up the third."

"I'm sure he'll be fine. You and Liz both have a lot of experience with him."

"Yes we have. I'm curious how you think the crew will handle switching ships all the time."

"It's become more common. The biggest complaints have been about increased maintenance cost, but that's not going to be a problem for you since you're always coming back to the home port. The ships are going to be identical so the crew won't get confused."

"We thought about all that. But what about making sure the crew does all their maintenance chores just before the switch. Won't they be tempted to let things slide?"

"That's always the danger with crew rotations. But I always made it a challenge for the new crew to find what the last crew missed. That motivates both crews to keep things up to snuff."

"Ah, I like that idea. Did you impose a penalty or was it enough to rely on their pride?"

"Pride worked pretty well. Different officers, so imposing a penalty was difficult, except in egregious cases."

"Okay, we should go over this with Liz when we get back. We need to come up with planetside work assignments for them."

"Prepping the next cargo should work. I assume you want the pods in orbit and ready to attach."

"Definitely. We're going to require the customers to have the pods waiting for us so we can shorten the turnaround time. But we need to add training and other stuff."

"I'll think about it. Now, I have a question, why are you going to let this ship sit for a week after this run?" Commander Griggs asked.

"We'll do a deep maintenance and inspection while we're back. But there's something that Liz and I need to be able to attend to when we get back. And it might change the objective for our next run."

"Something you care to share?"

"MacKenzie board secrets," Catie said. "Sorry."

"Don't worry about it. 'Need to know' is a pretty common answer in the Navy, so I'm used to it."

◆ ◆ ◆

"ADI, you shared the video with Liz?!" Catie asked as she headed back to her cabin. She felt offended that ADI had shared a video of Sophia with Liz that she wouldn't share with her.

"Of course, Liz is my friend," ADI replied.

"Are you still mad at me for not telling you what the plan was?"

"Yes! I spent a lot of time trying to figure out what you were going to do."

"And you didn't figure it out?"

"NO!"

"Are you mad at me or at yourself?"

"Both."

"Didn't you have fun trying to figure out what I had planned?"

"Hmm, fun? Possibly."

"Probably more fun than if I had just told you."

"Maybe. You are devious," ADI said.

"Not a vindictive bitch?"

"No. I've never heard anyone refer to you that way."

"I guess I have to lighten up, or they might?"

"But not too much so we still can have some fun getting even," ADI said.

"We want to keep our friends on their toes."

"Hi, Jimmy," Catie said as she joined Jimmy Gaines in the conference room on Gemini Station.

"Hi, Catie. Did your passengers behave themselves?"

"Mostly. 1.5G tends to keep people from chasing around causing problems."

"But then they have all the pent-up energy when you do the 1G rest period."

"There is that. I never got called by security, so it must not have been too bad."

"Good. Having the Dutchman making runs is going to simplify things for us. I assume you heard we're closing down the operation in Earth's orbit. We'll send those asteroids back here."

"No, I hadn't heard that. Are you happy about it?"

"It was our idea. More efficient for the miners. Gemini Station is a nice place to live. Rotating back to Earth once or twice a year seems to make everyone happy. And it's more efficient. With the co-op, our miners really hate to be idle."

Catie laughed, "Greedy?"

"Not greedy, just wanting to have nice choices," Jimmy said.

"I'm glad to hear it. So that explains the four pods of methane we're taking back."

"Yep, might as well keep you as full as possible, empty cargo pods don't help anyone."

"How is your smelter working?"

"Pretty good. It's a lot better than the one we were using at Delphi Station. I assume they're upgrading that one."

"Yes, it should be online about the time I get back," Catie said.

"Good. Half the pods we're sending back are full of unrefined ore, so it's all mixed up. The new smelter makes it easy to deal with. You'll be taking a bunch of engineers and engineering students back. They just finished tuning our smelter. I think they'll be tuning the one at Delphi Station before they start running ore through it."

"Oh," Catie said, wondering if Braxton would be among her passengers.

"Speaking of cargo and stuff, we have some interesting items we brought along."

"Such as?"

"Fresh fruit, some extra furniture for the cabins, things like that."

"You must be coordinating with Artie."

"He does manage our side-book cargo." Catie was referring to the cargo that they bought and hoped to sell at the destination site. Artie was an exceptional judge of what would sell in another location having honed his skills using excess lift capacity to ship speculative cargo to Delphi Station.

◆ ◆ ◆

"Catie, these are your passengers," Jimmy said as he led a small group to the boarding ramp for the Dutchman.

"We just loaded passengers," Catie said.

"I know, but these are the engineers I told you about."

"Oh, the ones staying in the guest cabins."

"Right."

"What are guest cabins?" the older man with Jimmy asked.

"Catie, this is Professor Haskell, he's the one that designed the smelter."

"Hi," Catie said.

"Catie McCormack?" Professor Haskell asked.

"Yes, and to answer your question, we have passenger cabins, which the miners are using, and we also have a limited number of guest cabins. They're a little nicer and are intended for dignitaries and guests of the crew," Catie explained.

"Well, I'm pleased to meet you. And honored to merit the guest cabins as well as such a distinguished captain. What did we do to deserve such an honor?"

"The Dutchman belongs to my company," Catie said. "Right now, my partner and I are the only captains. So you had to get one of us. I was stuck at the Academy last year, so this is my first chance to captain the Dutchman."

"Weren't you Alex MacGregor?" one of the students asked.

"Yes," Catie said. "I had to go by an alias while at the Academy. We didn't want my presence to upset the experience for me or my fellow cadets."

"Hey, Braxton, didn't you date an Alex MacGregor?"

"We went out a few times," Braxton said, trying to hide his embarrassment.

"Oh, hi Braxton, I didn't see you back there," Catie said. "You people should board, we push back in one hour."

Board Meeting – July 4th

"I call this meeting to order," Marc said. "I know we're all focused on what will happen when we finally enter the Fazullan ship next week, but we have to keep the company running. Fred, where are we?"

"The company's doing fine. We sent the first fusion core to Egypt, the next three will be a month apart. We'll slide the one for Somalia in between the second and third. Catie's bringing a load of platinum metals back with her as well as a bunch of ore. The smelter at Gemini Station is working like a champ. We'll be building one here at Delphi Station up as soon as Catie shows up with the designers."

"Any issues, Catie?"

"No, we just left the station at 0600."

"Blake, how is the U.N.'s mission in Africa going? We heard they're getting the fusion reactors."

"It's going about as expected. They've isolated Mogadishu and are expanding into the countryside. All indications are that the arms embargo is holding, so there's optimism that they might get it right this time."

"We can keep our fingers crossed," Marc said. "What about the federation of planets?"

"That's become a big hullabaloo. Nobody likes the idea of having one and nobody likes the idea of not having one, so they just argue. It's been endless debates. Margaret swears she's ready to resign."

"Tell her to appoint a sub-ambassador to sit in on the debates," Samantha said.

"Why don't you call her up and talk about it?" Blake said. "I'm within striking distance, so I'd rather you handle it."

"Chicken."

"Discreet."

"Alright, I'll call her."

"Do we have a plan for the Paraxean asteroid yet?" Marc asked.

"I think we should wait," Catie said.

"What?! You know Governor Paratar will have a fit if we tell him we want to wait,"

"I'm sure Catie has a good reason," Samantha said. "Now, Catie, why don't you share it with us?"

"Dr. McDowell and I did some experiments where we proved that we could combine wormholes. Just like you did when you jumped the Victory next to the Fazullan starship. But what you might not remember is that we can combine them in a sequence so that there would only be one wormhole to pass through to get from Earth to Mangkatar. I think it would be better to prove that, and then only have one jump with the asteroid."

"How long will that take?"

"We need to make more solar explorers. We would then move one into each of the systems we have to pass through. Then we can open a wormhole between the jump ships in Sol and a set in Mangkatar Prime. We can push a few things through it to verify that it works. Then when we're ready, we can open it again and push the asteroid through in one go."

"I agree with your concern," Marc said, "but that is a big delay. Is it really worth it?"

"I think so, and to make it easy on the Paraxeans, we can start accelerating the asteroid now. We can still jump it when it's moving, but then it won't take so long to reach the planet. I think we can make the delay a wash."

"Okay, what do you need?"

"Permission to make the solar explorer probes. I think we can open the wormhole at the exit with just a probe, but I need to run a few tests to prove it."

"Wouldn't you crash into the probe when you exited the wormhole?" Admiral Michaels asked.

"I don't think so. We can open the wormhole in front of the probe. That way, even though you're passing through the probe, you're still in the wormhole, so there's no physical contact."

"Okay, so how long?" Marc asked.

"Four weeks to make them, then two weeks to get them in place."

"Okay, start making them. We'll talk at the next meeting about some of the implications and how we want to manage them."

"I think we need a new design for a frigate-sized starship," Blake said. "Having to use the jump ships for the Victory could have created problems."

"Something the size of the Roebuck?" Catie asked.

"Yes, but with more firepower and flight bay capacity."

"I'll work on a proposal if that's okay with the rest of you."

"You're our ship designer. Work with Ajda," Marc said.

"Okay. I should have a proposal ready in four weeks."

"Welcome everyone," Blake said. "We jumped the alien ship back to Artemis one hour ago. We're now getting ready to board her."

Liz, Catie, Kal, and Admiral Michaels had joined Blake in the boardroom on Delphi Station. Marc and Samantha were attending via Comm link.

"Captain Clements, a status update if you please," Blake ordered.

"Yes, sir. The Marines are ready to enter the ship. The Fazullans did not offer any resistance. Captain Lantaq is meeting them in the airlock."

"Good."

Everyone was on edge; this was the first time they had ever boarded an alien starship. Although they had boarded several Paraxean starships during the war, they were intimately familiar with their designs since all the Delphi starships were based on Paraxean designs.

"The pressure has been equalized," the Marine major announced. "Opening the airlock now."

They watched as the major rotated the handle and pushed the airlock door open. Standing in front of the now-open door, Captain Lantaq was alone. The Marines were all in full exosuits, nobody was interested in testing out the alien air. Even if it was breathable, who knew if it was safe.

"All of my crew are confined to their stations, and unnecessary crew are in stasis," Captain Lantaq informed the Marines.

"Good, please lead us to the bridge," the Marine major's Comm was handling translations for him. He spoke in a quiet voice, allowing the Comm's translation to be the dominant sound.

"Of course. Follow me. I assume your boots are attaching themselves to the deck. As you can tell, this is the zero-gravity section of the ship."

"We're good."

"The ship's center is rotating about two revolutions per minute, so with a sixty-meter diameter, it should have 0.15Gs at the outer hull," ADI informed everyone.

"Looks kind of normal," Liz said.

"That's what I expected. Bulkheads, floors, doors, and passageways seem to have a galactic standard," Blake said.

"This lift will take us to the bridge. When it engages, there will be an abrupt change in speed, then it will settle," Captain Lantaq said.

"We understand," the Marine major said.

A few seconds later, the door to the lift opened showing the bridge that they had all seen on the videos. The bridge crew were all sitting quietly at their stations and there were no bodyguards hanging around.

"If you will step to the command chair, I will turn the ship over to you," Captain Lantaq said. This was the point that everyone was terrified of: Would the transfer of control go smoothly or was it a trap? Would Captain Lantaq have the ship self-destruct? It was even possible that a self-destruct would be automatic when the ship was surrendered.

"This is Captain Lantaq, command code Delta, Omega, Epsilon, Four, Three, Nine, Two."

"Command code recognized," the ship's DI replied.

"I am handing command control to Major," he looked at the Marine major.

"Prescott."

"I am handing command control to Major Prescott. Please acknowledge change of command."

"Major Prescott, please state your full name," the DI requested.

"Major Gregory James Prescott."

"Command codes are changed. Major Prescott, please enter a security password."

"It will record your voice, so it doesn't matter if anyone else hears it," Captain Lantaq said.

"Omega, Delphi, Alfa, Gamma, Five, Nine, Eight, Seven."

"The ship is under your command. What are your orders?" the DI asked.

Major Prescott looked at Captain Lantaq with a puzzled expression.

"The DI is conversant in your language, thanks to the language files you shared with us. You can give your commands in English."

"Hold position."

"Hold position acknowledged."

Major Prescott detailed two Marines to stay on the bridge and then had Captain Lantaq take them to engineering.

"I have guards in each of the critical sections. Everything we've seen so far matches what we got from the three prisoners we captured from the shuttle," Major Prescott announced. "I'm now having Captain Lantaq take us to the stasis pods."

"Very well," Captain Fitzgerald said.

Everyone watched as the team headed back to the zero G section of the ship. The tension had dropped considerably once control had been handed over and the ship didn't explode, but there was still a general fear that something bad would happen.

"These are the crew stasis chambers," Captain Lantaq indicated. ADI reported that there were one hundred twenty chambers and most of them were occupied.

"I see," Major Prescott said as he surveyed the room. "You said crew stasis chambers, are there others?"

"Yes, we have the laborers we brought with us. Those pods are in the section over there," Captain Lantaq said, indicating a door at the back of the room.

"Let's check them out," Major Prescott said.

"Follow me."

As they entered the second chamber it was immediately obvious that there were far more stasis chambers in it than in the crew section.

"How many chambers are there in here?"

"Five thousand," Captain Lantaq said.

Major Prescott whistled. Then he started to walk down the aisle to check out a few chambers.

Major Prescott pulled up short, shocked at what he was seeing. "Sir, there are Paraxeans in some of these stasis pods."

"Hold on Major. Admiral?" Captain Clements asked.

"Get a doctor over there and wake up a Paraxean or two," Blake ordered. "Call us when they're able to talk."

"What do you have for us, Major?" Blake asked once they had regathered to review the intelligence.

"Captain Lantaq confirms what the Paraxeans have said. They are prisoners, virtual slaves. They appear to be descendants of the Paraxeans captured from the colony mission that the rebel Paraxeans came from."

"How many races were there?"

"Three, besides the Fazullans," Captain Clements said. "Apparently they were to be used as labor to mine the asteroids for metals."

"But how can that be?" Catie asked. "That's over two hundred light-years."

"I have not been able to get a satisfactory answer from anyone. One of the others swears that they were living on a planet in a trinary star system. They were used as farm and manufacturing labor."

"Did Captain Lantaq confirm any of that?"

"He refused to say. We're interrogating the rest of the crew and digging into the ship's logs. They're encrypted so it may take some time."

"Very well. Keep us informed," Blake ordered.

"Yes sir. By the way, in case anyone is interested, these Fazullans are ugly looking, but if you didn't notice on the video, the tall ones are only about 175 cms, or five foot nine."

Catie laughed. "So yours is bigger, Uncle Blake."

"Well, you never know," Liz said.

"You two, get your minds out of the gutter," Blake said.

After reviewing the data from the interrogations of the crew and a few of the prisoners, Catie moved to the display at the back of the room and brought up a map of star systems. She had Artemis marked as well as the region of space where the Paraxean Colony ship was attacked. She was slowly highlighting the stars between the two points.

"What are you thinking?" Blake asked Catie as he joined her at the display.

"I don't know. I'm looking for a quaternary star system between the two points, our location and the one where the aliens attacked the Paraxeans. Unfortunately, there seem to be six of them."

"Why a quaternary star system, the Paraxeans said it was a trinary system?" Liz asked.

"A quaternary system with a binary star would look like a trinary system to the naked eye. And a quaternary system might create a natural wormhole," Catie replied.

"Are you serious?"

"It's the only thing that makes sense. I'm looking at all the star systems between Artemis and the location where the Paraxean Colony mission was attacked."

"What do you get when you backtrack their course?"

"It doesn't lead to one of the quaternary systems, besides they're all too far. But it does lead to this system, which is almost in a direct line with that quaternary system. And that system is also in an approximate straight line to the system where the Paraxeans were attacked."

"But that's over 200 light-years," Liz said.

"I know, but it's the only thing I can think of that makes sense," Catie said. "I need to talk with Doctor McDowell."

"Then get after it," Blake said. "We need to figure this thing out."

Afterword

Thanks for reading Delphi Challenge!

I hope you've enjoyed the ninth book in the Delphi in Space series. The story will continue in Delphi League.   If you would like to join my newsletter group go to ⬚https://tinyurl.com/tiny-delphi. The newsletter provides interesting Science facts for SciFi fans, book recommendation based on books I truly loved reading, deals on books I think you'll like, and notification of when the next book in my series is available.

As a self-published author, the one thing you can do that will help the most is to leave a review on Goodreads and Amazon.

Acknowledgments

It is impossible to say how much I am indebted to my beta readers and copy editors. Without them, you would not be able to read my books due to all the grammar and spelling errors. I have always subscribed to Andrew Jackson's opinion that "It is a damn poor mind that can think of only one way to spell a word."

So special thanks to:

My copy editor, Ann Clark, who also happens to be my wife.

My beta reader and editor, Theresa Holmes.

My beta reader and cheerleader, Roger Blanton, who happens to be my brother.

Also important to a book author is the cover art for their book. I'm am especially thankful to Momir Borocki for the exceptional covers he has produced for my books. It is amazing what he can do with the strange PowerPoint drawings I give him; and how he makes sense of my suggestions, I'll never know.

If you need a cover, he can be reached at momir.borocki@gmail.com.

Also by Bob Blanton

Delphi in Space

Starship Sakira

Delphi City

Delphi Station

Delphi Nation

Delphi Alliance

Delphi Federation

Delphi Exploration

Delphi Colony

Delphi Challenge

Delphi League – coming in April 2021

Stone Series

Matthew and the Stone

Stone Ranger

Stone Undercover

Made in the USA
Las Vegas, NV
28 October 2022

58286347R10148